W9-BUB-866

A PLACE *to* HANG *the* MOON

A PLACE *to* HANG *the* MOON

KATE ALBUS

MARGARET FERGUSON BOOKS
HOLIDAY HOUSE • NEW YORK

Margaret Ferguson Books

Printed and bound in December 2020 at Maple Press, York, PA, USA.

www.holidayhouse.com

First Edition

1 3 5 7 9 10 8 6 4 2

Library of Congress Cataloging-in-Publication Data

Names: Albus, Kate, author.
Title: A place to hang the moon / by Kate Albus.
Description: First edition. | New York : Holiday House, [2021] | Audience: Ages 9 to 12. | Audience: Grades 4–6. | Summary: In World War II England, orphaned siblings William, Edmund, and Anna are evacuated from London to live in the countryside, where they bounce from home to home in search of someone willing to adopt them permanently.
Identifiers: LCCN 2020039711 | ISBN 9780823447053 (hardcover)
Subjects: LCSH: World War, 1939–1945—Evacuation of civilians—Great Britain—Juvenile fiction. | CYAC: World War, 1939–1945—Evacuation of civilians—Fiction. | Orphans—Fiction. | Brothers and sisters—Fiction. Family life—England—Fiction. | Villages—Fiction. | Great Britain—History—George VI, 1936–1952—Fiction.
Classification: LCC PZ7.1.A432 Pl 2021 | DDC [Fic]—dc23
LC record available at https://lccn.loc.gov/2020039711

ISBN: 978-0-8234-4705-3 (hardcover)

For Luke and Olivia . . .

who hung the moon

A PLACE *to* HANG *the* MOON

Chapter One

Funeral receptions can be tough spots to find enjoyment, but eleven-year-old Edmund Pearce was doing his best.

He was intent on the iced buns. Some of them had gone squashy on one side or the other, some had lost their icing when a neighboring bun had been removed, and a few had been sadly neglected in the icing department from the start. Undaunted, Edmund picked through the pile, finding two that met with his approval. He shoved one into each of his trouser pockets and, scooping up a handful of custard cream cookies to round out the meal, navigated through the crowd until he found a vacant armchair. There he settled, quite content despite the occasion. It helped that he'd never cared much for his grandmother, anyway.

On the other side of the room, Anna Pearce sat cross-legged on the floor between a corner cabinet and a brocade settee. The settee's occupants didn't notice the nine-year-old tucked under the weighty scroll of its arm. Anna had nearly finished *Mary Poppins,* and she preferred its company to that of the unfamiliar elderly ladies perched on the settee, or any of the other guests. Like her brother, Anna had managed to find enjoyment at the funeral reception. Also like her brother, Anna felt little grief at her grandmother's passing.

William Pearce, the eldest of our threesome, made his way through the throng, thanking people for coming. He had spent a particularly long while with the vicar, who was quite deaf. Everything had to be repeated before the dear man understood, and this took some time. William was cross and tired. The corners of his mouth felt tight with smiling. But funeral receptions, after all, were not events to be enjoyed. Even when one didn't much miss one's grandmother.

William glimpsed the toe of Anna's shoe by the corner cabinet. He smiled. His first real smile that day. Crossing the room and nodding to the elderly ladies on the settee, he nudged Anna's foot with his own. She looked up from her book and smiled back at him.

William crouched low and squeezed between the furniture to join his sister. It was a tight spot, and none too comfortable for a tallish boy of twelve, but this is what one does when one loves one's sister very much. Especially when one hasn't any parents who might make themselves uncomfortable on behalf of their children.

William eyed the slim handful of pages remaining to be read in Anna's book. "Last chapter?"

Anna marked her spot with a hair ribbon and nodded. "Mary Poppins has gone away, and the children are so sad."

William pulled Anna close.

"Is the reception nearly over?" she asked.

"Nearly." William surveyed the crowd. "People are starting to leave. They've got to get home before the blackout."

"Where's Edmund?"

William sighed. "Last I saw, he was taunting the vicar."

Anna's eyes went wide. "Taunting?"

"Standing behind him, trying to figure how loud he had to shout before the vicar noticed he was there."

"Oh, dear."

"Mmmmm. I should find him." William squeezed Anna's shoulder. "Stay here and finish your book."

Anna took her brother's hand. "I'll come with you. I'd rather finish it in bed tonight."

With that, the pair began to search for their brother in the crowded room. This took quite a while, as they were stopped at every turn by well-dressed strangers wishing to list their grandmother's many fine qualities. Anna found herself collecting words along the way. *Principled. Dignified. Formidable.* She wasn't entirely certain what *formidable* meant, but it sounded like *forbidding,* which was a word that described their grandmother nicely. Certainly more so than a word like *grandmotherly.*

"Thank you, sir," she heard William say, as he shook the hand of a brittle-looking man in a gold-buttoned jacket. "You're right, sir. She was formidable, sir."

William spied Edmund in the armchair. He was tossing bits of cookie into the air and catching them—most of them—in his mouth. William excused himself from the gold-buttoned man and pulled Anna along behind him. The pair reached Edmund just as a piece of a custard cream bounced off his chin and skidded across the floor to lodge itself against the base of a standing lamp.

William put his hands on his hips. "Must you, Edmund?"

Edmund grinned. "There were only boring cookies left. You've got to do something to make them more interesting."

Anna eyed the piece by the lamp. "I like custard creams." She thought it a shame to waste them, even if there hadn't been a war on. Which, in fact, there was.

William scowled at Edmund's feet. "Edmund, put your shoes back on."

"Why?"

"Because the guests are leaving. We've got to see them out."

"I'm in my own house. Why do I have to wear shoes?"

"Just—" William retrieved his brother's shoes from the floor. "Please, Edmund."

Edmund grunted his indignation but took the shoes.

As the children waited for Edmund to do up his laces, they caught snippets of conversation here and there.

"Lovely sermon," a woman in a blue suit said—twice—to the vicar.

". . . blasted Germans . . . ," a ruddy-faced man grunted as he made his way toward the door.

". . . if only they weren't rationing bacon," said a plump woman being helped into her jacket by an even more plump woman.

"Whatever is to be done about the children?"

This last came from the dining room.

William, Anna, and Edmund exchanged glances. They recognized the voice of their elderly housekeeper, Miss Collins. They could hear no more of her conversation, but they didn't need to. They were only too aware that nobody had yet come up with an answer to the question of *what was to be done about the children*.

At the moment, however, there was no time to dwell on this rather terrifying unknown, as a heavily ringed hand landed on Anna's shoulder. "I'm sorry for your loss, children. Your grandmother was a paragon, as you no doubt know."

"Thank you, ma'am," Anna said. Anna didn't know the ringed woman. She also didn't know what *paragon* meant but thought it sounded rather like *pagoda,* which couldn't be right. She noted, silently, that the woman smelled of mothballs.

"Yes, thank you," William said, recoiling with some dismay as he saw Edmund remove an iced bun from his pocket—his pocket!—and shove it into his mouth, whole.

The ringed woman looked to Edmund for his response. It was perhaps for the best that his mouth was filled with iced bun, for this made his answer unintelligible. The woman raised her eyebrows in distaste and brushed a spray of crumbs from her lapel. She carried on toward the front door, muttering something about the world and what it was coming to.

"Charming, Ed," William said.

Edmund swallowed the last of the bun. "She *was* a miserable old cow, and you know it. Why must we all of a sudden pretend to have adored her?"

"It's what people do?" Anna said.

"Yes, but *why*?"

Anna considered this but could find no sense in it. Frankly, she was preoccupied with hunger, and a bit jealous of Edmund for having got the last of the custard creams. She picked out a finger sandwich from the buffet and nibbled it, wishing it were a cookie.

As the door was closed on the last of the guests, Miss Collins appeared and asked the three of them to join her in the dining room. There, she lowered herself into a chair.

"You'll remember, children, that your grandmother's solicitor, Mr. Engersoll, will be here early tomorrow?"

William, Edmund, and Anna knew the meeting with the solicitor was to be about their FUTURES—somehow the word always sounded capitalized when adults said it—and all three felt rather sick at the bleak uncertainty.

For June of 1940 was, even for those who had not recently

become orphans, a time of most uncertain futures. The country's worst fears about Mr. Hitler had been realized the previous fall when war with Germany had been declared. While no bombs had yet been dropped on London, the overheard conversations of adults suggested that it was only a matter of time.

William smiled a stalwart sort of half smile. Edmund looked at the floor. The sides of Anna's nose were beginning to go pink, warning of oncoming tears. "Miss Collins," she whispered, "can't you just stay on with us?"

"Don't be daft," Edmund said. "She's ancient."

William grimaced. "Ed."

Miss Collins laid a wizened hand on William's. "Children. How I wish such a thing could be. I'm afraid, though, that an old bird like me"—she directed a smile at Edmund—"is in no position to become mother to anyone."

"But we don't need a real mother," Anna said, only a hint of a whine creeping into her voice. "We just need someone to watch us when we're home from boarding school at the holidays. We wouldn't be any bother." Her eyes darted briefly toward Edmund. "Truly, we wouldn't."

William thought of hushing his sister, but the fact was that he wished for precisely the same thing she did. Indeed, if he was to be honest about his heart's desire, he wished for more. He wished Miss Collins *would* volunteer to be a mother to the three of them. He wished she would stop

Edmund from sneaking sweets after dinner. He wished she would read Anna—all of them, come to that—stories at bedtime and tuck the covers about their necks before saying *Sweet dreams* and switching off the lamp. He wished she would praise him for his top marks in history. He wished she would take him in her bony old arms and tell him she'd be in charge and he needn't worry any longer. Truth be told, he had wished all of this for a very long time, though he knew a housekeeper's job was cleaning and cooking, not tucking in and hugging.

Miss Collins dug in her apron and produced a spotless handkerchief. She dabbed at her nose, now gone pinker than Anna's. "I'm afraid there's nothing for it, children." She gripped William's hand. "What you need is a proper guardian." She faltered, gave a sniffle. "And while I wish things were different, that's more than I'm . . ." She sniffled again. "That's more than I'm able to give you." With that, she rose and fled through the doorway to her own quarters as quickly as her aged bones would carry her.

Left to themselves, the children trudged upstairs to the nursery for their own private council of war.

Edmund perched on the window seat, which was rather useless just now, as the blackout shades were tightly drawn and eclipsed any view of the dusky London streets below. He picked up a rubber ball and began tossing it into the air and catching it again. "I suppose that was supper," he said.

William sat cross-legged on the floor, paging through a book. The rhythmic riffling of the pages was soothing. "Honestly, Edmund," he said. "Do you really need more food?"

Edmund shrugged. "What do you think the solicitor will have to say, Will?"

"I don't know. Hopefully Miss Collins will stay on until we go back to school in September. And then . . . maybe the grandmother had some sort of plan thought out for us."

"I'm fairly certain the only thought the grandmother had about us was that we were a right pain in the neck."

"Ed."

Edmund hesitated only a moment. "She did think that, though."

William sighed. "I know, but you needn't say it out loud." He fanned the pages of the book again. "Maybe there was a plan left over from Mum and Dad."

Anna lay down on the nursery rug. "Tell me something about them, William."

William gave her ankle a squeeze. "Mum always said her children hung the moon."

"You tell us that one all the time," Edmund complained. "We know that one."

"I know you know it." William frowned. "But it's a good one."

"Yes, but tell us something else anyhow," Anna pleaded.

For you see, of the three of them, only William had any memory of their parents. Nothing too detailed, mind you, as he was not yet five when they died. He remembered being led by the hand through the back garden. A cool palm on his forehead when he was ill. A few notes from a tune sung to him at bedtime. And with this handful of fleeting memories plus a great many more he concocted from his own imagination, William had made it his business, some years ago, to paint for his brother and sister a vivid, if largely fictitious, portrait of their parents. Anna would, with some regularity, turn to William and say *tell me something about them.* Edmund never asked but always listened. Whether the memory about hanging the moon was real or whether William had made it up such a long time ago it had become so, well—did it matter?

William thought for a moment. "I've got another. I've only just remembered this one. When she was small, Mum got her little finger run over by someone's roller skate, and she broke it."

"The skate, or the finger?" Edmund asked.

"The finger!"

Edmund narrowed his eyes. "You actually remember her telling you that one?"

"I do."

"Must have hurt, mustn't it?" Anna said.

"I'm sure it did," William agreed.

The children sat in silence for a long while, pondering broken fingers and uncertain futures, until finally William rose, shook himself, and mustered a confidence that was almost believable.

"Mr. Engersoll will have a plan for us, and everything will be all right."

CHAPTER TWO

There are those adults who possess a rare gift for explaining complex subjects to children. Harold Engersoll, it may safely be said, was not one of these. He and Miss Collins sat on straight-backed chairs in the parlor. The children bunched together on a sofa opposite them.

Mr. Engersoll cleared his throat. "It goes without saying, I suppose, children, that your situation is both unique and precarious?"

This was not the opening any of them had hoped for.

"Yes, sir. I mean . . . no, sir." William stumbled. "I mean, we understand . . . that we're . . . unique and . . . precarious."

"Yes. Well. As you are no doubt aware, the three of you are heirs to a comfortable inheritance." The children only blinked at him. "However, that inheritance is of little use in the procurement of the one thing you require—a guardian to watch over you until you are grown." He offered an awkward smile. "Your grandmother did not name such a guardian in her will." He paused. "It is rather a bitter irony, isn't it?"

William reached for Anna's hand, aware that she hadn't

a clue what irony was. He wasn't sure he understood it himself, truth be told, but he knew what Mr. Engersoll was getting at. "He means that we have money but we don't have anyone to take care of us."

Edmund, for his part, was studying the tufts of hair sprouting from the solicitor's ears. *And none on top,* Edmund thought. *Rough, that.*

The solicitor cleared his throat again. "Miss Collins has agreed to stay on until alternative arrangements can be made, but—I'm sure you understand—she has served your grandmother here for over forty years and it isn't her job to—ehm—well, she is of such an age that . . ." He faltered for a moment. "It's time for her to retire to her own lodgings. Her own family."

Miss Collins dabbed at her nose with a handkerchief.

Anna wasn't quite prepared to give up on Miss Collins. "We don't need a real guardian, though. Only somebody to watch us on school holidays."

Mr. Engersoll gave the three of them a long look. "I hardly think a just-for-the-holidays guardian seems the right solution, do you?"

The children saw the sense in this. They shook their heads.

"Therefore," Mr. Engersoll continued, "I believe now is the time to proceed to a discussion of other—ehm—*external* options?"

Anna's eyes met William's. "He's talking about adoption," William explained. He looked at the solicitor. "Is that right?"

"Perhaps," Mr. Engersoll replied. "Let me continue, however, as I fear circumstances may make adoption... challenging. First, I assume you would prefer to remain together?"

This question Anna understood perfectly. A fat tear slid down her cheek.

"What sort of question is that?" Edmund fairly bellowed.

William stiffened. "Yes, sir." He took a deep breath. "We would prefer to remain together."

A sniffle escaped from Miss Collins.

"Of course," Mr. Engersoll said. "I am sorry. What I mean to say is—" He removed his spotless spectacles to polish them. Anna climbed onto William's lap, where she buried her wet face in his shirt. Edmund's fists were clenched as Mr. Engersoll proceeded gingerly. "It's only that... three is rather a lot to adopt, especially with the war going on. Families aren't sure they can keep their own children safe, let alone take on more." The solicitor replaced his spectacles and leaned close to the assembled siblings. "Which brings me to my recommendation for the three of you..."

William thought he saw the old man's eyes twinkle. But that couldn't be right. This was not an occasion for twinkling.

"I wonder whether," Mr. Engersoll said, "in this very

special case . . . the war might, in fact, be seen as rather . . . an opportunity?"

William assumed he had misunderstood. "An opportunity?"

Mr. Engersoll's fingers met in a steeple under his chin. "You are aware of the latest round of evacuations currently being carried out in London and other—ehm—*imperiled* locations around the country?"

The children nodded. They knew that thousands of children had already been evacuated from London to the countryside last September, after war was declared, in the hopes of keeping them out of harm's way should the Germans bomb the city.

"I should like for you to consider," Mr. Engersoll continued, "the possibility of being evacuated yourselves."

William frowned. "But . . . wouldn't we be safe at school, sir?"

The solicitor looked from one to the other of them. "You probably would, William, but as it doesn't solve the problem of finding you a proper guardian, I'm not sure going back to school is what's best for you."

Not going back to school. Edmund was beginning to like the sound of this.

Mr. Engersoll leaned even closer, his voice a near whisper now. "What if . . . the three of you were to be evacuated with the rest of London's schoolchildren? Off to the country with you, where you would no doubt make a most favorable impression on whatever family was lucky enough to have you? Is it not possible that an arrangement intended as temporary could evolve into something . . . permanent?"

William glanced at Edmund, then Miss Collins. "You mean," he said, measuring each word, "that we should be evacuated and hope that whatever family takes us on wants to keep us forever?"

Mr. Engersoll leaned back and folded his hands in his lap. "Precisely."

Edmund snorted. "Right. So . . . we're to ship out to the wilderness, where we just happen to be scooped up by some kindly . . . farmer and his wife . . . who've been waiting all their lives for three half-grown children to drop into their laps?"

Mr. Engersoll sighed. "It does sound preposterous when you say it that way." He was not to be put down so quickly, however. "Is it outside the realm of possibility, though? You would be doing just as nearly a quarter of a million other children are doing, so it's not as if you'll be put on a train alone to seek your fortunes. And at the very least, evacuation will offer you the *possibility* of a permanent guardian." He cleared his throat again. "You would need to be circumspect, of course. You couldn't tell anyone the truth about your grandmother, or your inheritance, at least until you were sure you'd landed somewhere that you all agreed was a suitable home. We don't want anybody taking advantage of you."

William wrinkled his nose. "So . . . we'd be lying?"

"Well," said Mr. Engersoll, looking rather guilty at the mention of *lying*, "I wouldn't want you to lie, so much as to . . . omit the truth, I suppose. That is, you needn't tell anyone that you left London because your grandmother died . . . only that she sent you away for your own safety."

"Which is lying," Edmund said.

The solicitor gave a sad sort of smile. "It isn't a perfect plan, children. I understand. But among the limited options I see for you, this one offers the best hope, in my imagination."

Hope and imagination. How funny that the dour old solicitor should choose those words. For children—above all other creatures—are naturally endowed with extraordinary capacities for both. Indeed, having grown up in the care of a grandmother who lacked much in the way of warmth, William, Edmund, and Anna had spent untold hours *imagining* what a real family might look like and *hoping* one day to find themselves in one. And now, in the silence of the parlor, each of the children could *imagine* the faintest glimmer of *hope* in the solicitor's admittedly preposterous plan.

"What if we don't find a suitable place?" William asked. He thought, but didn't say out loud, *What if we do find one, but they don't want us, even if we do come with an inheritance?* He wasn't sure which of those was worse.

Mr. Engersoll sighed. "Why don't we cross that bridge when we come to it?"

The children sat for a long moment, considering.

Edmund set his teeth in a grimace. "It'll never work."

And yet the children found themselves in the nursery the following week, packing their suitcases. Mr. Engersoll had contacted a colleague in the Ministry of Health and arranged for William, Edmund, and Anna to join the students of St. Michael's, a North London primary school, when their evacuation occurred.

For the most part, the wartime evacuations of London were accomplished through the schools. Children packed their things and boarded trains with their teachers, to be delivered to the relative safety of the countryside. There, willing strangers gathered in churches and schools, in village halls, even in theaters and cattle markets, to select evacuees to host until such time as London was safe again and the children could return to their families.

"It's an awfully small suitcase," Anna said, reading aloud the official packing list Mr. Engersoll had obtained for them. " 'Nightgown, handkerchiefs, face cloth, toothbrush, comb, sturdy walking shoes'—right, I've got those. 'One small family memento.' "

"No worries there," Edmund said. "That'll save you some room."

Anna ignored him, continuing down the list. " 'A small bag or rucksack for school materials . . . if possible, a coat . . .' "

"If possible?" Edmund wrinkled his nose.

"Not everyone's got a coat, Ed," William said absently. Edmund paused a moment in his packing to digest this notion.

" 'A favorite storybook,' " Anna went on. "One?" she asked.

The very idea. To pick just one favorite book seemed as impossible as—well, as finding a family through a mass wartime evacuation. But there you have it.

Anna surveyed the nursery shelves, taking down books here and there, considering each, then moving on.

The Arabian Nights?

"Far too heavy," Edmund advised, "and I'm not carrying it for you."

Peter and Wendy? All those lost boys looking for a mother. A bit too close to home.

Heidi? Agh. More orphans.

A Little Princess. This one, Anna hadn't read. She paged through the book, catching phrases: *warm things, kind things, sweet things*... *nothing so strong as rage, except what makes you hold it in*... *a princess in rags and tatters*... Anna snapped the cover shut and nestled the book in her suitcase.

William's selection was decided by an assignment he had made himself two years ago. On his tenth birthday, William announced to no one in particular that he planned to read the *Encyclopaedia Britannica* straight through, beginning to end. He read other things along the way, of course—heavens, to think of reading nothing but the *Britannica* for years and years—but had carried on with his quest. He had just started the fourth volume: *HER(cules) to ITA(lic).* He hefted it off the shelf. Surely the war would be over and done before it was time to move on to volume five and the doings of *ITA(liysky, Aleksandr Vasilyevich Suvorov)*?

Edmund, retrieving a well-worn copy of *The Count of Monte Cristo* from the topmost shelf, marveled at his brother's utter lack of sense. He poked William in the stomach with a corner of *The Count.* "You can borrow this, if you like, once you realize what a stupid choice you've made."

Miss Collins joined the children toward the end of their packing. Her eyes were red-rimmed, and she pocketed her handkerchief as she entered the nursery. "Now, children—shall we go through your suitcases and ensure you've not forgotten anything?"

"Mine hardly latches," Edmund replied. "Even if I had forgot something, I don't know where I'd put it."

"Even so—let's have a look, shall we?" Miss Collins opened Edmund's suitcase to reveal an impressive selection of sweets. Dairy Milk chocolate bars and jelly babies, Cadbury Roses and wine gums, even a roll of Parma Violets. A weary smile played at the housekeeper's lips. "Edmund, dear, hadn't you better use your suitcase for essentials?"

"These *are* essentials, Miss Collins. What if they haven't got jelly babies in the country?"

"Hmmm. The horror. Perhaps if we just...edited... a bit? Don't you think that by wintertime you might fancy some extra socks more than jelly babies?"

"I can't imagine ever fancying socks over jelly babies."

"Indeed. Well, let's have a look-through, and if all the necessaries are there, I suppose some extra sweets aren't going to hurt anyone." Miss Collins set to work on Edmund's suitcase as Anna and William silently considered slipping down to the kitchen to see what sorts of treats they might fit into theirs.

Making her way through each of their cases in turn, Miss Collins looked up. "Have you got your gas masks?" The children hesitated for a moment, none of them certain where theirs had got to. The masks had been distributed throughout England back in September. The children had received theirs while they were away at school, and they seemed novel at the time. Edmund had especially enjoyed the way the mask amplified rude noises made with one's mouth. With time, however, even this became tiresome, and the masks were forgotten. Edmund and William found theirs, at last, on the topmost shelf of their bedroom closet. Anna's was discovered under her bed.

The packing done, Miss Collins gathered the children and handed each a slip of paper inscribed with addresses and telephone numbers. "Right, then, children. Fix these to the insides of your suitcases. I'll be staying with my sister near Watford."

"Why aren't you getting evacuated, Miss Collins?" Edmund asked. "They're not just doing children, you know. They're sending the elderly—" He stopped, midsentence. It had sounded more rude than he intended.

William sighed, but Miss Collins didn't fuss. "My sister's is evacuation enough for me, Edmund. Now—you're to contact me and let me know your whereabouts straightaway, all right? I'll pass the information along to Mr. Engersoll, but his address and telephone number are here as well. Should you need anything at all . . ." Here, the old housekeeper faltered. She rummaged in her apron pocket for her handkerchief and pressed it to the end of her nose. "Oh, children . . . I'm sorry."

William went to her side. "It's all right, Miss Collins. We know you'd carry on living with us if you could." Anna was blinking back tears. Edmund stared resolutely at the nursery rug. He made it a point of pride that he didn't cry. Not ever.

Miss Collins laid a hand on William's shoulder. "If you only knew how I wish I were twenty-five years younger."

She pocketed her handkerchief with a sniff and squared her shoulders. "Now—while I rather agree with Edmund's assessment of Mr. Engersoll's scheme—namely that it's a bit far-fetched—if there were ever three children who could make such a thing happen, it would be you." At this, the children gave wan smiles. "But remember—you're not to advertise your situation to anyone—not until you find yourselves in a place where you all three agree the time is right to let someone in on your secret. Do you understand?"

Edmund smiled in a macabre sort of way. "So, we're not to introduce ourselves by saying 'We're the Pearces, and we'd like you to adopt us straightaway . . . and by the way, we've got a bit of money that could be yours if you took us on'?"

Miss Collins gave a dark chuckle. "Indeed, Edmund. I wouldn't advise it."

Chapter Three

The next morning, Mr. Engersoll arrived at seven to drive the children to the schoolyard from which they would embark.

Miss Collins presented each of them with lunches to stow in their rucksacks. "Sandwiches, apples . . . and the little that's left of the chocolate," she said, offering Edmund a tiny smile. She embraced each of the children in turn, alternately wiping Anna's eyes and her own as they said their goodbyes. "Best behavior, now," she whispered to Edmund, who dodged her attempt to smooth a rogue cowlick with her palm.

She held on to William an extra moment. "Take good care of them," she said.

William swallowed a hard thing at the back of his throat but found that this accomplished nothing. This is what happens, sometimes, with hard things at the back of one's throat. "I will," he said.

With that, the children proceeded—rather like Sherpas—wearing their winter coats, rucksacks slung over their shoulders, suitcases in one hand, gas masks hung round their necks, to Mr. Engersoll's waiting car.

In gentler times, the children had always adored drives through London. This morning, however, dreadful weights lodged in the pits of their stomachs, and none of them took any notice of the waking city as it passed. Anna sat between her brothers, squeezing William's fingers so tightly they went white. Edmund, though he would never admit it, was prone to motion sickness and was just hoping he wouldn't have to ask the solicitor to pull the car to the side of the road. He distracted himself by concentrating hard on how remarkably shiny Mr. Engersoll's bald head was.

Regent's Park passed in a blur of green. William noted a small sign for the zoological park and wondered whether he would ever go there, now that he was leaving London. It seemed an awful shame, he thought, never to have seen the zoo. He recalled reading, somewhere, that the elephants and pandas had been evacuated already. *Just like us,* he thought.

Several miles on, Mr. Engersoll startled the three of them from their reveries. "Here we are, children." He parked the car at the side of a large building bordered by an iron fence. Unfolding themselves from the back seat and retrieving their things from the trunk, Anna, Edmund, and William made their way along the fence line until they could see into a paved schoolyard where seventy or eighty children milled about.

The solicitor walked his charges past the swarm of

children to a young woman with a clipboard. She had kind eyes, William noted. Mr. Engersoll inquired after a Miss Carr, whom he understood to be the directress of operations.

The kind-looking lady pointed out a hawkish woman near the side gate. "That's Miss Carr." She smiled at Mr. Engersoll, then offered the children a wink as they walked toward the woman in charge. She was waggling her finger at a boy about Anna's age.

The solicitor cleared his throat. "Miss Carr?"

She turned. "Yes?"

"Harold Engersoll. I'm here with the Pearce children?"

The woman hesitated, then gave a nod. "Ah, yes. I was advised you were coming." She looked the children up and down. "Twelve, eleven, and nine, I recall?"

"Yes, ma'am," William replied.

"Wait here, please. You'll need to be checked."

"Checked for what?" Edmund asked. The woman's suit, he noted, was the color of a stagnant pond. To his credit, he did not say this aloud.

"For nits," Miss Carr replied.

Anna wrinkled her nose. William took a step backward.

"We haven't got nits," Edmund said.

Poor hygiene had been one of the complaints among host families from the first wave of evacuations. Official memoranda had been distributed, indicating that children should be thoroughly inspected prior to evacuation.

Judith Carr was not a woman who disregarded official memoranda. She offered Edmund a tight-lipped smile. "We'll just make sure, then, won't we?"

Edmund looked to Mr. Engersoll, but the solicitor raised his eyebrows in an expression of defeat.

Thankfully, it was the woman with the kind eyes who was charged with their inspection. She greeted them with a smile, introducing herself as Mrs. Warren.

"We'll just get this over and done quickly, shall we?" She gave another wink as she used her index finger to part Anna's hair down the middle and bent to look closely. Anna's eyes burned at the indignity.

"You three are from outside the school?" Mrs. Warren asked. They nodded. "That must be a bit of a challenge, I expect? Not knowing anyone?" The children gave another silent nod as she moved on to William.

"Well, you know someone now." It was a thoughtful thing to say, and it warmed the children's hearts.

"You're being evacuated as well?" William asked.

"I am," she replied, turning to Edmund, who gritted his teeth and bent his head in submission. "As a teacher, I'm expected to facilitate the evacuation. My husband is away fighting, so it almost doesn't even feel like leaving home, the way things are."

Giving their heads the all clear, Mrs. Warren nodded. "Now—if the three of you need anything on the journey, don't hesitate to find me." She turned with a wave and crossed the yard.

Mr. Engersoll took this moment to offer a reminder. "You'll take care, then, children," he said, "to be circumspect in divulging the particulars of your situation?"

By now, Anna had given up trying to understand the solicitor. *Circumspect* sounded like *circumference,* but that made no sense. It was enough for her to hear William say that they understood and would be *circumspect.*

At this, Miss Carr reappeared and produced labels for the children. Each had a large black number at the center, and the children's names had been penciled in below. "You're to wear these. Attach them to one of your shirt buttons, please. It's unlikely any of us will be separated, but you're not to remove these, in any case. We can't have anyone going missing, can we?" She thumbed through the papers on her clipboard. "Young lady," she said to Anna, "you will be with the group that is on that side of the yard." She turned to Edmund. "And I assume you, young man, are the eleven-year-old? Your group is in the rear corner."

Edmund looked up at her. "We're staying together." He didn't mean to be defiant, but it came out that way nonetheless.

Miss Carr lowered her clipboard and stared hard at him. "Children," she replied, "are to be grouped by age. Your group"—she gestured to William—"is at the back of the yard there."

Edmund crossed his arms. "We're staying together," he repeated. This time, he did mean to be defiant.

To the children's relief, Mr. Engersoll stepped in. "Miss Carr, I understand the importance of organization; however, I did speak with my colleague regarding special considerations for the Pearce children. Given that they are unknown to your school, I should think it in everyone's best interest that they remain together."

Miss Carr's eyes darted from Edmund to the solicitor. A commotion from the other side of the schoolyard drew her attention. "Right," she said. "Then we shall have to make . . . accommodations, won't we?" She pursed her lips. "If you'll wait here, I need to attend to other students." She went to manage a group of smaller children, two of whom were crying.

Mr. Engersoll let out a long breath. "I suppose that's that."

"Thank you, sir," William said.

Mr. Engersoll's cheeks flushed. He removed his spectacles and rubbed at them with a handkerchief. "I wish you the very best, all three of you," he said. "Rest assured that you can contact me, should there be any matters with which you require assistance. Remember our discussion . . . and do take care of yourselves." He extended a hand to William, who shook it firmly. "Best foot forward, now."

With that, he was gone.

William turned to his siblings. Edmund was looking hard at the ground, pushing a toe between the wide stones paving the schoolyard. Anna gripped her lower lip in her teeth in a determined effort not to cry. William took her hands in his.

"This is going to be a great adventure, right?" He forced lightness into his voice, but anyone could tell that he viewed their situation as neither great nor adventurous.

"That woman is horrible," Anna said, her voice cracking.

William knew there was nothing but truth in this. "She is," he conceded. "Perhaps we should just think of her as some sort of villain that we'll need to vanquish on our adventure, right?"

"Right," Edmund said. He didn't really mean it.

William, Edmund, and Anna knew the evacuation of London's schoolchildren was referred to by some as Operation Pied Piper. No doubt, whoever coined the phrase pictured children skipping over verdant hills in time to the music of the beloved piper. Those who read like our threesome, however, may recall that the piper in the original tale was, in fact, leading the youngsters of Hamelin away from their home as a punishment to the townspeople, who had failed to pay for his services as the town's rat catcher. This knowledge did little to settle the children's stomachs as they joined the end of the long line trudging toward Kings Cross train station.

They walked in silence for a good many blocks, past unfamiliar storefronts and through a tiny park dotted with flowering shrubs. The morning sun gave a brilliant flash through the stained glass of St. Pancras Church.

Just then, William felt someone's eyes on him. Ahead was a gangly girl with long braids. She had stopped walking, apparently waiting for the Pearces to catch up to her.

The girl addressed William. "You're not from St. Michael's, are you?"

"No," William said.

The girl smiled and shifted her suitcase to her left hand. "I'm Frances."

I think she wants me to shake her hand, William thought. For some reason he couldn't quite name, his cheeks felt hot.

Edmund grinned, rather delighted by his brother's evident discomfort with the attention. "I'm Edmund Pearce," he said, extending his hand. "This is my sister, Anna, and that's my brother, William."

Frances shook Edmund's hand and glanced at Anna for the briefest of moments before turning her gaze again to William. "Pleased to meet you, William."

Edmund stifled a giggle. "My brother's a bit shy, Frances. Don't take it personally."

William wanted to stomp on Edmund's foot.

"Why are you being evacuated with St. Michael's?" Frances asked.

"Our grandmother—ehm—arranged it," Edmund said.

Frances nodded as if this explained everything. "Oh." Her eyes lingered on William. "Well," she said, "I'm awfully glad to meet you."

"You as well," William said. His voice was higher than usual.

"Yes, very glad to meet you, Frances," Edmund chimed in.

Frances saw Miss Carr checking the lines and said goodbye, hurrying to rejoin her group.

William knocked his suitcase into the back of Edmund's leg and took no small pleasure in watching his brother's knee buckle a bit.

The group arrived at the busy station a little the worse for wear. The morning was unusually warm for June, and most of the children were dressed in layers in an effort to bring as much clothing as possible. William, having carried both his suitcase and Anna's, pulled a handkerchief from his pocket to wipe perspiration from his neck.

Edmund set his suitcase down and stretched his fingers. "My feet hurt."

William had little sympathy. "Everyone's feet hurt, Ed. Don't complain."

"Right, then," Miss Carr trilled, herding the children toward platform three. "Follow your groups," she called, walking down the line of evacuees, glancing at her clipboard every few moments and directing children to the waiting train.

Her eyes landed on William, Edmund, and Anna and she marched toward them, her low heels a staccato. "You'll be expecting your own car, Your Highnesses?"

William swallowed. "No, ma'am. I mean, we'll be fine wherever there's room. And thanks—I mean, thank you for—for accommodating us."

Miss Carr glanced at her roster, at the train, then at the children. "Last car, last compartment, you lot."

The children did have a compartment to themselves, as it turned out, and whether this was accidental or not, they were glad to travel in the familiarity of their own bedraggled family. They took off their winter coats with a sigh of relief and surveyed their accommodations.

"Sit on that side, Edmund," William said. "The train'll be going this way and if you're traveling backward you'll be sick."

"I won't," Edmund said, collapsing onto the rear-facing seat.

William shrugged. "Suit yourself." He retrieved his book from his suitcase, then Edmund's and Anna's from theirs, before stowing their things in the rack above the compartment's window. None of the children opened their books just yet, however. It is often the case that, at times of great anxiety, when the diversion of a good story should seem most welcome, one is least equipped to focus one's mind on reading. This was so for our threesome, who now sat in tense silence, waiting for the train to move.

A brisk knock from the corridor announced the arrival of Mrs. Warren. She slid open the compartment door. "Hello, children. I wanted to make sure you got your postcard. To send home to your family once we've arrived . . . to let them know the address of your billet."

"What's a billet?" Anna asked.

"It's another name for a place to stay," Mrs. Warren explained. "A temporary home for you, until the war's over."

William took the outstretched card. "Thanks very much."

"Certainly." Mrs. Warren smiled at the children as the train suddenly gave a lurch. "Oh! We're off! I'm just two compartments down the corridor, at the other end of this car. In case you need anything." She heaved the door closed behind her.

The children went to the window, where Anna sat on William's lap, pressing her forehead to the glass. The brightly lit platform soon gave way to the starless midnight of a tunnel. The darkness didn't last long, though, for presently they emerged into the helter-skelter jumble of tracks and spare train cars just outside Kings Cross. The train gathered speed, and the children were whisked past the backsides of the rather shabby establishments usually found near railway stations.

In twenty minutes' time, the pewter of London began to give way. Patches of green emerged like rabbits venturing from their warrens, quick and few at first, then mustering courage and appearing in greater numbers. England's rain, infamous though it may be, begets the most extraordinary array of greens. The yellow greens of new grass met the purple greens of heather, and these tumbled toward the emerald hills beyond. The children took all this in somewhat absently, their minds occupied with the vast unknown that lay beyond that shifting green.

Anna moved from William's lap and picked up *A Little Princess*, ready to leave dark thoughts for the time being. She opened it with reverence, careful not to crack the spine. The first words of a new book are so delicious—like the first taste of a cookie fresh from the oven and not yet properly cooled. Anna settled in.

Once, on a dark winter's day, when the yellow fog hung so thick and heavy in the streets of London that the lamps were lighted and the shop windows blazed with gas as they do at night, an odd-looking little girl sat in a cab with her father . . .

Yes, Anna thought. *I like odd-looking little girls better than pretty ones. They're generally far more interesting.*

William, still too distracted to read, closed his eyes and let his mind drift. As the makeshift guardian of our threesome, his thoughts inevitably flew to the darkest of questions. *What if we get split up? What if we're taken in by someone awful? What if we're taken in by someone lovely but Edmund misbehaves and ruins things?* With time, though, the rocking of the train got the better of him, and he drifted into fitful sleep.

Edmund felt rather queasy, but he wasn't about to admit it. Like Anna, he picked up his book. He had read *The Count* before, and he welcomed Edmond Dantès, hero of downtrodden boys, taking pleasure in their similar names. Riding backward on a train is—as William suggested—ill-advised for those prone to motion sickness, but Edmund tucked into the story, unwilling to prove his brother right by succumbing to a touchy stomach.

He was able to manage this for thirty minutes or so but closed the book around page fifteen, his stomach churning. He closed his eyes and swallowed. He tried to sleep but couldn't. At no point did he consider changing seats.

Stubbornness can serve one well at times. This was not one of those times.

Nearly two hours outside of London, the train began to slow. Anna looked up from her book to peer out the window. She shook William awake.

"Are we there?" he asked.

Anna shrugged. "This doesn't seem far enough from London to be worth the trouble."

The compartment door opened, bringing Mrs. Warren's welcome face. "Not there yet, children. Just a moment to stretch your legs and use the facilities, if you need to."

Edmund's stomach gave a bilious lurch. He very much needed *the facilities*. However, as the evacuees were ushered off the train to a single, cramped privy at the far end of the platform, he eyed the line and could see he was in for a wait. His stomach roiled alarmingly. The thought of being sick in front of everyone, but most especially his brother, filled him with dread. Now gone quite pale, he gulped at the fresh air, hoping to stop himself from making a scene. Within a few minutes, though, it became quite clear that his stomach was determined to do just that. He stepped off the platform to the rock-studded hillside adjoining the railway station, seeking a spot to be sick without an audience.

William watched in dismay. "Edmund! Where are you going?"

Intent on his mission, Edmund didn't respond. The trees nearest the station were too scrawny to provide adequate cover, and none of the rocks were large enough to hide behind. He pressed on, up the hill. The sour tang was now at the very top of his throat, and his forehead was cold and damp. His eyes watering, he didn't notice a bulging root and was suddenly brought to his knees.

He could hold out no longer and was luridly sick.

Being luridly sick is never enjoyable, but it does bring

a certain measure of relief. Edmund remained kneeling on the slope, heaving deep breaths. When he was sure the scourge was over, he swiped at his mouth, then rose slowly. He brushed the dirt from his trouser legs, one of which was now torn, the frayed hole rimmed with a growing red stain from the skinned knee within. Edmund sighed and made his way back down to the platform.

None of the children appeared to have noticed the show on the hillside, except, of course, for Anna and William, who had watched it all with alarm. William took in Edmund's shirtsleeves, soiled with sick, and his torn trousers. He felt the heat of his brother's shame. "Are you all right?"

Edmund didn't have time to answer. His return had apparently not escaped the attention of Miss Carr, who approached them at a clip. There was fire in her eyes.

"Who gave you permission to leave this platform?"

Edmund neither looked at her nor answered. A charged silence followed, ultimately broken by a welcome voice.

"I did, Judith," Mrs. Warren said. "Just needed a bit of a stretch, the boy did." She smiled at Edmund, who could have hugged her, had he approved of such things.

Miss Carr leaned over Edmund, taking in his torn trousers and the unmistakable stench of sick, and wrinkled her nose. "In a few hours' time, the lot of you will be lined up in front of a hall full of people who will choose which of you they are willing to take into their homes." She fixed her gaze on the top of Edmund's downturned head. "You would do well to remember that a billet for three is a challenge, even for evacuees not in such states of disrepair."

Edmund's knee stung, and hot tears threatened, but he blinked them back and willed the moment to end.

At last it did. Miss Carr turned with a huff to shepherd all the children back to the train.

Edmund looked at Mrs. Warren. "Thank you," he whispered.

"Glad to be of help," Mrs. Warren replied. "She can be a bit grim, Miss Carr. Best to toe the line with her, if you know what I mean?"

Edmund nodded.

"And best to ride forward-facing, don't you think?" She winked at Edmund, who returned to the train with Anna and William, seating himself on the sensible side of the compartment without another word.

CHAPTER FOUR

The remainder of the journey passed without incident, save for the children's mounting anxiety. They slept—ten minutes here, twenty minutes there—heads tipped at uncomfortable angles. Anna and William ate the lunches Miss Collins had packed. Edmund thought it best to leave his stomach alone.

It was midafternoon by the time the train began to slow again. The children peered out the window, where the steeple of a church pierced the sky in the distance. A few cottages could be seen, then more, and now the train was well and truly stopping. The three looked at one another in wordless acknowledgment. This must be their destination.

Miss Carr, Mrs. Warren, and two other teachers led the evacuees from the train to a grassy area outside the station. Some of the smaller children were asleep on the shoulders of older brothers and sisters. A few more looked as if they would like to be.

Edmund, on steady ground at last and recovered now from the episode on the hillside, was hungry. He rooted out the chocolate Miss Collins had packed. As he did, he noticed a smallish boy looking up at him, wide-eyed. Edmund took in the boy's mended jacket, the eyes underlined in shadows, the skin above his upper lip chapped raw from a dripping nose gone unattended, and saw the sort of hunger whose endlessness digs a pit in a person. Being eleven, Edmund wouldn't have put it in quite those words, but he recognized it nonetheless. He looked from the boy to the chocolate now slightly melted in his palm. It was so awfully tempting to simply pop it into his mouth and have done with it. Instead, Edmund extended the precious ration to the boy, who snatched it and swallowed it, seemingly without chewing. Edmund felt uncomfortable, suddenly, and began to study the hole in his trousers.

Miss Carr stood on the steps of the station. "Children!" She clapped her hands for attention. "Let me commend you on your management of the journey thus far. We will now proceed to the village hall, where you will be served refreshments while you wait for your new foster families. Stay in your lines and follow me, please!" She set off, glancing back now and again to ensure there were no stragglers.

This last leg of the journey proved challenging. Sweaty hands lost their grips on heavy suitcases. One poor child held up the whole procession when her case—in truth, a sofa cushion cover held together with twine—split and spilled its contents into the road. One of the teachers scurried to help her gather her things and retie her bundle.

Bringing up the rear of the parade were Anna, Edmund, and William.

"How's this going to work?" Edmund asked his brother.

William shrugged. "Dunno. Tuck in your shirt before we get there."

Ahead of them, they could see the first children in the line walking through the double front doors of a large building bearing a hand-lettered banner: WELCOME, EVACUEES. As they reached the doors themselves, the children could see their companions gathering around a long table laden with cookies, fruit, and milk. The boy who had accepted Edmund's chocolate was filling his pockets. One of the teachers put a stop to this with a gentle hand on the boy's shoulder.

There were others in the hall, and the children assumed these must be the foster families. Most were women—so many men had already been called up to fight in the war. Some of the adults had children of their own with them. Some were quite elderly. Most appeared kind.

William poured cups of milk for the three of them as he watched Miss Carr climb the steps to a stage at the far end of the hall. The schoolmistress was accompanied by a stately woman in a peacock-colored suit.

Peacock approached a small podium, where her mere presence commanded silence. "Good afternoon, everyone," she said. "I am Mrs. Norton, president of the Women's

Voluntary Service and your billeting officer." A few people clapped their hands before realizing that this was unnecessary. "I know I speak for the whole of England when I say to all of you who are doing your bit by opening your homes to evacuees . . . thank you!" She offered her own personal round of applause to the assembled adults, then cleared her throat. "We at the WVS recognize what an undertaking this is, and we are here to support you. While it is June, evacuees shall nevertheless have morning lessons at the village school, to relieve billeting families of some of the, ehm . . . burden . . . of their care."

A groan made its way through the evacuees. Edmund, especially. The war had interfered with a great many things, but the summer holidays? That seemed a step too far. Anna thought school in summer didn't sound so awful, but she didn't at all care for being referred to as a *burden*.

Mrs. Norton waited for silence. "In addition, lunches will be provided to evacuees after school each day." She glanced at Miss Carr. "Now, children. Rest assured that your teachers and I shall see that appropriate billets are found for all. Toward that end, I would like to introduce Miss Judith Carr, who will direct the proceedings from here."

Miss Carr took her place at the podium. Her voice was shrill—perhaps because she was trying to make herself heard, or perhaps because shrillness was in her nature. "Children! Please form a line around the perimeter of the room, youngest over here in front of the stage, continuing on to oldest. Brothers and sisters"—she glanced briefly at the Pearces—"may remain together for the time being."

With that, the adults in the hall began to survey the evacuees.

It was all terribly odd and more than a little terrifying. The children wondered what the selection criteria might be. Age? Cleanliness? Was red hair an asset? *Likely, no one's looking for a boy who smells of sick,* Edmund thought. Positioned near the end of the line, he, William, and Anna watched as their traveling companions were looked over, evaluated, and either accepted or rejected.

Anna thought the first woman to pass looked rather stern. She breathed a sigh of relief when the lady proceeded down the line without a second glance.

Next was an older couple with gentle, well-lined faces. Anna felt a surge of hope.

The woman smiled at her. "Hello, dear. Are you all by yourself?"

Anna's voice quavered only a little bit. "No, ma'am. I'm with my brothers."

"Oh." The woman regarded the children with tenderness. "Only room for one, I'm afraid. You'll find a nice family, though, sweet as you are." She brushed a finger under Anna's chin.

Anna managed a smile. "Thank you, ma'am."

Again and again, the children were passed over. "My wife was hoping for younger ones," one man said. "What, three of you?" another questioned, as if the very notion were absurd. Edmund saw that by now even the scruffy recipient of his chocolate was gone . . . chosen, he hoped, by some kind lady who happened to own a sweet shop or a bakery.

Next in line was a couple with two big boys trailing behind them. The man was fat, with red cheeks. The woman was slight and wore an elaborately flowered frock. She seemed anxious to make a choice, her eyes darting from one evacuee to another.

When she saw Anna, she brightened. "Aren't you lovely!" The woman smiled kindly, though Anna noted that her lips were a rather alarming shade of pink. "I've always wanted a little girl," the woman said. "Only boys in my family!"

Anna hesitated. "I'm with my brothers." She gestured to Edmund and William, who did their best to look upstanding.

The woman's smile faded a bit. "I see," she said, looking at the boys, then back to Anna. "You'd not consider coming with us, just yourself, then?"

"No, ma'am." Anna gulped. "I'm sorry, ma'am." Edmund and William shifted uncomfortably from one foot to another.

The woman turned to the ruddy-faced man. "Perhaps the boys would be good companions?"

The man looked at his sons, fleshy like their father. Both averted their gazes. The man offered a tired sort of a smile. "How old are you, children?"

"I'm twelve, my brother is eleven, and my sister is nine," William answered.

The furrow in the man's brow deepened as he turned to his wife. "Where would they sleep?"

The woman's face brightened. "We've the spare room for the girl—what's your name, pet?"

Anna answered, and introduced William and Edmund as well, thinking they must feel rather like the third wheel on a bicycle just now.

"And we have the pallets in the attic," the woman continued. "The boys could all bunk in together, couldn't they? Just like when your sister and her lot come from Cardiff?"

The man turned to his sons. "What do you think about that, boys?"

Neither offered more than a shrug. The man sighed resignedly.

The woman seemed to take this as a sign of agreement. She clasped Anna's hand with an eager smile. "I'm Nellie Forrester. This is my husband, Peter, and our twins, Simon and Jack." She squeezed Anna's fingers. "This will be lovely, won't it?"

Anna looked at her brothers, barely able to breathe, the moment seemed so important. Was this the family Mr.

Engersoll had imagined for them? More to the point, was this the family they had imagined for themselves? The children glanced around the shrinking crowd and came to an unspoken agreement that there seemed no other choice.

"Thank you, ma'am . . . sir . . . Mr. and Mrs. Forrester," William said. "We appreciate your accommodating all three of us."

"Call us Auntie Nellie and Uncle Peter." The woman gave Anna's fingers another squeeze. "This is going to be just lovely," she said again.

The children mustered the very best smiles they could and gathered their belongings.

The three male Forresters were fairly mute on the mile-long walk to their home, but Mrs. Forrester's chatter more than made up for their silence. She pointed out the village school—to which the children would return in the morning—the church, the haberdashery, the newsagent, a pub called the Slug and Cabbage.

It all passed in a bit of a blur. The children's feet hurt, and William, who was still carrying his own suitcase and Anna's, felt the beginnings of blisters on his palms. All three were keen for their journey to end.

The main road through town bent uphill as they passed into a residential area. Down one tree-lined lane and up another, at last they arrived at a comfortable-looking Tudor house with a garden full of neat roses and sweet peas, pale blue hydrangeas and garishly pink azaleas. Simon and Jack unlatched the gate and disappeared unceremoniously into the house. They were nowhere to be seen by the time Mr. Forrester bustled the rest of them through the front door.

"Here we are!" Mrs. Forrester exclaimed. She led them into a small foyer where the walls bore framed photographs of the family, all looking rather stiff, Edmund thought.

To the left was a parlor with an arrangement of tufted chairs. *No bookcase,* Anna noticed. She supposed bookcases were not necessarily requirements of good parents.

To the right was a dining room, neat as a pin. Edmund noted that the smell coming from the kitchen beyond was excellent. This was encouraging.

"Would you like to put your things away?" Mrs. Forrester asked. The children nodded. "Perhaps Uncle Peter can take you boys while I show Anna her room?"

She took Anna's suitcase and led her to a set of stairs at the back of the house. Mr. Forrester trailed behind with Edmund and William, their cases thumping.

Anna stole a glance at her brothers as they parted ways at the top of the stairs. She followed Mrs. Forrester, who opened a door at the end of the hall.

"I hope this will be all right for you, pet?" She switched on a lamp.

Anna peeked in. "Yes, ma'am," she answered. "It's lovely."

"Oh, good." Mrs. Forrester breathed a sigh of relief. "I do hope you'll be comfortable here, pet. I've always wanted a little girl like you."

"Thank you, Mrs. Forrester—ehm—Auntie Nellie." Anna wasn't certain she cared for it, being called *pet,* but having little experience being mothered, she supposed it must be part of the bargain. In any event, she was certain she could get used to it.

The boys, meanwhile, were being introduced to their new arrangements in Jack and Simon's room.

"You boys can leave your suitcases here while I collect the pallets," Mr. Forrester said. "I'll just pop up to the attic." With that, he disappeared into the hallway. Given the man's bulk, Edmund didn't guess it was easy for him to *pop up to the attic*—or anywhere, come to that. He and William glanced at each other, unsure how to tread with Jack and Simon, who reclined on their beds and offered no conversation.

"Thanks for sharing your room," William said.

Neither boy did more than shrug.

"How old are you?" William asked.

It was Simon who replied. "Twelve."

"Oh." William paused. "I'm twelve, as well, and Edmund is eleven."

"We heard," Jack said. He and his brother withdrew *Beano* comics from under their pillows.

Edmund's eyes lit up with interest. "You like *Beano,* then?"

"Obviously," Simon answered.

Edmund was undaunted. "Is that the latest one? I missed the latest one back in London because of"—he faltered—"because of—the way things are."

"Uh-huh," Simon answered from behind the comic, which he did not, it should be noted, offer to loan to Edmund when he had finished.

Edmund and William felt as if they'd been on their feet for hours. There were no chairs, however, and no offer of a seat on Simon's or Jack's bed. Standing in the awkward stillness, the boys were relieved when they heard Mr. Forrester returning from the attic.

"Here you are." Mr. Forrester lowered the thin mattresses into the space between Jack's and Simon's beds. "These will go nicely here, won't they?"

"Thank you, sir," William and Edmund chorused.

"You're welcome, boys. I imagine you're tired and hungry after your travels?"

Edmund's stomach growled in reply.

Mr. Forrester smiled. "Nellie will be putting supper on the table anytime now. Come downstairs and I'll show you to the bathroom so you can wash your hands. It'll be tight, seven of us sharing one washroom, but we'll manage."

William and Edmund followed Mr. Forrester downstairs, all too happy to leave the thick silence of their new bedroom.

The table in the Forresters' dining room had been laid with a damask cloth and seven matching china settings—white, with pink flowers round the rims.

Mr. Forrester seated himself at the head of the table as Mrs. Forrester appeared with a roasting pan of what Edmund hoped was Yorkshire pudding.

"You must be famished, all of you. Sit wherever you like," she said, setting the pan on a trivet.

The children chose seats. "This looks delicious, Mrs. Forrester," William said.

"Auntie Nellie, please!"

"Ehm—Auntie Nellie. Right. Thank you. You needn't have gone to such trouble for us." Truth be told, it felt rather nice to have someone go to trouble for them.

"Oh, it's no trouble, pet! We didn't know we'd have three coming home with us, did we? Lucky I put roast enough for a crowd in the oven this afternoon!"

Edmund's stomach gave a leap of delight.

Heavy footsteps were heard on the stairs, and Jack and Simon appeared.

Simon narrowed his eyes at William. "That's where I sit."

William stood, rapping his knee on the table. "Sorry." He moved to an empty chair on the opposite side.

"Now, boys," Mr. Forrester said, clucking, "we're all just going to need to make some adjustments, aren't we?" Simon and Jack grunted. Mr. Forrester turned back to the table, said a cursory blessing, and began to pass dishes.

Anna swallowed her first bite. "It's delicious, Auntie Nellie. Thank you."

Mrs. Forrester smiled. "Uncle Peter is a butcher, you see, so we're well placed when it comes to meat, even with it going on the ration and all."

Edmund wondered whether this was fair, exactly, that the village butcher should be above the rationing scheme, but as the tender roast melted in his mouth, so did any misgivings he might have had.

Mr. Forrester took a heaping forkful. "You'll want to write your postcard to your parents, won't you, children? Let them know where you are? What are their names, your parents?"

Here we go, William thought. He took a deep breath. "Their names were Ellen and David, but they've both passed away. We've been raised by our grandmother . . . Eleanor." This was not a lie, he reasoned. He had simply neglected to mention the fact of the grandmother's no longer being part of the arrangement, living-wise.

Mrs. Forrester clasped her hands over her chest. "Heavens, losing your parents at such young ages. What a blessing your grandmother must be to you."

All three children looked at their plates. "Yes, ma'am."

"You'll want to let her know you're safely arrived. Would you like me to telephone and speak to her myself?"

It took William a moment to answer. "Oh . . . thank you, ma'am. But—no, thank you . . . the—the postcard will be just fine."

"She's pretty independent, our grandmother," Edmund added.

Seated on Edmund's right, Jack turned to him and wrinkled his nose. "What's that smell?" Edmund froze as Jack leaned closer. "It smells sour," he said. "Is that you?"

"Jack," Mrs. Forrester said, "you're imagining things, I think."

"I'm not," Jack said. "It smells of . . . it smells of . . . of sick."

The silence became a living thing hovering above the table, heaving its hot, foul breath down Edmund's back. He wanted to dissolve into nothingness, to sprout wings and fly through the dining room window. Anything, he thought, to avoid this humiliation.

William cleared his throat. "Edmund gets motion sickness," he said. "He was ill on the journey." He could see his brother's face go crimson. "We washed up for dinner, but his shirt..." He trailed off. "Sorry." He meant this last for Edmund.

The rest of the table seemed to think it was directed at them. "Nothing to worry about, my boy," Mr. Forrester said. "Happens to all of us at some time or another, doesn't it? I'm sure Auntie Nellie will be able to clean you up. Isn't that right, Nellie?"

"Of course! Poor pets—it must have been a dreadful trip, mustn't it? We'll just give your things a good wash, shall we? And mend those trousers?"

So she'd noticed the hole. Edmund willed the burning in his cheeks to subside. "Thank you, ma'am."

"Can I be excused?" Jack asked.

Simon nodded. "Me too? I seem to have lost my appetite."

"Oh, dear, boys," Mrs. Forrester said. "Of course you may be excused. I'll just wrap your plates and put them in the icebox, in case you're peckish later." She looked at Edmund and whispered, "The boys have sensitive stomachs."

As the Forrester boys rose from the table, Edmund felt Jack's shoe graze his shin in a way that couldn't be accidental.

Mrs. Forrester brightened. "Perhaps you'd all three like baths before bed?"

It is unusual, indeed, to find a child who would *like* a bath, but on this night, Anna, Edmund, and William all welcomed the opportunity. They retrieved their nightclothes from their suitcases and took it in turns to wash off the dust of the road. Mrs. Forrester took Edmund's offending shirt and the remainder of their traveling clothes and set them to wash in a tidy scullery behind the kitchen.

The children emerged from their baths scrubbed and tired, all of them ready for bed. Mr. Forrester bade them good night from his chair in the parlor, where he sat listening to the low chatter of the radio. Mrs. Forrester accompanied them upstairs, where she said good night to the boys, then followed Anna down the hall to her bedroom.

She pulled back the coverlet on the bed. "Heavens, it's been an age since my boys were willing to have me tuck them in. What a treat to have a little one in the house. I hope you'll be happy here, pet."

Anna decided she was willing to forgive the irksome nickname in exchange for being *tucked in,* as Mrs. Forrester put it. She'd never had a proper tucking-in. At school, there was no such thing, of course, and when they were home at school holidays, the grandmother thought the practice vulgar. William had sometimes taken on this most grown-up of responsibilities, and admirably so, but Anna imagined that to be tucked in by an actual grown-up must be an entirely different experience.

Mrs. Forrester pulled the coverlet over Anna's shoulders. "I'm sure you're tired, pet."

Anna yawned. She wondered when the bedtime story would be forthcoming.

"Oh! And I'm sure it won't be necessary, but the Anderson's just out back," Mrs. Forrester said, stepping into the hall. "Pleasant dreams, now." She pulled the door shut behind her.

An *Anderson*—in case you've never heard of one—is a bomb shelter. Many families had dug holes in their back gardens and buried these small metal rooms under the sod in preparation for air raids. Needless to say, the thought did not lend itself to pleasant dreams. Not in the least.

Down the hall, Jack and Simon had returned to their comics and did not look up when the boys entered. Knowing better now than to try to strike up a conversation, William and Edmund simply climbed onto their pallets, sandwiched low between the twin beds of their new foster brothers. William sought Edmund's gaze, but Edmund, who hadn't forgiven his brother for the suppertime betrayal, rolled to his side and closed his eyes. More than ready for the abyss of sleep himself, William sighed and did the same.

In that half-dream place between waking and sleeping, both Edmund and William hoped they were imagining it when they heard one of the twins murmur, "Filthy vackies."

Chapter Five

The children were grateful for the night's sleep. Indeed, the Forresters' blackout shades would have allowed them all to sleep in, but Mrs. Forrester's singsong voice in the hall alerted them that it was time to get up. Simon and Jack didn't stir. Edmund and William dressed quickly, grabbed their rucksacks for school, and slipped down the hall to Anna's room. There, they found her dressed as well, sitting on the bed while Mrs. Forrester brushed her hair.

"Good morning, boys! I hope you slept well?" Mrs. Forrester set Anna's hairbrush on the bedside table.

"Very well," William said. "Thank you, ma'am."

"Wonderful! And you'll never guess what I found your sister doing when I knocked this morning!"

William and Edmund looked at Anna, who only shrugged.

"Reading!" Mrs. Forrester exclaimed. "Can you imagine?" She beamed at Anna. "Well then," she continued, "I'll have breakfast for you in two shakes of a lamb's tail." With that, she left the room.

William took the cane chair, while Edmund flopped on the bed. "Well done you, Anna. Imagine reading!"

Anna poked her brother with her toe.

William sighed. "I wish we could fit our pallets in here with you."

Anna looked at her brothers. "Are the twins horrid?" She surveyed her bedroom. "If we took out the wardrobe and chair, your pallets might fit."

Edmund shook his head. "Wouldn't give them the satisfaction."

William looked at Anna. "Mr. and Mrs. Forrester do seem nice, though. And she seems awfully glad to have a girl."

"Mmmm," Anna hummed, conceding. "But I wish we were all together. I almost snuck down the hall last night to ask you to tuck me in."

William cocked his head at her. "It looked like Mrs. Forrester was on the job."

Anna didn't wish to complain, sensing that her brothers' situation was far more unpleasant than her own. "She was, but—she didn't do it right."

Edmund sat up. He lacked experience with tucking in as well. If there were a right and a wrong way to do it, this was news to him. "What do you mean?"

"I mean, she didn't tell me a story. All she did was let me know where the Anderson was. And I couldn't very well ask her to tell me something about Mummy and Daddy, could I?"

William rose and joined his siblings on the bed. "It's going to be different, isn't it? But I'll sort out a way to get you tucked in from now on, all right? And I'll tell you loads about Mum and Dad. I thought of something last night, actually."

Edmund and Anna looked at him in anticipation.

"Dad liked his sheets ironed."

Edmund scowled. "That's daft. Why would anyone go to the trouble? You're only going to wrinkle them."

William shrugged. "I don't know." He was not entirely sure himself how the idea had come to him. "I just know that's how he liked them."

"Hmmm," Anna murmured, satisfied.

William produced the postcard given them on the train the day before. "We've got to write this and put it in the post. Miss Collins will worry if she doesn't hear from us."

"I'll do it," Edmund said.

This was uncharacteristically responsible, William thought, but he was glad to have the task taken off him. He didn't much feel like telling the story of their journey just now, and he hadn't spent enough time with the Forresters to know what to say about them.

Edmund did not find himself at such a loss for words. He scratched away for a few minutes, then handed the completed work to William, who read it aloud.

Dear Miss Collins,

Our address is on the front of this card. The train ride was long and I got sick and tore my trousers. Mr. and Mrs. Forrester seem nice enough. She's a good cook, but her lipstick is too pink. He's a butcher and is getting around the rationing scheme somehow but it's all right because it'll mean more meat for us. They have two sons who are horrid, but we'll manage fine. I hope you are having fun with your sister.

Your friend,

Edmund (and Anna and William)

William sighed. "Honestly, Ed."

"What?"

"Is it absolutely necessary to comment on Mrs. Forrester's lipstick?"

Edmund shrugged. "I thought Miss Collins would want to know. Girls care about lipstick."

"I don't," Anna protested. "But you're right that hers is far too pink."

Outnumbered on the lipstick issue, William carried on with his critique. "And you don't sign a letter to an old lady 'Your friend.' "

"How am I supposed to sign it?"

" 'Sincerely'? 'Fondly'? 'Cordially'?"

"I'm eleven. I would never actually say any of those words."

"I'm only a year older, and I would."

"Well, that's the difference between you and me, isn't it?"

One of many, William thought, resigning himself to Edmund's note.

As the children ate breakfast, Mrs. Forrester outlined the plan for the day. "They've made arrangements for evacuated children to have lessons in the morning." *To take the burden off,* Anna thought, indignant. "And then the WVS will have sandwiches and milk for you in the village hall, all right?" The children nodded, swallowing their fried eggs and bacon. "Simon and Jack are on summer holiday, but they'll be glad to show you the way to the school this morning."

This bit seemed highly dubious to the children, but they thanked Mrs. Forrester for breakfast and settled in to wait for the twins. Mrs. Forrester called twice from the dining room to no avail, then bustled upstairs to retrieve her sons.

They appeared some minutes later, rumpled and scowling.

"Come on," Jack grunted at Anna, Edmund, and William. "What are you waiting for?"

"Jack and Simon will be excellent guides," Mrs. Forrester said, "but I'll come to collect you at the village hall this afternoon, shall I?" She held the door wide for them. "Just to make sure you've learned the way?" The children nodded as she waved goodbye to the five of them, then closed the door.

At this, Simon raised his eyebrows at his brother and gave a leering grin. The two of them took off at a run. "Keep up!" Jack shouted over his shoulder.

Given no alternative, our threesome gathered themselves and ran after Jack and Simon, who got to the end of the lane and picked up speed as they turned left. Reaching the corner themselves, William, Edmund, and Anna turned, keeping their unwilling guides in their sights. The twins passed several corners before banking right at a decrepit cemetery. William and Edmund reached the graveyard first, from which point they could see Jack and Simon some way ahead, making a left at the far side of a green.

The boys put their hands to their knees, gasping, as they waited for Anna to catch up to them. "Come on, slowpoke!" Edmund shouted. "We're losing them!"

Anna arrived, her cheeks red with exertion, or anger. More likely both.

" 'S'all right." William rolled his eyes at his siblings. "I'll run ahead to that next corner and see if I can see them."

Edmund had no intention of being left behind. "I'm coming, too!"

Anna took off after her brothers, understandably unwilling to be left alone next to a cemetery.

By the time the children arrived at the far end of the green, Jack and Simon were nowhere in sight.

Coughing with exhaustion, the children wiped perspiration from their foreheads and continued down the lane, hoping they might pass someone who could offer directions. Neat rows of houses soon gave way to businesses . . . they recognized the Slug and Cabbage from the day before. The village was stretching itself awake, the greengrocer and baker opening their doors to the morning. William spotted a newsagent's, where he was able to get directions to the village school at last.

The children carried on, peering through shop windows as they went. They passed a butcher shop and assumed it was Mr. Forrester's. A sweet shop on the corner drew Edmund's attention. He looked longingly through the window, wishing they'd been allowed to bring pocket money, but he supposed it would have looked rather suspicious for the three of them to throw coins about anytime they fancied sweets. William pulled him away from the window at last, fearing they'd be late for school.

On the next block, they passed a postbox, where William mailed their postcard to Miss Collins. Not much farther on, a small but solid stone building on a corner overlooking the square bore a sign announcing itself as the village lending library. Anna peered through the window even more hungrily than Edmund had at the sweet shop. She stood on her toes for a better view, making out a warren of shelves stretching from floor to ceiling, crammed with a comforting blur of books. Anna painted a picture of the spot in her mind's eye and filed it away as a place of refuge. Should the need arise.

* * *

Across the square, the village school was easily identifiable by the imposing presence of Miss Carr standing sentry at the door.

She leafed through the roster on her clipboard as the children arrived. "We're making do as we can, given too many children and not enough teachers, so we'll be combining classes. Same room, all three of you. Upstairs, on your left. Mrs. Warren."

The children breathed a collective sigh of relief. All three in one class? Mrs. Warren? Delightful news. Only Edmund felt the tiniest pang at the prospect of sharing a classroom with his older and—it must be said—more academically inclined brother.

The children climbed the stairs and found a door with a paper sign in neat print: MRS. WARREN. They entered to find a hive of boys and girls, and Mrs. Warren calling out for the children to take their seats.

Her eyes lit upon them. "Welcome, children! I was wondering if I might have you lot in my class. Are you all right, then? Have you been billeted together, I hope?"

Glad of her interest, William smiled. "Yes, ma'am."

"And all is well?"

"Yes, ma'am. Thank you. Have you found someplace pleasant?"

Edmund marveled. *Pleasant,* he thought. *Who says* pleasant?

"I have," Mrs. Warren replied. "I'm billeted with a lovely old couple not far from here." She glanced over the children's heads and took in the restless students behind them. "Find seats." She winked. "Time for school."

The children took seats near the back of the room, Anna's next to the recipient of Edmund's chocolate from the day before. He was wearing the same clothes he had worn then, but his pink cheeks had the look of a recent scrubbing, and the raw patch under his nose shone with some sort of ointment. Anna introduced herself in a whisper.

"I'm Hugh," the boy replied. He nodded at Edmund. "Is that your brother?"

"Yes. That's Edmund, and my other brother's William."

Hugh said no more, only looked at Edmund with wide eyes.

As William and Edmund settled themselves, a heavyset boy in front of them turned and introduced himself as Alfie. "You're not from our school, are you?" he asked.

"No," William answered. "We just got evacuated with you."

"Right," Alfie said. "You've come into some luck, being put in Mrs. Warren's class. As have I. Back home, I was in Carr-buncle's class last year. Good thing for us that she's been moved up to lord it over everyone else instead of teaching. Not meant to be with children, that one, if you ask me."

Mrs. Warren clapped her hands. "Good morning, children! Welcome to what will be your classroom until... until... well—you're all most welcome." She cleared her throat. "For those of you who don't know me, I am Mrs. Warren, and I look forward to working with you. Now—I realize it's unconventional to be at school during the summer holidays, and to have nines through twelves together, but there are a lot of things that are unconventional these days, so we'll all just need to make the best of it, won't we?"

A few children grumbled.

"Does anyone have any questions before we begin?"

Frances, the girl who had taken such interest in William during the previous morning's walk to Kings Cross station, raised her hand. "Where are we to go if the Germans attack while we're in school?"

That one gets right to the point, Edmund thought.

Mrs. Warren hesitated. "That's a very good question, Frances, and one that will be—ehm—answered shortly. We haven't yet received the details on air raid precautions."

"But what if the Germans bomb us today?" Frances asked insistently. A smaller girl next to her let out a squeak.

Mrs. Warren seemed to realize that this line of questioning was likely to lead to panic. "Remember, children... the reason we've come here is to be out of harm's way. It is highly unlikely that the Germans would—"

"But what if they did?" Frances asked.

She's a bulldog, Frances is, Edmund thought with no small degree of admiration.

Mrs. Warren sighed and offered a shaky smile. "In the *highly unlikely* event"—she looked at the now-whimpering girl next to Frances—"that we should be bombed this very morning, we shall proceed in an orderly manner down the stairs to the boiler room, where we should be the safest."

William had the distinct impression that Mrs. Warren had made up the boiler room. Not that he blamed her for it. There are times when the making up of boiler rooms is precisely what is necessary. In any case, Frances was satisfied. The girl next to her rubbed at her eyes with her fists.

"Now. Let's begin, shall we?" Mrs. Warren said. "We'll start with geography. Youngest students—my nine- and ten-year-olds—if you would please bring your chairs to the front of the class." There was a scraping of chair legs as she continued. "Elevens, please retrieve pencil and paper from the shelves under the windows and copy the European capitals from the board. Twelves, you're each to collect a geography textbook from the bookcase near the door. Please take notes on the chapter titled 'Understanding Topography.' And please take care with the materials, as they aren't ours!"

Thus the school day began. Grousing about school in June notwithstanding, the evacuees were glad of the familiarity of a classroom, where well-worn textbooks released a comforting perfume of ink and must. Their pages spoke of the past, a reminder that the battered old world had whirred for a very long time indeed, and that even this latest buffeting would likely be withstood.

Geography gave way to mathematics, then reading and writing, and with that, the children's first day of school in the country was done. They returned books to shelves, then followed Mrs. Warren downstairs to the entry hall, where other evacuees were gathered. Miss Carr directed the restless regiment down the street to the village hall, where the good ladies of the WVS had laid out sandwiches and milk.

Mrs. Forrester arrived to collect Anna, Edmund, and William just as they finished their lunches. She surveyed the teeming hall until her eyes lit on her charges. She picked her way over children sitting cross-legged on the floor. "There you are, you three! Was it a good day at school? Did the boys help you find your way this morning?"

William chose to respond to only the first question. "School went well, thanks. And thank you for coming to collect us."

"Happy to, pet. I had some shopping to do, but the lines are dreadful. I still need to register your ration books with the greengrocer, and while I'm there I'll see whether there are any onions this week. Shall we do that together?"

The children wondered whether this was meant as an actual question. Perhaps it was one of those statements adults put as a question when they only mean to inform one that one is going onion shopping.

Edmund ventured a response. "Actually—er—our teacher's given us an assignment. We're to read something." He glanced sideways at his siblings. "Would it be all right if we went to the lending library while you're at the greengrocer?"

Anna and William gaped at their brother, delighted by the imaginary assignment he had conjured. Fibs, you must know, are entirely acceptable when they serve the purpose of getting one to the library.

"The lending library!" Mrs. Forrester looked as though the very notion had never occurred to her. "Goodness, such a thing! The only books we have in the house are those comics the boys love so. Yes, of course, children—you go and make your selections, and I'll retrieve you once I've done the shopping. Good?"

Edmund grinned. "Good."

Chapter Six

William pushed his shoulder into the heavy door of the lending library. It gave way with a satisfying creak. Inside, the children were greeted by the sort of cool and reverent silence known only to places that house books—well, and perhaps artwork and religious artifacts. Mismatched bookcases stood back to back and side to side, making raucously wobbly passageways of words. A fireplace in the corner was unlit on this warm afternoon, but the collection of overstuffed chairs gathered around it was no doubt delightful in winter. The children followed a sign pointing them to LITERATURE AND FICTION, then another to CHILDREN'S BOOKS.

And they were home.

William, Edmund, and Anna knew, somewhere deep in the place where we know things that we cannot say aloud, that they had never lived in the sort of home one reads about in stories—one of warmth and affection and certainty in the knowledge that someone believes you hung the moon. The grandmother had provided for them. When they were small, before they'd been sent off to boarding school, there had been kind nannies. Miss Collins had always been dear and affectionate. But affection is not the same thing as proper family love. This sort of love, the children knew only from one another—and from books. Over many pages, each of them had cobbled together a sense of what the family of their dreams might look like.

When Edmund thought about such things, there was a good deal of swashbuckling involved. His storybook father was a cowboy in the Wild West, though he did some pirating when his travels took him seaward. Mum was not much different. She cared little for the washing of ears—or of anything, come to that—and she allowed him both his own horse and his own rifle. Edmund's only nod to tradition was that his storybook mother was the greatest cook this side of the Rio Grande—wherever that was.

In William's vision, cookery was also a priority, though the dishes he dreamt of were less fanciful than his brother's. Where Edmund envisioned chocolate cake for breakfast, William wished for a perfectly poached egg on buttered toast—served in bed if he was ill, and in the garden if the weather was fine. The storybook mums and dads he coveted were the reliable ones. The ones most likely to think it wrong for a boy of twelve to be responsible for anything more than excelling at his studies, keeping his bedroom tidy, and being polite when company came to call.

Oddly—or perhaps not oddly at all if you give it some

thought—the mum Anna pictured was not unlike William. She was kind, of course. She read stories—that goes without saying—and she was comfortable to sit upon while she read them. She abided no nonsense unless nonsense was precisely what was required. She was there with a fervent embrace when a fervent embrace was the only thing that could make it better. And she was there with—well, she was *there.*

"Can I help you?"

All three startled at the voice behind them, turning to find a woman looking at them expectantly. Her chestnut hair was pulled back in a low bun. She wore a nubby cardigan over a delicately-flowered dress. The pile of books balanced in her arms suggested that this might be the librarian.

"We were just looking," William answered.

The woman's voice was soft—whether it was in her nature or something required of a librarian, the children couldn't tell. "We specialize in *just looking.* Are you some of the children who've come from London? I don't believe I've seen you before."

William nodded. "Yes, ma'am. We arrived yesterday."

"Well, welcome. Will you be wanting library cards?"

"Yes, ma'am. Would that be possible?"

"Certainly. Guest bibliophiles are quite welcome."

While she wasn't sure of the precise definition of *biblio-phile,* Anna was certain that it meant something she wanted to be.

"Well, carry on choosing your books," the librarian continued, "and when you've made your selections, come to the desk and I'll have cards for you to fill out." With that, the woman retreated with her pile of books.

The children set to browsing. Anna and Edmund chose quickly and sank to the floor to delve into their selections. William took longer. While he would never admit that Edmund was right, his choice of the *Britannica* from the nursery shelf back in London had been shortsighted. Now that he faced the reality of life as an evacuee, William did not want to read about the Polish astronomer *HEVELIUS, Johannes,* even if the man *had* mapped the surface of the moon. He found he had no interest whatsoever in the poetry of *HOPKINS, Gerard Manley.* William wanted escape, not enlightenment, and he scoured the shelves for something that might fit the bill.

Perhaps twenty minutes passed. Perhaps two hours. Anna looked up from her book at her brother's still-empty hands. She unfolded herself from her seat on the floor and stretched. "Mrs. Forrester's likely going to be here soon. Shouldn't you choose something?"

William shrugged. He offered a hand to haul Edmund up, and the three made their way to the main reading room, where they found the librarian at the lending desk.

Edmund handed over his book first. The librarian grinned. "*The Incredible Adventures of Professor Branestawm,*" she said, riffling the pages. "I haven't read it. Will you tell me about it once you've finished?" Edmund nodded. The woman turned to Anna, who was holding up her choice—*The Yellow Fairy Book.* "Is this your first *Fairy* book, or have you read any others?"

Anna answered with some pride that she had read the *Lilac.* "And I'm also reading *A Little Princess,*" she said, "but it's the only one I brought from home, so I want to make it last." She was confident that a lady who worked in a library must be interested in such details. "Edmund brought *The Count of Monte Cristo,* and William brought the encyclopedia."

The woman stamped Anna's book. "You're reading the encyclopedia?"

William nodded, his cheeks warm.

"All of it?"

"I'm only up to *H.*"

"As in *HORRIBLY boring,*" Edmund said.

The librarian raised her hand to her mouth to hide a smile. "Well. Extraordinary, all of you," she said. "You must be true connoisseurs."

Anna couldn't for the life of her say what *connoisseur* might mean, but it sounded awfully elegant.

The librarian looked at William's empty hands. "Did you not want to borrow anything today, then?"

He shrugged. "I couldn't decide."

"Hmmm," murmured the library lady. She narrowed her eyes at him. "Have you read any Agatha Christie?"

William shook his head.

"She's not meant for children, typically, but it seems to me that a boy who chooses to read the encyclopedia isn't your typical child."

"That's certain," Edmund said under his breath.

The librarian grinned. "Shall we find one for you?"

"Thanks very much," William said, following the woman to the mysteries and feeling a thrill that his selection was coming from outside the children's section.

The librarian pulled a book from the shelf and handed it to him. "It's one of my favorites. A train full of people trapped in a snowstorm with a murderer aboard."

William's spine tingled. "A murderer?"

The lady raised her eyebrows. "Indeed."

William smiled. "It sounds perfect."

"Enjoy it," the librarian said. "Well done you, on the encyclopedia. I hope you keep it up, but I suppose when one is set adrift in an unknown land, a bit of diversion might not be such a bad thing?"

William's eyes widened at the lady's mind reading. "Thanks very much."

He followed the librarian through to the main reading room. Mrs. Forrester had arrived, sagging under the burden of her parcels. "Ah, there you are, children," she said. "Lovely. You've chosen, then?"

"Yes, ma'am," Anna replied. "We just need to get our library cards."

Mrs. Forrester's eyes lit on the librarian. "Mrs. Müller."

"Good afternoon, Nellie," the library lady said. "I hope you and Peter and the boys are keeping well?" She glanced at the children. "I gather you've quite a billet-full, haven't you?"

"Indeed," Mrs. Forrester replied. Her usual chirpiness seemed to have drained from her. "Will you be needing anything from me, Mrs. Müller, to complete the children's transaction?"

The librarian—Mrs. Müller, the children supposed—offered them a tight smile. "Just your names, children, and your signature as the responsible adult, Nellie."

William spelled their names for the librarian, who took down the information, then looked at Mrs. Forrester. "And your address, please, Nellie. I don't recall that your family has library cards on file for that information?"

Mrs. Forrester shifted her parcels. "No." She filled in the cards, then looked back at the librarian. "If that will be all?" The chill in her voice was evident.

"It will." The librarian's smile heaved under the weight of its own effort. "Enjoy your books, William, Edmund, Anna."

The children liked that the woman had already committed

their names to memory. A librarian seemed a good sort of friend to have.

Back at the Forresters', the children were eager to retire for some reading. They were nearly to the stairs when Mrs. Forrester called out from the parlor that perhaps Anna might like to sit with her and look at the latest *Woman's Weekly*.

Edmund snorted.

Anna watched her brothers retreat up the stairs. "Ehm, thanks, Mrs.—Auntie Nellie. That sounds lovely."

The twins were nowhere to be found, and about this Edmund and William had no complaints. They settled in for a delightful afternoon. William got quite lost in the murder mystery, interrupted only occasionally by Edmund's cackling at his own book. It was nearly five o'clock when the slamming of the front door announced the arrival of Jack and Simon.

"Here we go," Edmund muttered.

The twins could be heard barreling up the stairs, but they went silent at the bedroom door. Crossing their arms, they appraised William and Edmund.

"We're letting you sleep in our room," Jack barked, "but that's it. Get your things and shove off."

Edmund and William rose, their cheeks burning. William somehow managed a measured response. "Where are we to go, then?"

"I'm sure your sister and her dollies would like some company down the hall."

Edmund's blood boiled as William gathered their books and suitcases, then handed Edmund his, steered him into the hall, and closed the door.

"They can't do that!" Edmund growled.

"The thing is," William whispered, "I think they can. What are we going to do, tell the Forresters their precious boys are monsters?"

Edmund considered this, chest heaving, as Anna appeared at the top of the stairs. The trio made for her room, where the boys told her their tale of woe.

"We'll just make this our room, then, for all but sleeping," she said. "I don't want to be alone, anyhow."

The boys sat, Edmund on the floor and William on the bed.

"How was Auntie Nellie's *Woman's Weekly*?" Edmund asked with undisguised glee. His sister's misfortune was a welcome distraction from his own.

"Even worse than you could imagine," Anna said with a huff.

"Oh, I could imagine it being pretty bad."

Anna set her shoulders. "She read me a story about how to get on without nylon stockings now the war's made them so tough to get."

The boys couldn't find words adequate to this subject.

"You're supposed to draw a line down the backs of your legs with an eye pencil, to look like a seam," Anna explained.

William wrinkled his nose. "You're to draw on your legs?"

"That's not the worst bit," Anna said, sighing. "She wants *me* to draw the line on for her."

Edmund thought this might be the best thing he had ever heard. The bleak exchange with the Forrester boys forgotten, he could hardly speak for laughing.

Anna scowled. As it would be her holding the pencil, she failed to see the humor.

At supper that night, Jack and Simon wasted no time launching an assault.

"Charlie says loads of the vackies have got nits," Jack said, swallowing a mouthful of potatoes.

"Now, son, don't say *vackies,*" Mr. Forrester admonished. "Anna and Edmund and William are our guests."

Jack offered Edmund a patronizing grin. "I'm not saying *they've* got nits, Dad."

"Of course you're not, darling." Mrs. Forrester clucked.

Edmund's fists were clenched. "We haven't."

"Certainly you haven't, children," Mr. Forrester said. "Certainly. It's only that—well, you must understand that we read about an awful lot of problems with some of the children who were evacuated last fall. It was all over the papers, you know."

Edmund disregarded William's nudge under the table. "We were checked before we left London. We aren't lousy."

Mrs. Forrester gave a tight smile. "Of course you aren't."

Edmund gritted his teeth and spent the remainder of the meal soothing his nerves with the thought of the Dairy Milk bars he had brought from home.

But after supper, when the children retreated to Anna's room and he clicked open the latch of his suitcase, he found . . . nothing.

Well, not nothing. The socks, shirts, trousers, and other boring bits were in there. But no Dairy Milk, no jelly babies. Nothing that mattered.

"That's it," he said, eyes alight. "They're in for it now. They've taken my sweets!" He slammed the suitcase shut and stormed out the door.

"Edmund . . . ," William said, knowing he ought to stop his brother before he did something rash. But Edmund was already halfway down the hall. William and Anna followed, their hearts sick for their brother. The stealing of sweets, after all, is an act committed only by those with unspeakably black souls.

Edmund flung open the door to the twins' bedroom. It swung back on its hinges, hitting the wall behind with a terrific thwack.

"Where are they?" he bellowed.

Jack and Simon sat up from their comics. "Where are

what?" Simon asked. He smiled the most unpleasant smile. "And don't bang the door. Mum hates that."

"There were loads of sweets in my suitcase and they're all gone!" Edmund shouted. "Where've you put them?"

Jack and Simon didn't have time to answer before Mrs. Forrester appeared in the doorway. "Whatever is the commotion up here, children?"

Simon shook his head. "I told him not to bang the door, Mum."

Mrs. Forrester looked at Edmund. "What *is* going on?"

Edmund took a deep breath. "I brought sweets from home, and they're gone."

Mrs. Forrester looked from one to the other of them. "What do you mean?"

"I mean they're gone," Edmund answered. "They were in my suitcase this morning, and now they're gone." He glared at the twins. "They must have hidden them somewhere unless they've already eaten the lot."

Mrs. Forrester's reply left little doubt as to where her allegiance lay. "Jack and Simon would never do such a thing, pet. Perhaps you left your sweets on the train? Or ate more than you realized on your journey?"

"I didn't—" Edmund began.

"That's right," Jack said. "I bet you left them on the train. Bad luck, that."

"They were here—" Edmund started.

Jack cut him off. "You know what, Mum? I've got a bit of pocket money. I'd be glad to buy some sweets for all of us to share."

Mrs. Forrester looked as if she might weep. "Oh, Jack! I don't even know what to say. That's so awfully kind." She turned to Edmund. "See how things work out, pet? Perfectly understandable that you would have left things on the train, in all the commotion."

William answered before Edmund could respond. "You're right, Auntie Nellie. I'm sure that's what happened." He met Jack's and Simon's wicked grins for only a moment before taking Anna's hand and nudging Edmund. "We'll just finish getting ready for bed, then. Good night." He led his siblings down the hall to Anna's room.

Edmund's whisper only just contained his outrage. "What did you say that for?"

"What else could we do, Edmund?"

Edmund's eyes blazed. "You could have believed me!"

"I do believe you! But wasn't it obvious that *she* wasn't going to?"

Edmund's anger diminished not one bit. "Yes, but that's not the point."

"No. You're right. It's not the point," William whispered. "The point, Edmund, is that the three of us have nowhere else to go. I'm sorry about your sweets, truly I am, but I'm trying to keep us from getting chucked out! Can't you see that?"

Just then, Edmund couldn't see anything other than the unspeakable tragedy of his loss, but he gave up the fight and collapsed in a heap on his sister's bed.

William's words rang in Anna's ears. *Nowhere else to go.* She felt tears coming but sensed that her brothers' row had left no more space in the room for such things. She swallowed. "Tell me something, William."

"What?" William turned. "Didn't I just tell you something this morning?" The evening's drama had tapped him of his reserves, but when he saw his sister's face, the tears so close, he set to work on a new memory. "Right. Well, there's plenty more." He squeezed Anna's fingers as he thought for a moment.

"Dad hated radishes."

Anna nodded slowly. "I hate radishes, too." She turned to Edmund. "What about you, Edmund?"

Her brother folded his arms over his face and said nothing. It takes some time to let go of anger, especially when sweets are involved.

CHAPTER SEVEN

As their first week in the countryside marched on into a second, the children's days took on a familiar sort of order. They woke early and ate breakfast with Mrs. Forrester as Jack and Simon slumbered on. Mr. Forrester was often gone before breakfast, off to the shop to receive the day's deliveries and manage the growing lines for meat. Before the children left for school, Mrs. Forrester paid a great deal of attention to Anna's hair. Edmund expressed concern that such enthusiastic brushing might result in baldness. Anna hoped he was wrong.

The children knew their own way to and from school by now and looked forward to Mrs. Warren's reassuring welcome each morning. They had learned the names of their classmates, most of whom seemed to be settling in nicely to their new billets. Alfie reported that his foster mother did a bit too much praying for his liking. Frances complained about the unfamiliar foods here in the country. Hugh asked Edmund what their billet was like.

"Fine," Edmund said. He shot a look at his siblings. "I

mean, not sure if it's someplace we'd like to stay forever, but . . ."

William closed his eyes. Anna widened hers.

Evenings were spent gathered round the radio, anxiously awaiting news of the war. Most nights, it seemed a distant thing, but as June neared July, it crept closer. They listened in silence as the voice of Winston Churchill, the new prime minister, crackled through the wooden box, telling them that France had fallen to the Nazis.

Mr. Forrester shut off the radio. He shook his head. "Very bad news indeed."

"What do you mean, Uncle Peter?" Edmund asked.

"That leaves just the Channel between us and the Jerries, my boy. That's only thirty miles or thereabouts, if you're in Dover."

Anna grabbed William's hand. "How far is Dover from here?" she whispered.

"Far," William said.

Edmund looked at Mr. Forrester. "Do you think the Germans will attack us?"

He shook his head. "Likely not here, Edmund. They'd have little interest in the countryside, is my bet. But the big cities . . . London . . . I suppose evacuation was a good idea, isn't that right, you lot?"

The children swallowed at the sudden realness of it all.

Mrs. Forrester sighed. "I wonder if we'll still be able to get French perfume."

Anna, Edmund, and William chose a rainy Monday to return their books to the lending library on their way home from school. Mrs. Müller was at the desk when they arrived. She put down her knitting when she saw them.

"Hello, children... lovely to have you back! Did *The Yellow Fairy Book* meet with your approval, Anna?"

Anna was pleased that the librarian remembered both her name and the book she had borrowed. "Yes, Ma'am. Thank you very much."

"Which was your favorite of the fairy stories?"

Anna thought for a moment. She wanted her answer to be the right one. "I loved them all—well, nearly all—'The Steadfast Tin Soldier' was awfully sad. I suppose I loved 'The Tinder Box' best."

The librarian nodded. "I loved that one as well. Especially the part about the dog with eyes as big as saucers."

Anna thumbed eagerly through the book and produced a picture of the dog. The librarian ran a finger over the page and smiled, then turned to William, took the Agatha Christie from him, and marked it as returned.

"Well?" she asked.

William grinned. "Just what I was looking for."

"I'm glad," she said. "She's got loads more."

Edmund placed his book on the desk next. "And Edmund," the librarian said, "how was it?"

"Excellent," Edmund said. "Anna wants to read it next."

The librarian deftly rechecked the book for Anna. "I've just got a new one in this week, Edmund. I wonder if you might like to be first reader with it?"

Edmund liked the role of "first reader"—of first anything, come to that.

"It's called *The Enchanted Wood,*" Mrs. Müller continued, producing a book from a cart behind her. "It appears to be about three children who move from the city to the country." She smiled.

"Just like us," Anna said, beaming.

"Just like you," the librarian whispered. "And if the title is to be believed, I'm assuming they must happen upon some sort of enchanted wood." She winked. "Are you game for the assignment, Edmund?"

He smiled broadly and nodded.

The librarian marked the book as borrowed and handed it over the desk. "Would you like to borrow another as well, William?"

"Yes, ma'am. Please."

"Excellent. Let me know if you're in need of suggestions." With that, William set off to begin the hunt. Edmund followed him. Anna lingered by the lending desk.

"How is our Little Princess faring?" Mrs. Müller asked.

Anna wondered whether the librarian remembered what everyone was reading, or whether she was a special case. She hoped she was a special case. "She's quite well, only I think Miss Minchin is just being nice to her because she's got gobs of money."

"She is dreadful, isn't she?"

"Mmmm," Anna murmured. "Well, I don't want to keep you from your work." Really, in her secret heart, Anna wanted very much to keep Mrs. Müller from her work.

The librarian smiled. "The delightful thing is that talking about books actually *is* my work." She folded her hands. "So I'm glad of the company of such an astute reader."

Anna squinted. "What's *astute*?"

"It means clever."

"Oh." A blush of pride bloomed on Anna's cheeks. "Thank you."

It was at this moment that a white-haired woman pushed open the creaky old door. Shaking out her umbrella and depositing it in the stand by the entry, she looked toward the lending desk.

"Hello, Nora," she said. "I was hoping to chat with you."

Anna retreated to the chairs by the fireplace and opened her book, rather put out that the old woman had interrupted her *astute* conversation with the librarian.

"It's lovely to see you, Florence," Mrs. Müller said. "Are you here for a book?"

"I'm not, Nora—though I wouldn't mind perusing some cookbooks. So much food is unavailable these days, I'm in need of some suggestions as to how to get dinner on the table."

"You're here about dinner?"

The woman chuckled. "I suppose I am, in a way." She undid the top button of her raincoat. "You know as well as anyone, Nora, that with the war stopping food imports, we're all called upon to produce more of our own. I thought perhaps you'd consider doing a little gardening talk in the fall for the ladies of the village—and men, what's left of them?"

Mrs. Müller's voice went softer than usual. "Me?"

The lady nodded. "However much some of us may hate it, we're going to need to dig up our hydrangeas and boxwoods and put potatoes in their places. You've such a fine vegetable plot already, I think people could benefit from your expertise. You know—preparing their gardens to produce something next spring?"

"It's kind of you to say so, Florence . . . really, it is, but—"

"I'm not being kind, Nora. It's a fact. You grow more than anyone else in the village. Who better than you to offer advice?"

"Thank you, Florence. It's only . . ." Mrs. Müller's voice dropped so low that Anna had to tilt her head to hear. She knew she ought not to eavesdrop, but there is nothing so compelling as the sound of a whisper just within one's reach.

"I'm not exactly the most sought-after person in the village, am I?" the librarian said.

"Rubbish from a few small-minded people," the old lady replied. "You've done nothing wrong, Nora. Quite the opposite, in fact. It's you that's *been* done wrong."

"I know that, Florence. Well—on good days I know it. But it often feels as if it's more than just a handful of hard-hearted souls."

"Which is precisely why I think you ought to do this. Talk to people. Let them see you for the good soul you are. Show them you're doing your bit."

"I am doing my bit—or trying to. You know I am." Anna heard a tremble in the librarian's voice.

"I do, Nora. I do. Heavens, the scarves and socks you've knitted for our boys . . ."

William and Edmund appeared, selections in hand. "You haven't got very far, have you, Anna?" William said, noting that her book was only opened to the first page.

"What?" Anna said. "Oh, I haven't, have I? I was chatting with Mrs. Müller, and then I just . . ."

Anna wished she hadn't missed the end of the ladies' conversation, but by now Mrs. Müller was showing the older woman her knitting. She introduced the children when they approached. "The Pearces are staying with the Forresters," she said, "and they've already become my most astute customers."

Anna beamed—the boys did, too, come to that. Anna guessed they must already know what *astute* meant.

On the walk back to the Forresters', Anna told her brothers of the ladies' conversation.

William looked at her. "Anna! You know better than to eavesdrop."

"I know!" Anna cried. "But I was already there in the room! What was I to do?"

"I wonder what she's done to make people dislike her," Edmund said, kicking a pebble as they walked.

"She hasn't done anything," Anna said. "The old lady said so."

"She must have done something."

Anna's brow wrinkled. "It's something about the war. The old lady said if Mrs. Müller gave a gardening presentation, she could show she was *doing her bit.*"

"What could a library lady do that was against the war effort?" William asked.

Edmund considered this. "Stock too many books written by Germans?" He looked at his sister. "Didn't that fairy story book you just read have some stories by the brothers Grimm, Anna?"

"I don't—"

"They're German, I think." Edmund grinned wickedly

at her. "Can you be arrested for that? Reading stories by Germans?"

Anna narrowed her eyes at her brother.

"They're probably looking for you right now, ready to throw you in the clink." Edmund kicked at the pebble and missed, stubbing his toe on the roadway.

Anna gave a tiny smile. *The clink,* she thought. *Honestly.*

Chapter Eight

July brought news of bombings in Wales, Cornwall, and Dover.

"The Germans are hitting the ports," Mr. Forrester said, "trying to frighten us into capitulation."

"What's *capitulation*?" Anna asked.

William took her hand. "It means surrendering."

"We won't do that, will we?" Anna whispered.

"Of course not, stupid," Simon said, narrowing his eyes at her.

"Don't call my sister stupid," Edmund warned.

"Children—" Mrs. Forrester started, but Mr. Forrester cut her off.

"We won't capitulate. Not if Churchill has anything to say about it."

Indeed, Mr. Churchill did have something to say about it. The children listened to his rumbling voice on the radio as he said he would *rather see London laid in ruins and ashes* than give in to the Nazis.

Anna gulped. *Laid in ruins and ashes.*

"I'll tell you one thing," Mr. Forrester continued, "I may be a couple of years past being called up for soldiering"—*and perhaps a couple of pounds too fat,* Edmund thought—"but I'm going to join up with the Local Defense Volunteers straightaway."

"Oh, Peter—do you really think—" Mrs. Forrester began.

"I do, Nellie," he said, holding up a hand to indicate there would be no argument. "It's not as if I'll be in any great danger with the Local Defense. As near as I can tell, most of what I'll be doing is taking down road signs to confuse the Jerries. Perhaps if I'm lucky I'll get to manage some unexploded bombs?"

Anna thought this sounded anything but lucky.

Edmund tended to agree with Mr. Forrester. "How do you do that?" he asked.

Mr. Forrester chuckled. "I don't rightly know yet, but I expect they'll train me." He took Mrs. Forrester's hand. "You can do your bit as well, Nellie . . . they're turning cooking pots into planes, you know."

Mrs. Forrester glanced toward her kitchen. "First nylon stockings, now this."

The next day's post brought a letter. Mrs. Forrester handed it to William. "This must be from your grandmother, children."

"That would be something, wouldn't it?" Edmund muttered.

The children made their way upstairs to Anna's room, where William opened the envelope and read aloud.

Dear William, Edmund, and Anna,

I was delighted to receive your note and to know that you are all safe. I am forwarding your information to Mr. Engersoll, who will no doubt be glad of it as well.

I'm happy to hear that the Forresters seem kind people. Perhaps their boys are just adjusting to the new arrangements and by now you'll have made friends? I do hope so. And I wouldn't worry too much about lipstick, Edmund. One must choose one's battles in this life.

I am well here with my sister. I shan't say we are "having fun," as you put it, but we are comfortable enough.

Sending you all my very best wishes and hoping for the best with the "preposterous plan."

Yours,
Kezia Collins

"Her name's Kezia?" Edmund said. "It doesn't really suit her, does it?"

William was dumbfounded. "We've lived with her our whole lives and you didn't know her name was Kezia?"

"Well, it's not as if we were on a—what do you call it? First-base names?"

"First-name basis. But you still could have known her first name."

"Well, I know it now," Edmund said, "and I still say it doesn't suit her."

Anna had to agree. "It doesn't."

William sighed.

Edmund thought for a minute. "She's more of an Agnes." He thought some more. "Maybe Lavinia." He nodded, the matter decided. "Yeah. That's it. Lavinia."

Some afternoons after lunch, the teachers took the evacuees on outings. The children loved these rambles—skipping rocks in the stream that bordered the village to the north one week, watching sheep graze on the hill beyond the train station the next.

But none of these regular, ordinary outings compared with the surprise that awaited the children in late summer. One Friday, classes were let out early and the evacuees found themselves standing outside the village hall, waiting for buses that would take them to a theater in Coventry to see *Pinocchio.*

The children were beyond delighted. Anna, Edmund, and William had only ever been to see a movie once before, and all three agreed that one could hardly count seeing *Lassie from Lancashire* with Miss Collins.

Alfie was incredulous. "You never saw *The Wizard of Oz*?"

The children shook their heads.

Frances crossed her arms. "What about *Snow White and the Seven Dwarfs*?"

"No," Anna said.

"Why not?" Alfie asked.

Edmund shrugged. "Our grandmother doesn't really care for the cinema."

As the buses arrived, Anna couldn't stop herself from jumping up and down at the excitement of it all. Edmund shoved in front of her to be first on the bus.

William followed him. "We should sit in front, Ed—with you by a window so you don't get sick."

Edmund narrowed his eyes at his brother but lowered himself into a window seat in the second row. Anna slid in next to him, and William took the seat behind.

This proved an unfortunate choice, as it was Frances who boarded next. Her eyes glowed as she took the empty seat next to William.

"Ehm—H-hello, Frances," he stammered. "I—ehm—I think Anna wanted to sit there." He looked at his sister, who was quite comfortable and thought it would be terribly awkward to ask Frances to move.

Frances smiled. "She looks fine where she is."

Edmund hung over the back of the seat in delight. "Yeah, Will. Anna'll be fine with me. Don't worry."

William wondered whether it was too late for him to feign illness and flee the bus.

Frances smoothed the folds of her skirt. "Would you like to sit together in the theater as well?"

What to say? *I would rather throw myself under the wheels of this bus than sit next to you in a darkened theater?* "Ehm— thanks, Frances. It's only just . . . I think I should probably sit with my brother and sister, in case they—get scared or something."

Frances's eyes widened. "Oh! That is just darling."

This time it was Anna who peered over the back of the seat. "Scared of *Pinocchio*?"

It was an unexpected relief to William when Miss Carr boarded the bus and announced that she would teach them about Coventry as they made the journey westward. Green fields, browning a bit in the summer heat, passed in a blur as the children caught familiar names and phrases from history. King Richard II . . . King Henry IV . . . the Black Death . . . the Plague . . .

Edmund thought he might nod off for a bit.

"Miss Carr," came the voice of Alfie from the back of the bus, "Coventry's also where Lady Godiva lived, right? My grandad told me."

Miss Carr nodded. "Indeed, Alfred. Lady Godiva did live in Coventry."

"And did she really ride a horse naked?"

Edmund decided against nodding off after all.

"Yes, Alfred," Miss Carr said. "We all know the legend."

A small girl from the middle of the bus raised her hand. Evidently, she did not know the legend. "Why would someone ride a horse naked?"

"That's a fair question, Irene. And I would advise you all that the best way to ride a horse is, in fact, fully clothed." Miss Carr cleared her throat. "Lady Godiva was the wife of a lord, hundreds of years ago. The story goes that her husband was taxing the people unfairly, and when she asked him to be reasonable, he said that he would lower the taxes if she would ride through the streets of Coventry without any clothes on."

An audible gasp made its way through the bus. Frances looked at William, who could think of nobody he would like to look at less when discussing nakedness.

Frances returned her attention to Miss Carr. "So did she?"

"So the story goes, Frances. I'm fairly certain, however—"

Another voice came from the back of the bus. "And could people see her?"

Miss Carr gave a weary sigh. "According to legend...

she sent out a herald to tell the people not to peek. Now—let us get back to—"

"And *did* anyone peek?" Frances asked.

Miss Carr's shoulders sagged. "I don't know, Frances, whether anyone peeked. A poem called 'Godiva,' by Tennyson, tells us that one *low churl* did, and that his eyes shriveled and fell out of his head because of it."

"Excellent," Edmund murmured.

"Children," Miss Carr continued, "I should like to return to the subject of—"

Anna raised her hand in a moment of uncharacteristic boldness. "And did her husband lower the tax?"

Miss Carr nodded. "According to legend, he did."

Anna took this in. "It seems a funny way to make decisions about taxes."

The film was pure magic, even for William, who was—as feared—seated next to Frances. He was fairly certain that, when her hand accidentally brushed his during "When You Wish Upon a Star," it wasn't accidental at all. He crossed his arms over his chest as tightly as he could and was thus able to enjoy himself.

"That Walt Disney is brilliant," Edmund said as the children filed out of the cool, dim theater into the startling afternoon light.

On the way back to the village, William was strategic in

his choice of seats, sandwiching himself between Anna and the window. She fell asleep against his shoulder within a few minutes. Edmund was not long behind her, nodding off in his seat as the bus rumbled on.

The afternoon sun was low by the time the buses shuddered to a stop in front of the school. William gave Anna a nudge and she woke reluctantly, rubbing an eye with her fist. William turned to find Edmund with his head against the window, a thin line of drool making its way from the corner of his mouth.

William shook his brother's shoulder. "We're back, sleepyhead."

Edmund swiped at his mouth with his shirtsleeve. "That was fast."

By now, the children were regular customers at the lending library. They stopped in on their way home, eager for new selections. Mrs. Müller seemed ready to close up shop when they arrived but greeted them warmly. Anna, still rather twitchy with excitement, recounted nearly the entire plot of *Pinocchio*.

"I think she knows the story, Anna," Edmund said.

Mrs. Müller grinned. "I do, but I'm enjoying hearing your sister tell it, just the same."

Anna couldn't resist turning to Edmund with a rather self-satisfied smile.

"It *was* really good," William said. "Just as good as the book."

"Better," Edmund said, then looked at the librarian. "Sorry."

"That's quite all right, Edmund."

"I mean . . . it had songs. The book didn't have songs."

"I understand," Mrs. Müller said, stifling a laugh and turning to Anna. "And what news of our Little Princess? Still taking it slowly?"

"As slowly as I can," Anna said. "At least, I'm trying. But it's hard to put down. Sara's been locked in the attic by that horrid Miss Minchin."

The librarian studied her. "Do you need something a bit less . . . troublesome . . . to read alongside it?"

Anna nodded. The librarian closed one eye, considering. "What about *Anne of Green Gables*?" she asked.

"Is it another orphan story?" Anna asked.

The librarian chuckled. "I suppose there are rather a lot of orphan stories out there."

"Why do grown-ups write so many of them?" William asked.

"I hadn't really thought about it," Mrs. Müller confessed. "Perhaps they think children fancy the notion of living on their own, without adults to tell them what to do. It's quite daft, if you think about it, isn't it?"

"Mmmm," William said. "Daft."

* * *

The torture twins, as Edmund had dubbed them, still hadn't warmed to the presence of their foster siblings. Rather the opposite, truth be told. Since their arrival, Jack and Simon seemed to have made a project of playing tricks on the boys as often as possible. One night, Edmund's toothbrush was nowhere to be found. The next, it was William's comb. Forced, thus, to approach Mr. and Mrs. Forrester about the purchase of new things, the boys simply swallowed and shrugged when asked how such items could possibly go missing.

The worst attack was directed at William, who opened his rucksack at school one morning to find it had been liberally doused with tiny flakes of something that looked like charcoal. Upon closer inspection, the offending substance was determined to be pepper. For days, William was overcome with fits of sneezing when he opened his pack to retrieve something.

Anna shook her head. "You ought to tell Uncle Peter and Auntie Nellie."

"Don't be stupid," Edmund grumbled. "They'd never believe us." It seemed he had come around to this notion since the painful business with the stolen sweets.

"I think they would," Anna said.

Edmund only grimaced. "Mums and dads take the part of their own kids."

"But what if their own kids are awful?"

"Kids are never awful to their own mums and dads. To the mums and dads, they're perfect. And *filthy vackies* like us aren't going to convince anyone otherwise."

"Edmund's right," William said. "The Forresters think Jack and Simon hung the moon."

Anna was taken aback at the phrase she had only ever heard in reference to her own mother. "Must be lovely," she whispered.

Chapter Nine

The end of summer meant the village children's return to school. The evacuees kept their morning routine. The village children took over in the afternoons. Now that the Forrester boys were back in school, they were quick to find things to grumble about.

At dinner one night during their first week back, Jack swallowed a piece of sausage with a dramatic shake of his head. "One of their lot"—he gestured toward William, Edmund, and Anna—"has written *vackies* all over our history books."

"Oh, dear," Mr. Forrester murmured. "Vandalism."

"I know," Simon said. "Something like that would never have happened before they turned up. Shows what we get for sharing our classroom."

Edmund couldn't contain himself. "Why would evacuees write *vackies* on anything?"

Simon shrugged. "Haven't been taught proper manners, I suppose."

"Now, son," Mr. Forrester chided.

Edmund chose to ignore Simon's remark. "I mean," he said, "evacuees don't call themselves *vackies*. It's not exactly a term of—what do you call it, Will?"

"Endearment?" William said.

"Right," Edmund said. "It's not exactly a term of endearment—we don't call ourselves *vackies*, and we don't care for anybody else doing it, so why would we write it in a bunch of history books? That would be like you writing . . . *Simple Simon.*"

"Mum!" Simon whined. "You're not going to let him call me names, are you?"

"I wasn't—" Edmund began.

Mrs. Forrester gave Edmund a grim look. "Edmund. No more name-calling."

"But I wasn't—"

Edmund was silenced by the firm press of William's foot on his own.

"Everything was excellent, Auntie Nellie. Thanks." William rose to clear his plate. Anna followed quickly on his heels, and Edmund, not wishing to be left alone in enemy territory, did the same.

On the seventh of September, news arrived of a massive air attack on London. Gathered round the radio in the Forresters' parlor, the children listened for the names of streets they knew, parks and squares and buildings they'd heard of. Anna wept silent tears at the mention of casualties.

Jack sneered at her. "Don't be such a baby."

"Don't call my sister a baby," Edmund growled.

Mrs. Forrester hushed them. "Boys, please. Do you recognize any of those places, pet?" Anna only shook her head and sniffled.

William grabbed her hand. "They're mostly naming places in South London. We're from further north."

"Even still, pet," Mrs. Forrester said, "what about your grandmother?"

"The—ehm, our g-grandmother's . . . ," William stammered.

Long gone, Edmund thought.

"She's, ehm—with her sister near Watford," William said, recovering himself. "That's well north of the city."

"We're in for it now, aren't we, Dad?" Simon asked. "If they're bombing London?"

Mr. Forrester was ashen. He switched off the radio and wiped his brow. "I don't know, son. I just don't know."

The bombs fell on London again the night after, and the night after that. The children began to meet the nightly radio broadcasts with teeth gritted. On the fifth straight night of bombings, they listened to a reporter in the Piccadilly Tube station describing masses of Londoners seeking shelter a hundred feet underground as bombs wrecked their homes above. On the tenth straight night, they heard news of the sinking of the SS *City of Benares,* whose passengers included a hundred children being evacuated to Canada and the United States. *They're just like us,* William thought. *Only not anymore.*

On the thirty-seventh straight night, they listened as the king's daughter, the young Princess Elizabeth, made her first radio broadcast.

Thousands of you in this country have had to leave your homes and be separated from your fathers and mothers. My sister—Margaret Rose—and I feel so much for you, as we know from experience what it means to be away from those we love most of all. To you, living in new surroundings, we send a message of true sympathy; and at the same time, we would like to thank the kind people who have welcomed you to their homes in the country.

Mrs. Forrester puffed. "Did you ever imagine? The princess—thinking of us?"

Right. Edmund scowled. *She's been up all night, thinking of Nellie Forrester.*

Anna's mind lingered on the bit about missing those we love most of all. *It's easier for us, I suppose,* she thought. *We haven't left parents behind. It's just ourselves.* Perhaps this should have brought some comfort, but Anna found that it only filled her with a hollow sort of ache.

One bright fall afternoon, Mrs. Warren took the children to a hillside on the outskirts of town to forage the last of the wild damson plums.

"Delicious," Edmund murmured. He had come up with an especially sweet one. He lay on his back in the sun with Anna and William, his mouth full of perfect fruit, his hands smeared purple. Nearby, some of the younger boys were busy with sticks, digging on the crest of the hill.

Mrs. Warren called out to them. "Boys, whatever are you doing?"

It was young Hugh who answered. "Setting a trap."

"A trap for what?"

"Hitler."

Mrs. Warren sighed. "Oh, Hugh—"

"We're going to dig a trench," another boy chimed in, "then cover it with branches and such. That way, if the Jerries come, they'll fall in and we'll have 'em trapped."

Mrs. Warren had a vision of an innocent old-age pensioner meeting his death in the children's trench. On second thought, she doubted a gang of children would be able to inflict too much damage on the hillside. "All right, boys. Well done, all of you."

Edmund roused himself and set off down the hill for a second helping of plums. Under one especially fruitful tree, he spotted something that brought a flash of delight to his very soul. Coiled between the roots lay a dead snake. Freshly dead, from the looks of it—the creature retained its jeweled reptilian shimmer. It was missing an eye, which gave Edmund the curious impression that it was winking at him. He glanced around before slipping the creature into his rucksack.

That evening at dinner, even the sharp kicks Edmund received under the table from Jack couldn't dampen his spirits. He chatted with William and Anna about school assignments, with Mr. Forrester about the shortage of bacon. He complimented Mrs. Forrester on the meal, thinking all the while of the snake.

When it was time to get ready for bed, he took his time washing up, a fact duly noted by his siblings as he fiddled with the toothpaste.

"Come on, poky boots," Anna said grumpily.

William, too, was impatient for his turn. "Hurry up, Ed. Where's your head tonight, anyway?"

Edmund hadn't time to answer. Upstairs, one of the Forrester boys was suddenly squealing at a pitch that even Anna couldn't have matched. As they heard Mr. and Mrs.

Forrester bustle up the steps in alarm, William and Anna turned to their brother.

William's eyes were wide. "What did you do?"

Edmund only grinned. "What makes you think I've done anything?"

The children made their way toward the front hall as the screaming upstairs crescendoed, Auntie Nellie joining the chorus. Anna squeezed her eyes shut and tried to imagine what Edmund might have done to cause such a commotion.

The answer came to them as Mr. Forrester stomped past on his way to the front door, the snake in his outstretched hand. Anna recoiled as she watched him throw it into the hedge at the far side of the garden. Mr. Forrester closed the door and stood for a moment, gathering himself.

By now, Mrs. Forrester had come downstairs as well. Her hair was disheveled, her chest heaving. "A snake. A dead snake. In Simon's bed."

Anna gasped. "Oh, my."

A thick stillness filled the foyer. Edmund looked at the floor, grinding his teeth to stifle the giggle that was threatening to escape.

"Any . . . idea . . . how that got there?" Mr. Forrester asked, each word an effort.

William's voice came out a bit squeaky. "No, sir."

"No, sir," Anna said, genuinely appalled at the thought

of a snake in anyone's bed. Even someone as deserving as Simon.

"Nope," Edmund said, just a hair too glib. "No idea, Uncle Peter."

The toxic silence returned. Mrs. Forrester fanned herself with her hand, never taking her eyes from Edmund.

Mr. Forrester considered the children for what seemed an eternity. "Right. Off to bed, all of you." He looked directly at Edmund. "And there'll be absolutely no more nonsense. Do I make myself clear?"

"Yes, sir," the children chorused, and made their way upstairs.

Alone in Anna's room, William glared at his brother.

Edmund offered a lopsided smile. "C'mon, Will. I couldn't just take it all on the chin without doing anything."

William sighed, wishing for just a moment that he had pulled off the trick himself, before coming back to his senses. "This can't end well, Edmund."

For a few days, the twins were shadows of their former selves. Around the dinner table, they offered no complaints about evacuee hygiene. None of Edmund's or William's possessions went missing. Jack and Simon even stepped around the boys' pallets each morning, rather than treading on their pillows.

The first hint of trouble was not recognized as anything that might affect the children personally. Arriving at school one day, Anna, Edmund, and William stopped dead upon entering the front hall. There they found Miss Carr and another teacher staring at the back wall, where the word *VACKIES* had been painted large and inky black.

From where they stood, the children could make out only snippets of the teachers' hushed conversation.

"Whatever shall we . . ."

". . . think it was one of ours . . ."

". . . won't help matters . . ."

By now, the hall had filled with evacuees arriving for the morning's lessons. Gasps could be heard as children took in the ruined entryway. Miss Carr gathered herself and clapped her hands for attention. Her voice was especially shrill. "Children! Upstairs to your classes at once!"

Mrs. Warren greeted the children with a sad smile and a shake of her head.

"Do they think it was one of the evacuees?" William asked.

"I imagine so." Mrs. Warren nodded. "It's ridiculous to think any of you would have done such a thing." She sighed. "However, as guests in town, we are unknown and therefore the easiest to suspect." With that, she bade the children take their seats.

* * *

That afternoon, the children arrived at the library to find a sign on the door: DIG FOR VICTORY! BE PREPARED FOR SPRING PLANTING! Inside, three long tables bore trays of earth, worn spades and gloves, and envelopes announcing their contents in neat block print: CARROTS; PARSNIPS; BEETS; POTATOES; RADISHES. Anna wrinkled her nose.

Mrs. Müller appeared from the cloakroom, shining with perspiration. "Children! I'm afraid things are in a bit of disarray here. I'm to give a gardening presentation for the village . . . you know, encourage people to dig up their boxwoods so there'll be room for radishes, come spring." She wiped her brow with the back of her forearm. "But you're likely not here for a demonstration of radish planting, are you?"

"Anna hates radishes," Edmund said. Anna feared that her taste in vegetables would be found lacking by the librarian, whose opinions mattered rather a lot to her. Even on subjects as irrelevant as radishes.

Mrs. Müller only smiled. "I didn't care for them when I was nine, either. Rather spicy, as vegetables go."

Anna was relieved.

"Don't let us keep you, Mrs. Müller," William said.

The librarian swiped at her brow again. "I suppose I ought to gather the last of my things. Browse to your hearts' content, though—hopefully the gardeners won't be too disruptive."

The gardeners, as it turned out, could not have caused

much disruption, owing to the fact that there were only six of them, the librarian included. Florence—the old lady whom Anna had heard asking Mrs. Müller to do the gardening presentation—arrived first, followed by two women of similar age and a gray-haired couple.

"Nora, dear," Florence said, "I'm afraid Evelyn Norton has engaged a ministry speaker for the WVS at the end of the month. I've only just heard about it, and I'm awfully sorry if it means you don't have the turnout you ought to have today."

The librarian's face fell. "I see."

"Let's just sit for a bit and see who else turns up, shall we?"

"Of course." The quaver in Mrs. Müller's voice was unmistakable. "Make yourself comfortable, please, Florence."

Anna looked up from the shelves to find Mrs. Müller gazing out the window, twisting her fingers. At a quarter past the hour, Anna saw her talk in low tones with the older ladies. She thought her heart would break as she saw the librarian smooth her skirt, look at her wristwatch, and take a deep breath. With a last glance out the window, Mrs. Müller suggested they begin.

"Are children allowed, Mrs. Müller?" William asked.

Edmund resisted the temptation to protest. Anna, meanwhile, thought she had never loved her brother more than just now, as he came to the rescue of the librarian.

Mrs. Müller asked the children to have a seat.

* * *

"Honestly, how many sorts of potatoes does the world really need?" Edmund asked as the three of them made their way back to the Forresters'. The gardening presentation hadn't been as boring as he'd imagined it would be, but perhaps that was no great compliment, as he had imagined it being astonishingly boring.

"Come on, Ed, it wasn't that bad," William said. "And we did Mrs. Müller a good turn. She's been kind to us. I was just returning the favor."

"I liked hearing all the potato names," Anna said. "They sounded like royalty . . . King Edward the Seventh, Duke of York, May Queen . . ."

"Please stop," Edmund pleaded.

"She looked so awfully sad when so few people showed up," Anna said. "What could she possibly have done to make people treat her that way?"

Edmund sighed. "Probably talk about potatoes too much."

At dinner that evening, Anna brought up the gardening presentation.

Mrs. Forrester only pursed her lips. "Whyever would you children go to a gardening presentation?"

"We didn't mean to," William explained. "We were just there looking at books."

"Well," Mrs. Forrester continued, "there's to be a presentation by a ministry representative, and I'm certain it will be superior to anything Mrs. Müller has to offer."

"She seemed to know an awful lot about potatoes," Anna said.

"Indeed," Mrs. Forrester said. It was clear she wished to change the subject.

Jack and Simon were more than happy to oblige her, eager to voice their outrage at the defacement of the school building.

"It won't wash off," Simon informed the table.

"Thick and black, it was," Jack agreed.

"It has to be painted over. The old maintenance man was starting in on it this afternoon."

"It'll take more than one coat, probably," Jack added.

Mr. Forrester shook his head at his dinner plate. "What's this world coming to, anyway? Plenty of things to worry about already, and some hooligan goes and adds this to the mix. Who would do such a thing?"

"Well, Dad, all the teachers say it had to be one of the vackies." Jack looked at his mother. "Sorry, Mum. I mean one of the evacuees. Like Teacher says, a lot of them were never taught proper manners from the start."

Edmund felt the familiar pressure of William's foot on his.

* * *

After supper, the children retrieved their rucksacks to finish their homework in the parlor. Edmund was startled when a small but weighty item fell from his bag and landed with a metallic thwack on the polished floor. It took him a moment to realize what it was, but this he did, just as Mrs. Forrester appeared, wondering at the great thunk she had heard from the kitchen. "If someone has scratched my good wood floors—" she began, then stopped dead.

There, having rolled to nestle against the meeting place between floor and wall, was a tin of black paint.

For a moment Edmund only stared, wondering how somebody's paint had got into his rucksack. As he felt the heat of Mrs. Forrester's gaze, however, the reality of the situation became clear to him.

He looked at her, wide-eyed. "This isn't mine, Auntie Nellie."

Mrs. Forrester didn't even blink.

Edmund turned to Anna and William. "You know it isn't mine! You know I wouldn't!" His cheeks were on fire with the righteous anger of the wrongfully accused.

Mrs. Forrester's face, in contrast to Edmund's, had gone white. She looked from the paint to the children, then back again. Her jaw was so tightly clenched, she seemed to have difficulty forming words. "We—cannot—have—this."

Mr. Forrester arrived and took in the scene, his eyes landing on Edmund.

"It wasn't me!" Edmund cried. "I swear it!" He knew it was futile to blame the twins, but there was no defense other than the truth. "It was Jack and Simon. It must have been! They've had it in for us from the start. Please!"

Edmund cast a desperate look at Mr. Forrester, who looked first at his wife, then at the three children standing barefoot in the parlor. "Children," he said, "you don't really think Jack and Simon would do such a thing?"

Edmund reeled. "They had to have," he fairly screeched. "Because it wasn't me!"

Mrs. Forrester only glared at Edmund, her eyes somehow ice and fire at once.

Mr. Forrester heaved a weary sigh. "We'll have to speak to the school in the morning."

Edmund started. "You're not going to chuck us out, are you?" He glanced at Anna's tear-streaked face and thought his heart would split wide open. Never, when the snake winked at him from beneath the damson tree, had he imagined it would turn out like this—his sister weeping silently by his side as the realization dawned that they were likely about to be without home or guardian. Because of him.

"Nellie and I will need to sort this out between the two of us," Mr. Forrester said, every word an effort. "For now, bed."

The children made their way upstairs under the grim, silent stare of Mrs. Forrester.

Unable to face whatever gloating Jack and Simon might have in store for them, the boys followed Anna to her bedroom. Edmund sat on the floor, William and Anna on the bed. Tears continued to slide, one after the other, down Anna's cheeks. The silence of the room was broken only by her occasional sniffles.

Edmund was unable to bear it. "You both know I didn't do it, right?"

"Sure we do," William answered. "You've been with us the whole time."

Edmund glared at his brother. "But even if I hadn't been with you, you know I wouldn't do such a thing, don't you?"

The pause was just long enough to cut a hole in Edmund's heart.

"Of course," William said.

Chapter Ten

The walk to school the next morning was a solemn and anxious affair. Telephone calls had been made, and while Anna, Edmund, and William hadn't heard what was said, Mr. and Mrs. Forrester's tense silence as they marched beside the children told them all they needed to know. They no longer had a home with the Forresters.

William gripped Anna's hand tightly. Edmund walked behind, his heart pounding. While he had of course had nothing to do with the vandalism, he had done the bit with the snake. And if he hadn't done that—well, it was too late now, he decided. He tried, unsuccessfully, to shake the sick feeling from his stomach.

The glum party was met at the school by Miss Carr and the village's billeting officer, Mrs. Norton. Both women looked at the children severely, evidently believing that their culprit had been apprehended.

Edmund thought this might be his last chance to defend himself. "Miss Carr, it wasn't me!"

Miss Carr fairly spat her reply. "Not another word from you, young man."

Edmund looked at the floor. William and Anna were already studying their feet.

Mrs. Norton turned her attention to the Forresters. "Nellie. Peter. I'm terribly sorry about all this. You must be in an awful state."

Mrs. Forrester glanced at the children. "Really, Evelyn, it was quite a shock. Edmund says he had nothing to do with this, but when the evidence rolled out of his very own rucksack, what are we to do? I have my boys to think about."

"Of course, Nellie. Of course. You're no doubt ready for a bit of a respite. We'll carry on from here."

Mr. Forrester turned to the children. "We wish you the very best of luck," he said. "Really, we do." He looked at Mrs. Forrester, who gave nothing more than a curt nod. With that, the two of them made their retreat.

Mrs. Norton turned to Miss Carr. "Now there's the matter of finding another billet. Most of our available beds were filled when your classes arrived, but there's been some shuffling. Allow me until this afternoon to find a spot."

Anna sniffled. "What about Mrs. Müller—the lady from the library?"

Mrs. Norton raised her eyebrows. "Unsuitable."

Anna straightened her spine. "But I don't think she has any evacuees, and—"

Mrs. Norton put her hands on her hips. "Nora Müller is an unsuitable billet." She turned to Miss Carr, making it clear she had no intention of discussing the matter with the children. "As I said, Judith, give me the day to sort this out. I should have word to you by midafternoon."

"Of course," Miss Carr replied. "And thank you very much for your understanding. Most regrettable, all of it."

Mrs. Norton gave a nod and was gone.

Miss Carr gave Edmund a hard stare. "Do you have any idea the position your disgraceful behavior puts me in?"

"It wasn't me," Edmund whispered, his cheeks burning. "I didn't do it."

"The paint tin simply leapt into your rucksack of its own accord, did it?"

"Of course not!" Edmund was no longer whispering. "The Forresters' sons put it there. They've wanted us out from the start!"

"It's true," William said, stealing a glance at his brother. "Jack and Simon really did have it in for us—"

"Enough," Miss Carr said. "To accuse your foster family of such a thing is simply unconscionable. We'll have no more discussion on the matter. Do I make myself clear?"

Edmund lowered his head, resigned.

"Right," Miss Carr continued. "I'll expect you back here at three o'clock to learn of your new arrangements." She looked at each of the children in turn, then started down the hall, admonishing them as she disappeared. "If I smell one more whiff of trouble, you can be sure I shall speak with your family in London myself..."

"That would be a jolly interesting conversation, wouldn't it?" Edmund whispered.

"Look, Ed." William sought his brother's gaze. "I'm sorry about last night. I should have spoken up for you. I know you didn't do it—we both do."

Anna nodded her agreement. "We should have taken your part."

Still stinging, Edmund could muster little in the way of a response. "Let's go up. We'll be late."

Whether word of Edmund's alleged delinquency would spread or not, the children couldn't say, but for now all three were grateful for the normalcy of the day's routine.

After lessons and the usual luncheon in the village hall, their hearts were ripe for the comfort of the library.

Mrs. Müller was at the lending desk, knitting in hand. "Good afternoon, children! Back so soon?" She put down her needles. "Florence Hughes was just in... I gather there's been some commotion at the school?"

The words came out before William could weigh them. "It wasn't Edmund. Really and truly, it wasn't."

The librarian raised her eyebrows at the children. "Well, of course it wasn't. Whoever said it was?"

The children looked at one another as Edmund breathed

a sigh of relief. It was Anna who finally opened her mouth and found the entire story spilling out of it. Well, not all of it—she left out the bit about the three of them being orphans—but Jack and Simon's cruelties, the snake in the bed, the paint . . . all that, she told. Edmund trained his eyes at the floor, but as Anna came to the end of the tragic tale, he looked at the librarian and was alarmed to find she had tears in her eyes.

"Edmund. I'm terribly sorry." She sniffed. "To be blamed for something one did not do is a painful injustice indeed."

Hot tears threatened. Edmund bit his lower lip to stop them. "Thanks."

Mrs. Müller regarded him intently. "You really put a dead snake in one of those boys' beds?"

Edmund's gaze returned to the floor, shame burning his cheeks again. "I did."

Mrs. Müller considered this. She crossed her arms over her chest as a shadow of a smile crossed her lips. "Well done you."

Trudging toward the school a few minutes before three, the children made a gloomy trio.

"What if they split us up?" Anna asked.

"They can't," Edmund answered.

"If they try to, we'll ring Engersoll and ask him to fix it," William added. "And maybe—I mean, people say things happen for a reason. Maybe our new billet will be the right one. The one Engersoll was talking about."

"Sure," Edmund replied. "We're being put in whatever place is left over after the rest of the billets are used up. I'm sure in this one we'll find a new mum and dad just dying to adore us forever."

William pursed his lips. "It could happen."

Miss Carr met them just inside the school. "You're very lucky, children. Mrs. Norton has found you a billet. It will be cramped, but I expect you'll manage."

Anna gave an audible sigh of relief, and Edmund's shoulders relaxed the littlest bit. William thanked Miss Carr and told her that they would indeed manage.

Miss Carr simply raised her eyebrows. "Right. Mr. Forrester has delivered your belongings." She gestured toward their things, in a neat row by the door. "Let's be off. And I needn't remind you that you're to be on your best behavior, the lot of you. I've enough to manage without having to request new billets due to problems in deportment."

Edmund opened his mouth to defend himself, then shut it after a swift elbow in the ribs from his brother.

"Yes, ma'am," William said. "We understand."

The afternoon had turned cold. Edmund pulled up his socks and William buttoned Anna's coat. Gas masks hanging round their necks, the children picked up their suitcases and began their trek. Miss Carr led them to a narrow lane behind the school building. They passed a small park, a row of tidy homes, an ancient pub. Past three more lanes, and the landscape seemed to have lost much of its color, turned instead to a dun-colored warren of shabby houses. Miss Carr stopped at one of these and checked her clipboard to confirm the address—number four Livingston Lane. She gave a sharp rap on the door.

The squalling of a baby could be heard, getting louder as the children waited. Miss Carr gave them one last warning glance as the front door was opened by a woman bearing the source of the din on her hip.

The woman looked them over. "You'll be the new evacuees, then?"

She stepped aside and ushered them all into a dimly lit front room, its floor littered with clothing and bits of plaster from the ceiling, which bore a spider's web of cracks. An acrid tang of coal smoke and unwashed linens hung in the air above the meager furnishings—two threadbare chairs and a small, worn table. The room was little warmer than the outside air.

Two very small girls—still in diapers, both—sat on the floor gazing up at the children with wide, dark eyes. Another girl, only slightly older, looked on from the room beyond. The baby continued to shriek.

The woman shifted the child from one hip to the other. "The last lot went to an auntie in Devon and I was never paid for the last week with 'em."

Miss Carr was flustered. "Oh—ehm—so sorry, Mrs. Griffith. I can look into that for you. Thank you very much indeed for being willing to take on new evacuees."

The woman—Mrs. Griffith, the children supposed—said nothing but turned to them as if expecting an introduction.

William swallowed and stepped forward. "I'm William Pearce, ma'am. This is my brother, Edmund, and my sister, Anna."

"Right," the woman said, gesturing first to the wailing baby, then to the other children. "This is Robert Junior, these here are Jane and Helen, and that one by the kitchen is Penny, the oldest." She turned back to Miss Carr. "The pay'll be the same, will it? We need the money round here, you see. My Bob's away fighting, and it's all I can do to keep my own kids fed."

The children had been unaware, until now, that they were a source of income. They were suddenly grateful that the Forresters had never mentioned this fact.

Miss Carr looked taken aback herself. "Yes—ehm—you're to be paid ten and six for the first child, eight and six for each of the others. You will also receive rations for them, and they will continue to be provided with lunches."

"Good. Is that all, then?"

Miss Carr gave a stiff nod and gathered herself to leave. "Thank you very much again, Mrs. Griffith, for doing your bit." She handed William a postcard. "Post this to your family, to alert them to your new address." She opened the door, turning for one last look at the children. "I'll see the three of you at school in the morning."

Anna grasped William's hand and squeezed it tight.

Mrs. Griffith closed the door and sized them up as the shrieking of the baby continued. "Right. You'll sleep upstairs. Mine are in with me for now, so you've got the front bedroom. Come up with your things and get settled." She led the children through a tiny kitchen, notably warmer than the front room thanks to the coal-burning range. The children leaned toward its heat as they followed Mrs. Griffith to a narrow staircase at the back of the kitchen. The fourth step creaked alarmingly as they thumped their way up with their suitcases.

There were two doors at the top of the stairs. Mrs. Griffith opened one and showed the children inside. The room's single window was tacked over with tattered blackout paper, making it feel more like midnight than afternoon. Mrs. Griffith switched on a standing lamp. There was no other furniture, save a chamber pot, an empty apple crate, and three pallets on the floor. A single blanket was the only bedding to be seen.

"I asked the WVS lady to send over more blankets," Mrs. Griffith said, "but she hasn't got round to it." She looked the children up and down again. "You three look posh, don't you? You come from a fancy family?"

Unsure what response might be appropriate, the children only looked at the floor.

Mrs. Griffith narrowed her gaze at them. "Your family won't be coming round at every weekend, expecting me to feed them, will they? That's what happened with the last lot, and I won't stand for it. I'm not a hotel, you know."

"I'd be very surprised if our family turned up," Edmund said.

William gave a small cough. "Right. I don't think that will be a problem."

Mrs. Griffith gestured to the chamber pot. "Petty's out back." Judging from its association with the pot, the children assumed that a *petty* must be an outdoor toilet of some sort. This was not, Anna thought, a word she cared to learn.

"Settle in," Mrs. Griffith said. "I've got to tend to Robert before supper." The baby carried on wailing as they disappeared down the hall.

The children glanced around their new bedroom, then at one another. "Well, at least we're together," William said.

Edmund sat on one of the straw mattresses. "I wonder which of us is worth the ten and six. Probably you, Anna. Girls are likely worth more than boys."

This pronouncement did little to lift Anna's spirits.

William saw a tear slide down her cheek. He drew her close to him. "Anna—It'll be fine. Really, it will."

Anna brushed at her cheek. "This isn't the one, either."

"What one?"

"The one we're meant to be with. We haven't found the right family yet."

Edmund sighed. "Anna, you didn't really believe Engersoll's plan would work, did you?"

Anna's tearful stare at her brother was answer enough. In fact, she had believed just that.

The children's first dinner with Mrs. Griffith passed uneventfully. The baby had been fed and was sleeping quietly in a blanket-lined basket by the coal stove. Jane, Helen, and Penny had apparently already had their suppers—convenient, as there weren't enough chairs at the table for all of them. The girls sat on the floor on the other side of the stove, playing with a toy airplane and a bedraggled doll.

Corned beef and boiled cabbage quelled the gnawing in the children's stomachs as Mrs. Griffith outlined the household routines and expectations. "Monday's washing day. Friday's bath night. You lot are to help when I ask, and to keep the house tended."

Doesn't look as if it's used to much in the way of tending, Edmund thought.

"What can you do?" Mrs. Griffith asked.

Not certain as to the sorts of abilities she might find most agreeable, the children were at a loss.

I read, Anna thought. *I could read to the children.*

Edmund considered his own skills. *I put snakes in the beds of unpleasant persons. I get my brother and sister chucked out of places.*

William offered a diplomatic response. "We're glad to help any way we can."

"Do you know how to cook?"

Anna brightened. "I know how to make some things. Back in London, our housekeeper taught me."

Mrs. Griffith's face curdled. "Housekeeper? Well. Aren't we grand?" The children only twirled their forks in their bowls.

The meal done, William was anxious to show that they could earn their keep, as it were, and set to clearing the table. Mrs. Griffith filled the sink with water from what appeared to be the only tap in the house. A meager sprinkling of soap flakes, and William began scrubbing the plates with a torn strip of flannel, passing them to Mrs. Griffith to dry. Edmund used another strip to wipe down the table. He wrinkled his nose as the cloth came back dark with coal dust.

Anna, meanwhile, approached the children on the floor. It was unnerving, she thought, that they hadn't made a sound since she and Edmund and William had arrived. She knew little about small children, but she had always pictured them as noisier than these. Not baby Robert noisy, mind you, but certainly noisier than these.

"Hullo," she said tentatively. "That's a lovely doll. What's her name?"

Helen, who Anna guessed might be between two and three, did not respond but held out the doll. Anna took it tenderly. "She's beautiful."

"Bedtime, littlies," Mrs. Griffith said, setting the last of the bowls on a shelf, scooping up the sleeping baby in the basket, and beckoning to her girls. "G'night, you lot," she said to the children. The little ones toddled up the rickety steps with their mother, leaving Anna, Edmund, and William in the kitchen to ponder what came next.

"I suppose it's time to investigate the petty," William said with a grim set to his jaw. "I'll go first and report back."

Glad of their brother's willingness to perform reconnaissance, Anna and Edmund nodded encouragement. They sat at the kitchen table as William headed into the dark back garden.

"I wish we had a flashlight," Edmund said.

Anna's voice quavered. "Do you think there are spiders?"

"Probably."

William returned from his expedition in a few minutes'

time. "It's not so bad," he said, his nose pink from the chill. "But we should probably use the ones at school and the library when we can." Giving Edmund a bracing punch on the shoulder, William wished his brother luck and set to washing his hands in the cold water of the kitchen tap.

Edmund was back in half the time William had taken. "I swear I felt something move against my leg while I was in there." He shivered.

Anna's eyes widened.

Edmund ran his hands under the tap. "Your turn, then, Anna."

"I can't," Anna whispered.

Edmund dried his hands. "Of course you can, silly."

"I can't," Anna said again, her chin trembling now.

William wrapped an arm around her. "Edmund and I will go with you."

"What?" Edmund's indignation was fierce.

"We'll go with her."

"I'm not going out there again, and I'm certainly not tagging along every time she has to pee in the middle of the night!"

"I didn't say every time. For now, though. We'll go with her." William extended his hand to Anna.

Edmund stood, sputtering, until Anna's pleading stare got the better of him. "Just for tonight," he said with a huff. "But I'm not holding anybody's hand."

* * *

The children changed into their nightclothes by the weak light of the bedroom lamp. All three left their socks on as they crawled onto their straw mattresses, Anna in the middle with her brothers flanking her on either side. They pulled the single blanket over themselves. The room's temperature was bearable, but each wondered silently what it might be like once things had turned well and truly wintry.

"These beds are scratchy," Anna whispered.

"We'll get more blankets tomorrow," William said.

"I'm thirsty," Edmund said.

William sighed. "Go back downstairs for a glass of water."

"Not that thirsty."

The three were silent for a long moment before Anna spoke. "Tell me something, William."

William closed his eyes and concentrated. He found it was getting harder and harder to come up with things. "Right. I remember one. When she was a girl, Mum wanted to be a cabbie."

Anna smiled. "Really?"

"A cabbie?" Edmund scoffed. "Why would she want to be a cabbie?" In his secret heart, however, Edmund thought driving a cab sounded like an excellent career choice.

William sat up. "I forgot. We've got to write to Miss Collins." He rose with some reluctance and retrieved the postcard Miss Carr had left them. Crawling back under the blanket, he lay on his stomach to write.

Dear Miss Collins,

I hope this card finds you well. We wanted to let you and Mr. Engersoll know we are in a new home with a lady named Mrs. Griffith. Evacuees change billets quite a bit, as it turns out, but we are still together, the three of us, which is the most important thing.

Our very best regards,
William, Edmund, and Anna

Peering over William's shoulder, Edmund marveled once again at his brother. *I hope this card finds you well. Honestly.* He bit his tongue, however, glad that William had neglected to mention the reason for their change of billet.

"Let's have a bedtime story," William suggested. "What shall we read, Anna?"

"I don't want to listen to girls' books," Edmund protested.

Anna took offense. "I don't read *girls'* books!"

William chose the path of least resistance. "Fine. Let's start with the book Edmund got yesterday. That looked like a good one, didn't it?"

Pleased, Edmund reached into his rucksack for *Five Children and It.* He passed the book to William, who waited until the others had settled themselves before beginning. The title of the first chapter was certainly encouraging: "Beautiful as the Day."

Chapter Eleven

Despite being lulled to sleep by the lovely story of the great white house and the gardens and the promise of fairies, it was a restless first night for the children in their new lodgings. The straw pallets were scratchy, and they woke periodically to the piercing wail of baby Robert and the creak of floorboards as Mrs. Griffith tried to quiet him.

When the children heard the baby being carried downstairs in the morning, they dressed quickly and tiptoed after. In the kitchen, they found Mrs. Griffith stirring a pot of porridge while Robert whimpered on her hip.

"Sleep well?" Mrs. Griffith asked.

"Yes, ma'am, we did, thank you," William replied. Edmund and Anna were impressed at how convincing he was.

"Take the baby, one of you, and the others set the table."

"Yes, ma'am," the children said in unison.

Anna was pleasantly surprised when baby Robert let her take him without protest. He extended a wavering fist toward her face and began exploring her mouth with his fingers. It might have been quite nice, holding the baby, were it not for the greenish muck streaming from his nose and the decidedly swampy feeling of his bottom.

Mrs. Griffith ladled a bowlful of porridge for each of the children. "We've only enough milk for the girls. They'll be up soon," she said. "Ask your teacher about your ration books, as well as the blankets, would you? And do the washing-up before you go to school." With that unceremonious farewell, she took the baby and made her way back upstairs.

What a very great relief the school building was to the children that morning, at least until they met the unpleasant sight of Miss Carr behind the teacher's desk. They took their seats quietly, wondering when Mrs. Warren would arrive.

"Children," Miss Carr began, her voice uncharacteristically tremulous. "I'm terribly sorry to report that Mrs. Warren won't be with us for the foreseeable future. She received word last evening that her husband was killed in North Africa." A murmur moved through the classroom. "I don't know when she will be able to return to us. In the meanwhile, I shall take responsibility for the teaching of your class." Another hum snaked through the students. "Our first task, I think, should be the writing of letters to Mrs. Warren, to let her know she is in our thoughts." Miss Carr swallowed thickly. "Paper and pencils out, please, children. Deliver your letters to my desk when you've finished." With that, she turned her attention to a stack of papers in front of her.

Anna's eyes brimmed.

"I know you'll miss her, Anna," Edmund said. "We all will."

Anna sniffled. "I'm not crying for me, Edmund. I'm crying for her. How can you be so heartless?"

Edmund only crossed his arms over his chest and turned away, stung that Anna had misunderstood his attempt at being heartful.

Alfie turned in his seat. "I'll tell you what's heartless," he whispered. "Giving us Carr-buncle for a teacher. That's heartless." Anna gave him a withering stare.

One by one, letters to Mrs. Warren were brought to the teacher's desk. The children then set to their lessons—glad, in a way, to lose themselves in whatever tasks Miss Carr assigned their groups. The subtraction of fractions, the memorization of King Henry's wives, the drawing of topographical maps . . . all these were preferable to thoughts of loss and tragedy.

After lunch at the village hall, Miss Carr presented the children with a welcome surprise: their ration books and two woolen blankets from the WVS. More welcome, still, was their trip to the library—the third in as many days. The children had pressing business to attend to, concerned that their library cards might no longer work, now that their billet had changed.

Mrs. Müller greeted them with some surprise. "Goodness, children—back already . . . and you've brought blankets!" She smiled. "Will you be sleeping here, then?"

If only we could, Anna thought. William explained about the blankets.

Mrs. Müller's face shadowed. "Who is it you're staying with?"

"Mrs. Griffith and her children," William said. "Behind the schoolhouse, a few streets back. Her husband's off fighting."

Mrs. Müller didn't recognize the family's name. "Is she kind, I hope?"

This was not the sort of question the children were used to answering. Mrs. Griffith hadn't been unkind . . . but that, as you no doubt know, is a very different state of affairs than kindness.

William's pause spoke volumes more than his words. "Yes. She's been kind."

Mrs. Müller continued to regard the children with her eyes narrowed. "I hope it makes a happy home for you, children. You ought to have a good place to stay until you can go back to your family."

William took a deep breath and carried on with the business at hand. "We were wondering," he said, "whether it will still be possible for us to use our library cards, now that our billet has changed?"

Mrs. Müller nodded. "Of course. Just have Mrs. Griffith pop in to fill out new cards, and you'll be right as rain."

The children's faces fell. Mrs. Griffith seemed about as likely to make a trip to the library as a penguin was to go to the moon.

It was Anna who spoke up. "It's only . . ." She faltered. "It's only—well—Mrs. Griffith has little ones. I'm not sure she'd be able to come, and . . ." She trailed off.

Mrs. Müller took in their anxious faces. "I see," she said. "Well, I can't have my best bookworms do without, can I? All that's required is a grown-up, and seeing as I'm one of those, let's just have me be your grown-up for the time being, shall we?"

Mrs. Müller was only offering to vouch for their library books, but the notion of her being *their grown-up* was, just now, almost too delicious for Anna to consider. "Thank you ever, ever, ever so much," she said, resisting a very strong desire to throw her arms around the librarian and squeeze her.

"Yes, thanks loads, Mrs. Müller," Edmund echoed. "You're a brick."

Mrs. Müller blushed at the compliment. "Well, children . . . can I help you select anything more today, or did you just come about the library cards?"

Anna spoke up again. "I thought I might borrow some

books to read to Mrs. Griffith's little ones. I don't think they have any."

"Oh, dear." Mrs. Müller shook her head at the terrible sadness of such a thing. "Well, then they're very lucky to have you for a new sister." With that, she came from behind the lending desk to help Anna with her selections.

The children arrived back at Livingston Lane, where the closing of the door brought Mrs. Griffith from the kitchen, hands on hips. "I see you got the blankets. What about the ration books?" William reached into his trouser pocket and produced these.

"That'll mean three whole extra eggs round here, won't it?" Mrs. Griffith gave a chuckle. "Well . . . come in the kitchen. I need you to tear up newspaper for the petty."

Edmund grimaced, but the three of them set to work. Mrs. Griffith stirred a pot on the stove, turning away periodically to tend to the baby, who was growing increasingly restless in his basket. Penny lay in the doorway, humming a tune. Jane and Helen were fighting over a toy truck, until Mrs. Griffith turned to them and croaked, "Will you stop that racket? You're firing up the baby and giving me a headache."

Anna remembered the books. "Would you like me to read to them, Mrs. Griffith? I brought some books for them from the library this afternoon."

"They don't know words yet, but if it'll get them to quit that racket, have at it."

Glad to be off the newspaper-tearing job, Anna washed the ink from her fingers so as not to smudge the library books. She bent over the girls and used her most grown-up voice. "Would you like to hear a story?" She took Helen and Jane, one by each hand, and bade Penny follow. Leading them to the front room, she chose the larger of the two chairs, lifted Jane into her lap, and patted the remaining spaces on either side of her. The other girls clambered in. Clearing her throat with just the right amount of theatricality, Anna started. "Chapter One: In Which We Are Introduced to Winnie-the-Pooh and Some Bees, and the Stories Begin."

The girls seemed content to sit close to Anna, who only occasionally had to ask them to stop touching the book for fear its pages would get sticky. Edmund and William listened from their spot in the kitchen, and while neither would admit it, they savored every word. When Anna got to the bit about Pooh disguising himself as a small black cloud and using a blue balloon to float himself to the top of the honey tree, Edmund's lips, of their own accord, moved along with hers.

Silly old bear.

The next day, the children were awakened by a curious pattering. As William rolled over to investigate the sound, his hand landed in a cold puddle on the floor. The source, the children discovered, was a leak in the bedroom ceiling. Rain was seeping through a crack in the plaster and making its way across the floor to William's pallet. Its underside was now heavy and damp. Edmund and Anna's pallets seemed to have escaped the wet, but all three propped their mattresses against the wall farthest from the dripping ceiling. They dressed quickly, grateful that their clothes hadn't been in the path of the flood, and hurried downstairs. Mrs. Griffith was not yet up, so William chose a large pot from the shelf above the coal stove and carried it upstairs to contain the leak.

Anna started the porridge the way Miss Collins had taught her; she measured the oats and then the water, setting these to bubble atop the coal stove and stirring it every few minutes, glad to be near the heat. Edmund and William laid the table, then rinsed their faces under the tap as Mrs. Griffith appeared on the steps with her brood.

"Morning," she yawned, setting the baby in his basket and peering into the porridge pot. She scowled. "How much porridge did you use?"

Anna hesitated. "I just made it the way I learned back in London."

"You've used up today's porridge and tomorrow's, from the looks of it."

Anna's cheeks reddened. "I'm awfully sorry. I didn't mean to."

Mrs. Griffith crossed her arms over her chest and narrowed her eyes at Anna. "I don't know what your *housekeeper* taught you, but money's tight round here and the rationing isn't making things easier, you know." She ladled porridge into bowls, setting each on the table with an irate thunk.

Anna looked down at her breakfast, her eyes burning. "I'm sorry," she said again.

Mrs. Griffith offered no reply. William reached under the table and found Anna's hand. She took a tiny spoonful of porridge. It tasted bitter. Or perhaps that was just the taste of the morning.

It was a cross threesome that made its way to school in the still-pelting rain. Anna's unpleasant encounter with Mrs. Griffith had left them all irritable.

Edmund scratched his neck. "Those mattresses make me itch."

"At least yours is dry," William said.

"I don't like it here," Anna put in.

"None of us do," William said, "but we've got to make the best of it. Mrs. Norton made it sound like there aren't a lot of choices. Look," he added with a sigh, "we'll head to the library again after lunch, all right?"

By the time the afternoon had come, the library was indeed a welcome sight. A fire crackled in the corner, and the children thought they had never seen anything so heavenly. Anna, who had taken her time with *A Little Princess* as best she could, had only a chapter to go. She found she could hold out no longer and retrieved the precious book from her rucksack, intent on finishing there and then.

Mrs. Müller appeared from the history section, pushing a small rolling cart. "I say, children, I have my few regulars, but none so regular as you." She took in the children's dripping coats. "It's awful out there, isn't it? Why don't you warm yourselves a bit?" She retreated with her cart as the children fairly ran to the fireplace.

Edmund proceeded to remove his shoes. He lay on his back on the floor and propped his stockinged feet on the fireplace grate.

"Edmund!" William chided. "Put your shoes back on! And sit up! It's not as if you're in your bedroom, are you?"

Edmund stretched. "That's right, because our bedroom doesn't have a fire, does it? Only a hole in the roof letting the rain in. I'm half frozen, and my feet hurt in those shoes." He closed his eyes and rested his head on his hands.

Anna, who had already had more than enough reprimands for one day, watched with some trepidation as Mrs. Müller reappeared from the back room. She expected that reclining in one's socks in the library would be frowned upon.

The librarian took in the scene. "Well, I daresay this is the first I've seen anyone go stocking-footed in the library!"

Edmund tasted the all-too-familiar tang of shame as he sat up.

Mrs. Müller turned to William and Anna. "I encourage you children to follow your brother's example."

Anna breathed a sigh of relief and wasted no time in removing her shoes. William set off to choose a new book as Edmund raised his eyebrows, grinned, and stuck out his tongue at his brother's retreating form.

When the children arrived at Livingston Lane that afternoon, they were met by a red-faced Mrs. Griffith. "It's about time!" she shouted over the din of Robert's wails. "At it with the books again, were you?" She gestured toward the baby in his basket. "Watch the children," she said. "I've got to go to my neighbor lady about something."

Penny, Jane, and Helen appeared from the kitchen as Anna retrieved the shrieking baby from his basket. She did her best to quiet him, rocking and pacing, but the child was foul-smelling. She expected that this problem could only be resolved by a clean diaper; however, none of the children knew the first thing about such goings-on.

"Didn't you ever have to do this for me, William?" Anna said.

"I wasn't old enough to do this when you were still in diapers."

"Right." Anna sent Edmund to search for a clean cloth. She laid the shrieking child back in his basket and proceeded to inspect the construction of the existing diaper.

William looked over her shoulder. "Looks like how you wrap up a sandwich for a picnic."

Edmund, back with the clean cloth, wrinkled his nose. "Pretty awful sandwich."

"Well," Anna said, taking a deep breath, "I guess there's nothing for it." Removing the pins, she peeled the fetid thing back an inch or two and, unwilling to inspect the scene too closely, used the existing diaper to clean the baby's bottom as best she could. Holding her breath, she rolled the offensive cloth into a ball and held it out to Edmund to dispose of. He refused, leaving William to remove the mess to the scullery.

Hesitating over the writhing little body, the children learned a valuable lesson about the importance of speed when diapering a baby. A stream suddenly arced from the exposed infant, hitting Edmund squarely in the chest. He froze, then began to hop from one foot to the other in an outraged dance. Red-faced with disgust, he could only groan at the vile indignity of it all.

Penny, Jane, and Helen found this show tremendously

entertaining, and had it not been for their giggling, Anna and William might have been able to contain themselves. As it was, all but Edmund dissolved into hysterics, laughing until their sides hurt. This made it difficult for Anna to fold and pin the clean diaper, but she managed the job, and Robert was blessedly quiet at last.

That night was bath night, and while the notion of an only-weekly bath may hold grimy appeal to some, it is telling that even Edmund—who generally saw little harm in a thin layer of dirt—was glad of the opportunity. A good soak in warm water sounded lovely. Bath time at Livingston Lane, however, was hardly a cozy affair.

A tin tub was set by the coal fire and filled with water heated on the stove. The household took turns scrubbing themselves in the meager privacy provided by a sheet tacked to the ceiling. Mrs. Griffith went first with the baby. Then that water was dumped and a new batch heated for Penny, then Jane and Helen together, then our young threesome, each in their turn. The children had read stories about such baths and were at least glad to learn that they weren't expected to use the same water as the person before. All told, bath night was a three-hour affair for the cramped household of eight souls, and the children retired upstairs cleaner but shivering and exhausted. William's pallet was still damp from the previous night's rain, so he and Edmund pushed the other two together for the three of them to share. Edmund grumbled at the crowding but was secretly glad of their huddled warmth against the chill.

William read aloud to them, but even the magic of the story provided little distraction. When he finished, Anna's voice came from under the blanket.

"Tell me something, William."

William wanted only to close his eyes and drift away, but he searched the corners of his mind for something suitable. He found he could think of little more than bath night. "When they got married, Mum and Dad had towels with their names sewn on."

Anna's voice came from under the blanket again. "Their names?"

"Well, their initials."

"Why?" Edmund asked. "Were they afraid someone might steal their towels?"

"No, silly," William said. "That's just what grown-ups do."

The children fell asleep at last, wondering at the gross misalignment of adults' priorities.

Chapter Twelve

Saturday offered little opportunity for the children to lie about, as Mrs. Griffith announced that they were to do the shopping for her. "I've got a list. You're to go to the grocer and *green*grocer, as well as the bakery and butcher." *Mr. Forrester,* the children thought, with no small degree of anxiety at the prospect of such a reunion.

"Here's the money," Mrs. Griffith said, handing William a small coin purse. "And the ration books. Mind you carry back a receipt for everything you buy, and don't even think about getting anything extra." She looked at Anna, who felt cut through her heart.

"Yes, ma'am," she whispered. "I mean, no, ma'am. We won't buy anything extra."

The children had rarely been part of shopping days back in London, and when they had, it was always with Miss Collins in charge. None of them shared this inexperience with Mrs. Griffith as they buttoned their coats against the chill and set off.

William read the list as they walked, noting that Mrs.

Griffith had misspelled *margarine.* They began at the grocer, easily identified by the line snaking from the front door to the corner beyond. It was about three-quarters of an hour before they made their way inside. The children set to work finding barley, porridge oats, margarine, and milk.

"No jam?" Edmund asked, looking over William's shoulder at the list.

William double-checked. "No jam."

Edmund looked again. "Perhaps she just forgot to write that down?" After all, a boy can dream.

That stop done, the children carried on to the greengrocer, where a similar line awaited them. William was glad of the chance to set down the bottles of milk he was carrying, which were already twice as heavy as they had been at the grocer, he was sure. Once inside, the children found cabbage and potatoes. Onions, however, were nowhere to be seen.

The greengrocer, a rabbity man in a white apron, told them there were none. "We've got leeks, though, which can be substituted if your mum's creative."

Not the first word that comes to mind to describe Mrs. Griffith, Edmund thought.

"Do leeks cost the same as onions?" William asked.

"They're dearer."

William turned to Edmund and Anna. "What are we to do, then? Turn up with nothing, or substitute the leeks?" His siblings only shrugged. William swallowed and turned back to the counter. "We'll take the leeks."

The bakery was next. By now it was well past noon and the children's stomachs grumbled horribly as they opened the door and were met by the heavenly smell inside. "I didn't know this was going to take all day," Edmund said. "Surely she doesn't expect us to go till teatime without anything. Can't we just share a slice of bread or something?"

William shook his head. "Not unless you'd like to be the one to explain it to her."

Anna's stomach growled audibly.

Mr. Forrester's butcher shop was last. "She wants trotters and liver," William said, checking the list.

"Unspeakable," Edmund whispered. He felt rather ill, and he wasn't certain whether it was the idea of the trotters and liver or of seeing Mr. Forrester that was unsettling his stomach.

"I have to go to the toilet," Anna said. She looked at the line of shoppers ahead of them and shifted from one foot to the other.

"Can't you wait until we're back at Mrs. Griffith's?" William asked.

Anna crossed her legs.

It was nearly half an hour before the children got to the front of the line. Mr. Forrester was behind the counter in a white apron gone bloody from the day's work. He startled when he saw them. "Good afternoon, children," he said with a gruff sort of smile. "I hope you're all three keeping well in your new billet?"

"Yes, sir," William answered.

"Who are you staying with?"

"We're with Mrs. Griffith, a few lanes back, past the school."

"Ah, right. I know Sally Griffith."

"She's asked us to buy trotters and liver," William continued. He laid the ration books and what remained of Mrs. Griffith's money on the counter.

Mr. Forrester looked at the money. "That's not enough for both the trotters and the liver, children. Is that all she's given you?"

"It is," William said, looking at his feet. It was unpleasant, this sudden awareness of want. "This is the first time we've done the shopping ourselves, so perhaps we haven't chosen correctly. There were no onions, you see, and . . ." It occurred to William that Mr. Forrester likely didn't give two figs about the onions. He trailed off midsentence.

Mr. Forrester looked over the children's shoulders at the customers behind them, then leaned over the counter and lowered his voice. "We'll just let it go, then, shall we? I'll get you Mrs. Griffith's trotters, and we'll throw in the liver free."

None of the children knew how to respond, other than to

offer their bewildered thanks. Edmund couldn't believe he was thanking anyone for free liver.

Mr. Forrester disappeared for a moment, returning with two packages neatly wrapped in brown paper. "Right, children. Here you are." He paused, lowering his voice and leaning toward them again. "I'm sorry about what happened, back at the house."

What did Mr. Forrester mean, he was sorry? Had he had a change of heart? Did he know that Edmund was innocent? Did he know that his own sons were guilty? The children didn't suppose they would ever find out.

"It's only—well . . . ," Mr. Forrester continued, "if you ever need anything, just pop in and ask."

William nodded. "Thank you, Mr. Forrester." He hesitated just a moment. "There is one thing we might ask of you."

Mr. Forrester looked at them expectantly.

"May Anna please use your toilet?"

The children trudged back to Mrs. Griffith's, their arms aching with the weight of their parcels. Opening the door, they were greeted by the usual racket. The baby was crying, Jane and Helen were rolling over and over each other on the floor, and Penny was banging a steady rhythm on the bottom of a pot with a wooden spoon.

Mrs. Griffith unpacked the groceries on the kitchen table. William thought it best to explain about the leeks before she got to them.

"Who told you leeks could work as onions?"

"The greengrocer," William said.

Mrs. Griffith continued to pick her way through the contents of the shopping bags, consulting the receipts as she went.

"The liver isn't on the slip."

"Right," William answered. "We went to Mr. Forrester last, and there wasn't enough money left, so he just gave it to us."

"He did what, now?"

"He gave us the liver for free."

"Why would he do such a thing? Did you tell him I'd run out of money?"

"No, ma'am. We just told him it was our first time doing the shopping, and I think he felt sorry for us. He was our last billet, you know."

"Just so long's you don't go about telling people I haven't enough money."

"No, ma'am."

"Nearly two months my Bob's been gone now, and I've seen hardly a coin from the army. Only so many times you can borrow from neighbors, you know." Mrs. Griffith began putting the groceries away.

"I'm sorry, Mrs. Griffith," William whispered, "about your husband."

She gave no indication as to whether she had heard him, only set the tin of porridge oats on the cupboard shelf. Then she turned to Penny. "And quit that racket!" was all she said.

A few weeks after their arrival at Mrs. Griffith's, a letter came from Miss Collins. William read it to his brother and sister upstairs in the bedroom.

Dear Anna, Edmund, and William,

I was terribly glad when the post came with your letter. I suppose billets must change rather a lot, mustn't they, with the war keeping everyone on their toes?

My sister and I are holding up, though we've spent many a night in the Anderson in the back garden, and it's all taken rather a toll on my rheumatism. I can't complain, though, things being so very awful in London.

I do hope the three of you are keeping well at your new billet. You didn't say much about it in your letter. I hope all goes swimmingly with the preposterous plan.

Fondly,

Kezia Collins

Preposterous plan indeed, Edmund thought. *I tried to tell them it was utter nonsense.*

"What's rheumatism?" Anna asked. *It sounds rather like rhubarb,* she thought, *but surely that's not right.*

"Something old ladies get," Edmund answered.

Anna looked at the letter. "It's awful to think of Miss Collins sleeping in a hole in her sister's back garden."

"A hole in the back garden might be warmer than it is here," Edmund said.

"Mmmm," William murmured, his eyes gone far away. "I suppose that's one thing we haven't had to worry about, isn't it? Sleeping in an Anderson shelter?"

"Mrs. Griffith hasn't even got one," Anna said.

Edmund nodded. "Probably for the best. If her Anderson was anything like her house, the smell in there would be unbearable."

The talk of Anderson shelters was prophetic, somehow. Late that evening, as the children lay on their pallets, the stillness of the night was broken by a monstrous sound from far away.

Wrapping himself in his blanket, Edmund rose and went to the window, trying to peer through a tiny rip in the black-out paper. "I can't see anything." He used his index finger to widen the tear just an inch or so.

Anna and William joined him as the noise continued.

"Maybe it's thunder," Anna said.

Edmund shook his head. "It's not storming."

Peeking through the torn bit of paper again, the children could just make out a sort of glow on the horizon. In a different time and place, it might have been beautiful.

"Where do you think that is?" Edmund whispered.

William tried to keep his voice steady. "I don't know. It could be Coventry. There's manufacturing there, I think. Planes, munitions, that sort of thing."

Anna gripped William's hand. She made no effort to mask the shaking in her voice. "Do you think they'll bomb us here?"

"No," William said with as much certainty as he could muster. "They haven't any factories here. Nothing that's a worthy target." It took all he had to offer Anna a bracing squeeze, lost, as he was, in his own unnamed fear.

She squeezed back. "Should we wake Mrs. Griffith?"

"What would she do?" Edmund asked.

William thought Edmund made a fair point. Mrs. Griffith was unlikely to offer much in the way of comfort. "Let's just try and sleep, all right?" He tucked Anna back under her blanket and grabbed her hand again as they lay listening to the distant thundering.

Edmund stayed at the window for a long time, squinting at the beautiful, awful glow.

* * *

Mrs. Griffith didn't have a radio, so it wasn't until school the next morning that William's guess about the bombing was confirmed.

"Coventry." Miss Carr's face was gray. "I don't know details, but I gather it was bad."

"Coventry's only a few miles away," Frances said.

Miss Carr corrected her. "Twenty-five miles away, actually."

"But that's still really close," Frances said. "If the Jerries had missed, they could have hit us." Several of the smaller children looked close to tears.

"Twenty-five miles is really quite a long way, Frances," Miss Carr said, determined that the class not go down a rabbit hole of terror just now.

Alfie raised his hand. "It's not that far, Miss Carr. At my gran's, I rode almost that far on a bicycle once. Twenty-five miles would be easy for the Jerries to miss."

"That's enough, children," Miss Carr said, though her tone held little of its usual hardness. "We're really quite safe here."

Alfie raised his hand again. "Did they hit the cinema?" The students all thought of their lovely *Pinocchio* outing. It seemed such a long time ago.

Miss Carr sighed. "I've no idea, Alfred. And I should

think there are more important things to worry about than the cinema."

"Like what?"

"Like . . . factories, churches, people's homes, for heaven's sake."

"My mum says the cinema is important for keeping up morals."

"I think you mean keeping up *morale,* Alfred."

"What's the difference?"

"*Morals* means a sense of right and wrong. *Morale* means a positive spirit."

Alfie only shrugged. Just now, none of the children were able to conjure much in the way of positive spirit.

Chapter Thirteen

At breakfast the following Saturday, Mrs. Griffith gave the children their marching orders for the day. She asked Anna to mind the girls while she did the shopping, then turned to the boys. "You'll be helping with the ratting today, hear?"

Edmund and William glanced at each other.

"What's that?" Edmund asked.

"Big farm just outside town needs its rats exterminated once or twice a year. Ratcatcher'll pay for each tail, and we need the money."

Edmund considered the logistics of this. "How do we do it?"

"Farmer'll show you when you get there. Other boys from town go. My Bob always went before the war. Easy money."

"How do we get there?" Edmund asked insistently.

"You walk. Past the square, there's a road that leads south out of town. Hanover Street, it is, but they may have taken the signs down 'cause of the Jerries. The farms are strung along that road a couple of miles south. Like I said, boys from town go, so you'll fall in with some who'll show you how to get there. No dillydallying, though. They get started by midmorning." With that, she went upstairs to tend to the baby.

"I'm not sure I fancy being left alone," Anna whispered as William set to washing the porridge bowls.

Edmund crossed his arms. "I'm not sure I fancy ratting."

"I don't see as any of us has much of a choice," William said, setting down the rag he was using. "And you won't be alone, Anna. You'll have the girls with you."

"But I'm only nine. That's not old enough."

Truth be told, William was none too glad of his own assignment, which made it difficult to sympathize with his sister. "Just spend the day reading them stories. And be glad you're not murdering rats."

With that, the boys said a wide-eyed goodbye. They headed toward the square, pulling their coats tight against the chill. As Mrs. Griffith had predicted, they saw two boys ahead, one carrying a board and the other a piece of a thickish tree branch. Edmund and William ran to catch up and found that one of the boys was Alfie. He was with his foster brother from his billet—a plump and good-natured boy named Ernest.

Ernest reassured them that he knew all about ratting. "I've done this loads of times," he said. "Well . . . twice."

"How do you do it, then?" Edmund asked.

"They block up all the ratholes but two, turn a hose down one, and wait for the rats to come out the other."

"And then what?" Alfie asked, rapt.

Ernest shrugged. "We beat 'em."

The farm was impossible to miss. Several long cowsheds and some smaller outbuildings—Ernest said they were pigsties—were visible from the road, and as they made the turn into the farm they saw other boys their age, presumably there for the ratting as well. Dogs trotted in and out of the crowd. A handful of older men—too old to be fighting in the war, the boys guessed—milled about with pails and shovels, checking that holes had been adequately filled.

One of the men approached Edmund and William and their schoolmates. He wiped sweat from his brow, despite the November chill. "Have you boys brought clubs or sticks or the like?" The other boys displayed theirs, while Edmund and William shook their heads. The man directed them to a barn, where spent floorboards were piled in a corner. Edmund selected a board, then looked at William.

"Ever think we'd be doing something like this?" His eyes were lit with the glow of excitement reflected on fear.

William said nothing, only shook his head slowly. His heart was pounding, and he felt a bit sick to his stomach.

One of the men appeared from behind the barn, unfurling a ragged hose. He put the nozzle end into the ground near the barn door, as if plugging a lamp into a socket.

"Does everyone know what to do, boys?"

Of course we don't, William thought. He hadn't got anywhere near *R* in the *Britannica,* but he was certain it offered no advice on *RAT(ting).*

The gaggle of boys nodded. A sort of electric hum made its way through their midst as the anticipation peaked. One of the dogs let out a whine, twitching in eagerness at what he seemed to know was coming.

"Mind you don't cudgel each other in a mad dash to catch the buggers, lads," the man advised. The boys looked at each other, judging safe distances as they raised their weapons to their shoulders.

William bit his lower lip. Edmund closed his eyes, breathless. The thought occurred to both boys to simply hang back and let the others do the ratting, but they feared the punishment they might face should they return to Mrs. Griffith empty-handed.

"Right!" the farmer shouted, giving a sign to whoever was manning the hose bib at the back of the barn.

"On three, then, lads. Ready?"

No, Edmund and William thought.

"ONE! TWO! THREE!"

Nothing.

For at least a minute, the only sound the boys could hear was the frenzy in their own ears. The noises of the farm—the breeze through the apple orchard, the lowing of the cows in their sheds—were eclipsed by the pulsing heartbeat of fearful anticipation. Standing there, William and Edmund had the same succession of thoughts. *Perhaps the hose didn't work. Perhaps there are no rats after all. Perhaps they've forgotten some of the holes and the vermin are just now escaping to the fields beyond.*

It was then that the first rat emerged. It nearly flew out of the hole, then froze on the spot. The boys thought they could see terror in its beady eyes. For a moment, neither rat nor ratters stirred, only stared at each other. But when the creature at last made a move, the spell was broken and one of the bigger boys came down on it with an old cricket bat.

Even above the earthy thud of bat hitting ground, the sound of the animal's death was unmistakable. Edmund and William heard the sickening crack of the rat's body being broken in pieces by the direct hit from the boy's bat, and both took a step back, lowering their weapons in horror as the reality of the ratting became all too vivid.

There was no time, however, to mourn the hapless creature, as now more rats began to pour from the hole in the ground, their shrieks filling the boys' ears. All around them, ratters sprang into action, swinging at the panicked vermin with whatever implements they had. Many missed their marks, sending animals scattering this way and that, only to be pursued by other boys. The dogs seemed built for the task, snatching their victims and giving them a single whip-like shake, breaking their necks in one efficient and deadly maneuver, then dropping them to the ground.

William and Edmund watched, their breath stuck in their throats, as the boys around them brought one rat after another to its grisly death. Alfie appeared similarly paralyzed. Ernest had killed one already. Raising his weapon to seek his next kill, he caught sight of William and Edmund. His eyes were unfocused and wild.

"Come on, then, you two! What are you doing?" he shouted.

William looked at his brother, mute and still as the chaos swirled about them. His eyes shining with hot tears, William grabbed Edmund by the arm. "You don't have to do this, Ed. I'll get two and we'll have done with it. We'll bring the money to Mrs. Griffith and we won't need to think about this ever again. You don't have to kill anything."

Never had Edmund wanted so desperately to let his older brother be his older brother, to relieve him of the responsibility of taking a creature's life in such a gruesome manner. He set his jaw and inhaled deeply. "I can do it," he whispered. "We stick together." The boys stared at each other for a long moment, then turned and set to work.

A huge rat, just missed by one of the other boys, saw

an escape route between Edmund and William. Edmund swung, missing the moving target by nearly a yard. The rodent swerved toward William, who raised his plank, squeezed his eyes shut, and brought it down.

Even without looking, he knew he had found his mark. The crunch of the rat's body rang in his ears, and he heaved deep breaths to keep from being sick as he opened his eyes to find the creature's ruined body twitching at his feet. William looked up at his brother, his eyes flooded.

Edmund couldn't look away from William's victim, which gave another rat the opportunity to skirt by him. Blinded now by tears, William swung at the creature, hitting only its tail. This was enough to send the thing skittering back toward Edmund, who raised his own plank and brought it down with a thwack, missing again. Swiping at his eyes with one sleeve, William swung at the animal a second time and hit it squarely. The writhing creature joined its fellow at the boys' feet, and William promptly turned and heaved the contents of his stomach into the dirt behind them. He grabbed his knees and gulped for air. "Enough," he rasped. "That's enough. No more."

Edmund took a trembling breath and bent over his brother. "It's all right, Will. It's all right."

The boys stayed doubled over as the pandemonium began to subside. Some of the boys around them were similarly dismayed. One or two had been sick like William.

A handful of others seemed in their element, on fire with bloodlust. Edmund thought briefly that the battle in this field must not be too different from those in other places, other fields, far away from this one.

William swiped at his streaming nose. "Not a word to Anna."

"No," Edmund whispered, hugging his own arms as a chill made its way through his sweat-soaked shirt.

The boys collected sixpence from the ratcatcher and left the farm. Neither was keen to relive the morning's events with Ernest and Alfie. They trudged back to town in silence.

It was only when the steeple of the church became visible over the crest of the hill that Edmund spoke. "I could have done it, you know. I tried. I just . . . missed."

William didn't look up. "I know, Ed. It's all right. I'm glad you didn't hit any. Nobody should have to do such a thing."

There was a long silence before Edmund spoke again. "Thanks."

"I told you, you didn't have to."

"I know you did, and I just . . . thanks."

"It's all right," William said, fresh tears threatening.

"Honest. Thanks. Not just for today, but . . . I don't know . . . for everything. For taking care of us, me and Anna."

William sniffled. "It's all right," he said again.

Edmund dug his fists into the pockets of his coat. "Do you think we'll ever find a proper grown-up, so you don't have to anymore?"

"Not exactly lining up for us, are they, the proper ones?" William's voice was bathed in a tiredness that came from the deepest part of him.

Edmund gave a bleak chuckle. "Maybe we should ask that farmer. Now you've proven yourself a champion rat murderer, I'll bet he'd think himself lucky to have us."

William managed a half smile. "Let's just hope we can ride things out till the war's over, and then we'll sort out what to do."

"Sixpence?" Mrs. Griffith fairly shrieked when the boys deposited their earnings on the kitchen table. "Where's the rest of it?"

Edmund glanced at William, waiting for him to respond. He didn't.

"This is all of it," Edmund said.

"That can't be all of it—what's that, one rat apiece?"

"Yes, ma'am."

"Gone half the day, for one rat apiece?"

"Yes, ma'am."

"Turn out your pockets," Mrs. Griffith hissed.

"What?" Edmund looked at William, who still said

nothing. Anna watched the volley from the bottom of the stairs.

"Turn out your pockets. Squirreling the rest of it away, are you?"

"We didn't take anything! This was all we got!" Edmund's rage was mounting now, his voice growing louder with each word.

"Did you spend some on the way home? Stop for sweets?"

By now Edmund was nearly shouting. "This is all we got!"

"What were the two of you doing the whole time? Larking about?"

Edmund stole a glance at William, who only swiped at his nose. "No, ma'am," Edmund said, trying to lower his voice. "We both tried . . . it was just . . . hard."

"I'll tell you what's hard," Mrs. Griffith said. "Feeding six children plus a baby on no money. That's what's hard." She paused but got no reply. "Get upstairs, the lot of you, and don't come down again till I tell you."

Edmund and William were mostly glad to be banished, though both felt fairly desperate to wash their hands of the sticky film of death. This seemed not the moment to ask for such favors, however, and the boys wasted no time in clambering up the stairs. Anna followed behind them.

"Was it awful?" she asked, once the bedroom door was closed. "Was it as dreadful as I'm imagining it to be?"

"William did all the work," Edmund said.

"I couldn't even think of doing such a thing," Anna continued. "Not that I care for rats, mind you, but to think of killing one . . ." She gave a little shudder. "Did you just hit them over the head?"

Edmund glanced at William. He was beginning to feel alarmed, now, at his brother's silence. "Yes."

"And you had to watch their insides come out, and—"

"Stop it, Anna," Edmund said.

"I just—"

"Stop it, Anna. I mean it."

The three sat in tense silence for a long while before Anna piped up again. "Do you think she's going to let us come down for supper? I'm hungry."

"I'm hungry, too," Edmund sighed. "But I think I'm more tired than hungry."

Anna brightened. "Do you want to read to us, William? Take your mind off things?"

William spoke at last. "I don't feel much like reading, Anna. Sorry."

"I'll do it," Edmund said.

Anna and William stared at their brother.

"Really. Will's done enough." Edmund rummaged through his things and retrieved *Five Children and It.*

William watched as Edmund opened the book, studying his brother like a person he had only just met.

* * *

By now the weather had gone well and truly cold. The trees ringing the village square were bare, the dry click of their branches heralding the approaching winter. Leaves gathered in doorways. The air was scented with earth and clove.

Meals at Mrs. Griffith's being what they were, the children were beginning to grow accustomed to the gnaw of hunger in their bellies. None of them had been especially choosy eaters to begin with, but now they found they would inhale anything put before them. When mealtimes were over, they would run their tongues round the rims of their plates and bowls, knowing this was terribly rude, but—needs must, as they say.

One afternoon at the end of November, the children sat by the fire in the library reading room, losing themselves in their latest selections. Mrs. Müller sat at the lending desk, engaged in her knitting. All in all, it made quite a cozy picture.

Edmund was reading *The Wind in the Willows*. He had been initially opposed to it, as Anna had recently finished it, and he hated to follow his younger sister—or anyone, come to that—in anything. Mrs. Müller had convinced him to try it, however, and Edmund was thoroughly enjoying Toad's misadventures. At present, the creature had been tossed into prison for stealing a motorcar. Reading the bit where the jailer's daughter appears with tea . . . *hot buttered toast, cut thick, very brown on both sides, with the butter running through the holes in it in great golden drops, like honey from the honeycomb* . . . Edmund found himself nearly drooling on the very page. There came a grumbling from his stomach that could have been heard all the way in the biography section.

"Such noise in a library!" Mrs. Müller raised her eyebrows in jest, then studied the children for a long moment. Her voice went softer. "You three look a bit peaky. Is there enough to go round at your billet?"

The children were caught out by the directness of the question. Each silently considered telling her the truth, but it seemed somehow shameful to admit their hunger.

William offered a characteristically diplomatic response. "Mrs. Griffith does the best she can, what with the rationing and all . . ."

A shadow of understanding clouded Mrs. Müller's brow. She rose from her seat by the fire and disappeared without a word. She returned a moment later with a tin and pried up the lid with her fingertips. "I keep a tin of cookies in the cloakroom, for emergencies." She set it on the hearth. "Tuck in . . . please."

The smell of the cookies filled the children with a warmth that can only come from the magnificent alchemy of butter and sugar. They set to nibbling as Mrs. Müller rearranged herself in her chair and resumed her knitting, pausing periodically to steal glances at the children. At her insistence, they dug into the tin again and again, until it was empty. They swallowed thickly and thanked Mrs. Müller, bolstered by her offering in ways she never could have guessed. Or perhaps she could.

Chapter Fourteen

December marked six months that the children had been living in the country. All three had grown, as children will do, and by now their clothes were snug. Edmund's shoes pinched so awfully that he had taken to slipping out of them at the heels.

And so it was with some delight that the children met Miss Carr's announcement one morning that the WVS would be holding a clothing swap. Wartime shortages had been felt by evacuees and villagers alike. News of the swap brought sighs of relief all around the classroom as children envisioned comfortable shoes and coats that covered their wrists. Mrs. Griffith, likewise, greeted the announcement with more joy than the children had yet seen from her. She arranged for a neighbor to mind the baby so she and the girls could attend.

The event was held in the village hall during the children's noontime meal. Participants came with too-small items to be enjoyed by others, and eager to find new things of their own. William told Edmund he ought to make do with his hand-me-downs, but Edmund refused, preferring the thrill of the new—or at least new to him. All three children came away with new coats and shoes, plus shirts and trousers for the boys and skirts and blouses for Anna. She had been loath to give up her favorite sweater—it had such lovely roses stitched on the yoke—but it had begun to let in errant drafts across her middle when she raised her arms, so away it went.

Their grand shopping spree complete, Edmund, William, and Anna walked home with an ebullient Mrs. Griffith. She was so uncharacteristically joyful that she used some of the milk ration for a custard that night. It was rather lumpy, but the children relished its creamy weight. Anxious to prolong the goodwill, Anna read to the girls after supper while Edmund and William did the washing-up.

Anna was never sure whether Jane, Helen, and Penny were getting anything out of the stories she read, but the little ones certainly sat rapt as she read them *The Story of Ferdinand* that night. By the time Ferdinand had infuriated the banderilleros and the picadores and the matador with his sitting *just quietly,* Jane and Helen had both fallen asleep in Anna's lap. Penny looked close to it.

William smiled wistfully. "Look at that, Anna. We've been sent here to try and find ourselves a mum, and here you are acting like one your own self."

The children were glad of their new coats that night, as December's chill made its way into the front bedroom. Sleeping in a coat was uncomfortable, but not nearly so uncomfortable as the wind that rattled the glass, making the house sound haunted—at least, Anna thought it sounded that way. The children pressed their straw pallets together for warmth but still slept fitfully. In the wee hours of the morning, a sleeting rain began to pelt the roof, and the children awakened to find that all three of their mattresses were damp. The puddle had even made its way to Edmund's new things, piled helter-skelter on the floor rather than folded on top of the apple crate where William had advised him to store them. Grumbling and shivering, Edmund donned the least-damp shirt and trousers he could find and hurried downstairs to the relative warmth of the coal stove.

At school that morning, Miss Carr announced that the children were to perform a Nativity Play at the village's Christmas Eve service. "Our gift to the townspeople who have offered us safe haven from the war," she said. "I expect the whole village will turn out to see it, so we shall be certain to make it a Nativity Play to remember. Roles will be decided by lottery before we leave for lunch today." Some children's eyes lit up with excitement, others not.

Edmund was decidedly in the "not" camp. When it was his turn to reach into the pail and withdraw a folded slip of paper, he hoped for the role that involved the least possible stage time. He unfolded his slip and read the word *STAR*.

His eyes went wide. "The star of the show?"

Miss Carr gave a withering stare. "Wouldn't you just like to think so?"

"Not at all," Edmund replied.

"The *Christmas* star," the teacher explained, exasperated. "The star that lit the way to the manger in Bethlehem?"

Edmund set to pondering what monstrosity of a costume would be required of him. He pictured an enormous star-shaped box, his head poking through a hole in its lurid egg-yellow center.

"What kind of part is a star, anyway?" he asked the others as they sat in the village hall eating lunch that afternoon. "It's not even a living thing. It's a . . . what do you call an unliving thing, Will?"

William swallowed the last of his milk. "A zombie?"

Edmund only scowled at him.

"Do you mean an inanimate object?" William found the whole affair rather funny, given his own assignment. For a brief and uncomfortable moment, he had endured the fluttering of Frances's eyelashes as she confessed her hope that the two of them would play Joseph and Mary. "Then we'd have to hold hands," she'd whispered. William's relief was palpable when he had drawn *SHEPHERD* from the pail. Confident that a shepherd needn't hold hands with anyone, he could now turn his attention to teasing his brother.

"I would have thought you'd be pleased, Ed, being *the star of the show* and all."

"Well, what would you have thought that meant—*STAR*?" Edmund asked. "I mean, honestly, it's an intimate object. Was that what you said?"

"Inanimate."

Anna was delighted with her role as *ANGEL*. "It'll be fun, I think. We've never been in a Nativity Play before. I wonder how they'll do the halos?"

The icy rain continued, on and off, the whole of the week, making the library especially inviting when the children could visit after their midday meal. Edmund had started *The Call of the Wild*. William was making his way through a treasury of Greek mythology. Anna was starting her first Sherlock Holmes mystery. She lay on her stomach in front of the fire, *The Hound of the Baskervilles* before her. She was struggling with some of the longer words but enjoying it nonetheless.

She scratched absently at her neck. "What's *doli*... *dolichocephalic*?"

"No idea," Edmund grunted.

"Nor me, exactly," William confessed. "I think *cephalic* has to do with brains."

"Mmmm," Anna murmured. "Holmes certainly has one of those, hasn't he?"

"I s'pose he must," William agreed.

Anna put the book down, scratching her neck again.

"Anna, quit scratching, will you? It'll only make it worse," William said.

Anna sat up. "Those pallets make my head terribly itchy. Can you look at it?" It was only as she said the words that an awful thought occurred to her. It couldn't be nits, could it? "Ehm . . . never mind. I'm sure it's just . . . my imagination."

But William had already shifted his position for a closer inspection and was lifting strands of her hair.

"Is it . . . ?" Anna couldn't finish the sentence. Her cheeks burned pink with shame.

William met her gaze and gave the tiniest of nods.

Edmund inched backward on the hearthrug as tears spilled onto Anna's cheeks.

"It must have been the new coat," William whispered. He put his arm around his sister, glancing furtively at her head as he did so. "It's all right, Anna," he said. "Really, it's going to be fine. We'll go back to the house and I'll get them out straightaway." The fact that he hadn't the foggiest idea how to do such a thing, he kept to himself.

Mrs. Müller appeared from the science section to find Anna weeping, Edmund wrinkling his nose, and William looking as if he were lost at sea.

"What is it, children?"

Please don't tell her, Anna thought. *Please don't tell anyone.*

William felt the heat of his sister's shame. "Anna—ehm—Anna's just gotten to an especially weepy bit in her book, is all. It's fine. We've—ehm—got to be going now."

The librarian reached into her sweater pocket and produced a clean handkerchief for Anna. "A weepy bit?" she asked gently. "In *Sherlock Holmes*?"

There was an uncomfortable silence. It was Edmund who spoke, at last.

"Anna's got nits."

William turned sharply to his brother as Anna dissolved into tears, burying her face in the handkerchief. Edmund shrugged. "There aren't really any bits worth crying over in *Sherlock Holmes,* I don't think."

Mrs. Müller nodded. "Indeed." She turned to William. "Will your foster mum know what to do to get rid of them?"

"I'm sure she will," William answered. "And if not, I can do it." He squeezed Anna's hand. "Really. We'll be fine." He heard the lie in his own voice.

The librarian heard it as well. She looked from one to the other of them, then lowered her head. "Why don't we just take care of them right here and now?"

Anna looked up from the sodden handkerchief with an odd combination of horror and gratitude.

"Thanks, Mrs. Müller," William said. "But honestly—we'll manage." A part of him hoped she couldn't see the tears burning his eyes. Another part rather hoped she could.

The librarian's voice was nearly a whisper. "I've no doubt you would. But this seems to me rather unfair to expect a boy of twelve to manage."

William held her gaze for a long while. He swallowed hard. "Thank you."

Mrs. Müller gathered herself. "Right. So, you three stay here and man the lending desk. I'll pop over to the chemist for some things. It's just a few doors down, so it won't take a moment. We'll have you right as rain before supper. Yes?"

The children nodded. Mrs. Müller grabbed her coat and was off.

For a long while, the silence was punctuated only occasionally by a crack from the fireplace or a sniffle from Anna. Edmund and William both felt rather itchy themselves—this does tend to happen when one thinks about crawly things on one's head—but they checked each other over and found nothing.

"Jack and Simon were right," Anna whispered, "about us being filthy vackies."

"Anna," William said, taking her hands in his. "Don't think that. It has to have been the coat from the swap."

Anna said nothing, only stared into the fire and fought the urge to scratch.

It wasn't long before the librarian returned with a small parcel. "Right, then," she said. "We've everything we need." She disappeared into the back hall, emerging with a dish of liquid that smelled of bleach. Retrieving a fine-toothed comb from her parcel, she knelt before Anna. "You know it isn't your fault, don't you?"

Anna only sniffled.

"I had nits more than once as a girl, you know," Mrs. Müller confided.

Edmund wrinkled his nose. "You did?"

"I did. They would go round school, especially in the winter when our coats and hats were all crammed together in the coat closet. One year, my sister and I had them four times between the two of us," she said. "My mum nearly shaved us both bald."

Anna smiled in spite of herself.

Mrs. Müller set to it. She gathered Anna into her lap and parted her hair down the middle, then down one side, then down the other, bending her head this way and that, reaching every strand. Part and repart. Comb and recomb. Each time she found one of the dreadful creatures, she would pick it out and send it to its death in the bowl of caustic-smelling liquid.

It was an awful job, and Anna would have avoided it if she could, of course, but as she sat there by the fire, feeling Mrs. Müller's fingers work through her curls, it occurred to Anna that she was entirely content. She puzzled over this. At first, she thought it was only relief that the unpleasant situation was being resolved. It was more than that, though. It was an indescribable tenderness, and it brought fresh tears.

These were not lost on Mrs. Müller, who stopped working for a moment and brushed Anna's cheeks with her fingertips. "It's going to be all right, Anna. I'll get all of them out. I promise."

"It's not that," Anna said with a hiccup. "It's just... thank you."

Mrs. Müller looked at Anna for a long moment, her own nose gone pink now. "It's nothing. Really. I'm glad to. I wouldn't want you to suffer with this a moment longer than you had to."

Edmund raised himself to his elbows. "Do you have children, Mrs. Müller?"

"I don't, Edmund."

"Do you have a husband?" Anna asked.

"Of course she does," Edmund said. "That's why she's a *missus*."

The librarian gave a sad smile. "You're right, Edmund. I do have a husband."

"Is he away fighting?" William asked.

The librarian looked into the fire. "That's rather a long story, I'm afraid." She nudged Anna's head forward, picking out another of the foul beasts. "Perhaps you children have noticed that not everyone around here is especially friendly toward me?"

Unsuitable, the children thought, but said nothing.

Mrs. Müller looked down at her hands. "My married name, you know, isn't an English one," she said. "It's German."

Edmund knitted his brow. "Your husband's a Jerry?"

William elbowed him sharply.

"He is," Mrs. Müller continued. She didn't remark on Edmund's use of the slur. "He came to England some years ago. Worked in a bookshop over in Northampton. That's where we met. I went in for a copy of *Anna Karenina*." The librarian smiled faintly, her eyes far away. "We married a year later and settled down here." She paused as if gathering herself, then took a deep breath and continued. "When Hitler took over and the world started heating up, Martin—that's his name—was worried for his family. He'd already lost a brother in the Great War, but he had a sister still in Germany, as well as his mum and dad. He wanted to go home to see them." The librarian paused again. "That was almost three years ago."

William leaned forward. "Where is he now?"

Mrs. Müller took a shuddering breath. "I don't know."

Edmund was thoroughly confused. He'd never heard of a husband going missing. "What do you mean?"

Mrs. Müller looked at them, almost sheepish. "Just that," she said. "I don't know." She parted another section of Anna's hair. "We wrote almost daily for a while. Then his letters came only weekly. And then, somehow, it was only me writing."

"Why?" Edmund asked. "Why'd he stop?"

The librarian's eyes were on the fire again. It seemed it was difficult for her to find her words. "At some point, I suppose he must have decided"—she paused—"that he didn't want to come back to me."

"But he never wrote to tell you that?" Edmund was outraged at the cowardice.

"He didn't." A tear fell from the end of the librarian's nose. "Oh, look at me," she said, drawing another handkerchief from her pocket. "Please forgive me, children."

"No," William said. "It's just . . . we're really sorry."

"It's awful," Edmund said.

"It's too awful for words," Anna echoed. She twisted around to look at the librarian directly. "But why is it people are unfriendly to you? You haven't done anything wrong."

Mrs. Müller blew her nose. "Thank you, Anna. That means the world to me. Really, it does. But I suppose the question on everyone's minds is whether he's—whether he's working for the . . . for the wrong side."

"You mean that he's a Nazi?" Edmund asked.

William's and Anna's eyes widened.

The librarian gave a sad smile. "That is the question, isn't it, Edmund?"

The children let this sink in.

"I can't believe he is," Mrs. Müller continued. "But then again, I thought he was just going home for a visit. I never doubted for a second that he'd come back to me, and . . ." She trailed off.

"And he didn't," Edmund said.

Mrs. Müller lowered her head. Her voice was almost inaudible. "And he didn't."

The children searched for the right thing to say, but the subject at hand was so very grown-up, none of them could find the words.

It was Anna who broke the silence at last. "I still don't see why anybody would blame you. You've done nothing."

Mrs. Müller gave a tiny shrug and started on another section of hair. "Guilt by association, I suppose. People are frightened."

Edmund snorted. "Of you?"

"Dangerous librarian, eh?" Mrs. Müller dabbed at her eyes. "I suppose I should consider myself lucky. You read stories in the papers about Germans and their . . . associates . . .

being rounded up. Interned, even. There's a camp outside Liverpool."

Again, the children looked at her in wordless sympathy.

"It's like when everyone thought I painted on the school wall," Edmund said at last. "I hadn't done anything, but everyone thought I did—"

William interrupted him. "It's not the same thing, Ed."

Edmund's shoulders sank. "Seems the same to me."

Mrs. Müller mustered a wan smile. "I appreciate the show of solidarity, Edmund. Really, I do." Blowing her nose one more time, then pocketing her handkerchief, she gave Anna's hair another once-over. "Now—we're nearly done. I'm just going to rub some rather unpleasant-smelling oil into your hair, Anna. Yours as well, boys, just to be safe. Let the stuff work its foul magic till tomorrow, then have a good wash. And your coats should be washed straightaway. Do you think you can manage that tonight?"

The children nodded.

"Excellent. And your bed things as well?"

"Yes, ma'am," they chorused. *Not that we've much in the way of bed things,* Edmund thought. He'd never imagined he'd be grateful for that.

She gave them a bracing smile. "All of this will soon be a gruesome memory, and a grisly adventure for you to write to your family in London about, right?"

The children swallowed thickly. Mrs. Müller had shared her secret. Perhaps their own was safe to tell.

"Right," William answered.

The walk back to Livingston Lane was icy, and the children's reception at Mrs. Griffith's hardly warmed them. "Nits?" she fairly shrieked. "You've got to be having a laugh. That's all we need round here is nits. Have you not had a proper wash?"

Anna recoiled.

"It's nothing to do with that," Edmund protested. "It's her coat from the swap."

"We've got to wash them our coats. And our blankets," William added.

"You'll be up half the night, starting the washing after supper, and keeping me and the babies up while you're at it."

"If you'd rather we not," Edmund said hotly, "we'll just let things stay lousy."

Mrs. Griffith shook her head. "Just get it done, will you? We haven't enough soap flakes for this week's washing already, so you'll have to make do with the boiling. And be quiet, for God's sake."

After supper—an oily beef barley soup—Mrs. Griffith retired upstairs with the little ones, and the children set to their night's work. They had a vague idea of how copper boilers worked, but they were largely guessing. Edmund filled as many pots and kettles as he could find, hefted them into the tiny scullery behind the kitchen, and dumped them into the boiler. Anna threw in their coats and blankets. William collected coal from the bin and stocked the fireplace that heated the copper. It took forever for him to coax a flame, but when at last there was a steady glow, the children lowered themselves to the scullery floor and waited for the woolen soup to cook.

"How are we going to sleep tonight?" Anna asked. "The blankets won't be dry, and it's freezing upstairs."

"I don't know, Anna," William confessed. "I haven't worked that bit out yet."

"I'm sorry," Anna said, sniffling back tears that seemed to come from some sort of bottomless well.

"Anna, please don't start with the waterworks again," Edmund said.

William shot his brother a warning glance. "It's not your fault, Anna."

She swiped at her nose. "I wish we could have just stayed at the library and never come back here at all."

"Me too," William agreed, "but there's nothing for it."

"At least now we know why the WVS lady called Mrs. Müller unsuitable," Edmund said.

Anna sighed. "I don't think she's unsuitable. I'd live with her, gladly."

Edmund hugged himself in an effort to warm up. "What about her husband?"

Anna shrugged. "I don't care about that. I can't imagine he's a Nazi, and she's certainly not one."

"Of course," William said. "The husband probably isn't, either. But is *probably not a Nazi* enough for you?"

Anna sighed and said nothing more.

It was getting on toward midnight before the children decided that the lousy stew had cooked long enough. Anna was nearly asleep on her feet as she and her brothers heaved the coats and blankets out of the copper, wrung them out as best they could, and carried them one by one to the clothes mangle just outside the back door. Only ever having seen such contraptions in books, they made it up as they went. Anna fed their things between the rollers as Edmund and William turned the crank to squeeze out the water. Their wet hands froze in the icy night air, and no amount of blowing on them or shoving them in pockets seemed to help.

The job done at last, the children hung the damp things to dry on the line in the scullery, then huddled around the coal stove in the kitchen, thawing their chapped hands.

William's teeth chattered. "Let's just sleep down here."

Anna looked at him. "On the kitchen floor?"

"It's not perfect, I know, but I can't bear the thought of going back up to that icebox of a room tonight." He rubbed his hands together over the blessed heat of the coal stove. "Let's just think of it like a camping excursion."

Edmund shivered. "This is nothing at all like a camping excursion."

Chapter Fifteen

It seemed only moments until the children were wiping bits of sleep from their eyes and stretching their aching limbs. The floor had been every bit as uncomfortable as they'd imagined it would be.

Anna rose and made a watery porridge. This pleased Mrs. Griffith when she clumped downstairs an hour later. She seemed unaware that the three of them had slept in the kitchen, and since none of the children cared to linger on the subject, no one mentioned it. They ate a hasty breakfast and cleaned their faces and teeth.

"Bath night tonight, remember, you lot!" Mrs. Griffith shouted as they headed out the door. "None of your larking about with your books this afternoon!"

The children ran the whole of the way to school. Their damp coats still hung in the scullery, and the brisk pace served the dual purpose of warming them and bringing them more quickly to the comfort of the classroom.

The morning had been set aside for the making of costumes and sets for the Nativity Play. Supplies were meager, but *necessity is the mother of invention,* as they say. Meaning, *sometimes you've got to make angels' wings out of newspaper.*

"Do you think they'll have a real baby Jesus?" Anna asked.

Edmund yawned. "Maybe they could use Robert."

"Can you imagine?" William caught Edmund's yawn. "He'd shriek through the whole thing."

"Mightn't be so bad," Edmund said. "It'd take the attention off the rest of us." He was still anxious about the performance, although it had come as a very great relief that, rather than parading about in a yellow box, he needed only to dangle a star strung onto the end of a stick. This allowed him to view his role as more of a prop than an actual actor, and for this nuance, he was grateful.

By bath time that night, all three children were tired and cross. They were glad of the opportunity to wash the foul ointment from their hair, and the warmth of the tub by the coal stove was relatively appealing, but the thought of the cold bedroom was not. Retrieving their blankets from the line in the scullery, they retired upstairs, where their wet hair sent icy rivulets down their necks as they prepared for bed.

"Do we have anything warm to read?" Edmund asked. "I don't think I fancy *The Call of the Wild* tonight. Reading about Alaska seems a punishment." His throat had gone scratchy, and he wished for a cup of tea but knew there was none to be had.

Anna recalled a passage from *A Little Princess* that fit the bill. She retrieved it from her suitcase. Edmund scowled at the *princess* part but was too tired to protest.

"Listen to this bit," Anna said, thumbing her way to the right page. "It's perfect. Sara has been locked in the miserable, cold attic by the cruel Miss Minchin."

"Excellent." Edmund sighed. "I think I'll take Alaska, thanks."

"But listen, Edmund! She *imagines* someplace warm and comfortable with lots of food, and it *happens*!"

"Hmph," Edmund grunted, then sneezed.

Anna was not to be put off. "Just listen!"

In the grate there was a glowing, blazing fire, on the hob was a little brass kettle hissing and boiling; spread upon the floor was a thick, warm crimson rug; before the fire a folding-chair, unfolded, and with cushions on it; by the chair a small folding-table, unfolded, covered with a white cloth, and upon it spread small covered dishes, a cup, a saucer, a teapot; on the bed were new warm coverings and a satin-covered down quilt; at the foot a curious wadded silk robe, a pair of quilted slippers, and some books. The room of her dream seemed changed into fairyland—and it was flooded with warm light, for a bright lamp stood on the table covered with a rosy shade.

"And it's all real! All of it," Anna said.

William was curious now. "How did it get there?"

"Magic." Anna smiled. "Except, really," she whispered, "it came from the gentleman next door. She only thinks it's magic." Truth be told, Anna was rather giving away the ending, but sometimes one cannot help oneself.

"Hmph," Edmund grunted again.

Anna read on and on, only yawning every so often, until she found that both Edmund and William had dropped off. She closed the book and snuggled between her brothers under blankets that were by now almost entirely dry.

Before Anna opened her eyes the next morning, she wished fervently for the sort of miracle she had read of the night before. Concentrating very hard, she conjured a cheery fire in a grate, a table draped in white damask and piled high with warm buns and steaming mugs of hot chocolate. Opening her eyes at last, she felt a chill of disappointment that no such magic had occurred. Rising and peeking through the rip in the window paper, however, she found the next-best thing.

"Snow!" she exclaimed, shaking Edmund and William. "Snow!"

It took only a moment for the boys to extricate themselves from their blankets and join Anna at the window.

Their faces lit up as they peered into the lightening dawn, made ever so much brighter by the sparkling white carpet that shrouded the lane. The storm had had the good sense to arrive on a Saturday, and the children were giddy at the glorious December gift.

They crept downstairs and made the porridge, ate their own, did the washing-up, and left the rest on the stove for Mrs. Griffith and the little ones, who arrived downstairs shortly after nine. This seemed to the children a disgraceful hour for a snowy day, but the late start was not the worst of it.

"Play in the snow?" Mrs. Griffith scoffed at the very notion. "It's Saturday. I've shopping to do."

Anna's and William's shoulders sagged. Edmund's enthusiasm was not so easily squashed. "But it's snowed!"

Mrs. Griffith only scowled. "I can see it's snowed—I'm not blind, am I?"

"But—" Edmund began.

"Snow or no snow, there's still the shopping to do, and you'll either be taking care of that or minding the girls while I do it," Mrs. Griffith said.

There was a brief silence as the children considered their options.

"What if we took the girls to play in the snow with us?" Anna said.

Edmund was horrified. "What?"

"We could take them," Anna said. "They'd have ever so much fun."

Edmund only sputtered.

Mrs. Griffith looked at Penny, Jane, and Helen, her scowl softening. "If you'll take them with you and mind them properly, you can go." She sighed. "The baby can come with me."

"Thanks, Mrs. Griffith," William said. "We'll mind them properly."

Edmund only glared at him.

They lacked appropriate snow things, but what respectable child would give this a second's thought, under the circumstances? Neither lack of scarf, nor want of Wellington boots, nor Edmund's scratchy throat could dampen their spirits. Wrapping themselves up as best they could, the children set out toward the square. William carried Helen while Anna led Jane and Penny by the hands. This left Edmund free to pelt his brother's back with snowballs as they walked, a task he took on with great enthusiasm.

The village square was a hive of activity. The children, recognizing some of their classmates, joined the throng. Within an hour, the square had become a colony of snow people. Anna showed the girls how to swing their arms and legs back and forth to create snow angels. In truth, Penny,

Jane, and Helen made Anna quite popular, as the schoolgirls present thought it great fun to play at being nannies for the little ones.

Many of the children on the square had brought makeshift sleds—baking sheets, washtubs, and shovels. These were brought to the hillside north of the village, where the boys took turns careening from the crest of the hill to the frozen stream bed below. The sledding track grew slicker and slicker with the repeated runs, and the sting in the boys' cheeks as they flew down the hillside was the most glorious sort of pain.

When bits of earth and grass began to peek through the much-abused snow on the hill, the crowd returned to the square. Fat snowballs were hurled indiscriminately, until there was hardly a child who hadn't taken at least one full in the face. Penny, Jane, and Helen were notable exceptions, as there are surely special fires reserved down below for those who throw snowballs at small children. Snow fortresses were erected for protection, only to be infiltrated, again and again, by enemy forces.

The most noteworthy of these attacks was directed at Edmund as he crouched behind a battlement, molding reinforcements for his company's munitions supply. From out of nowhere came two strong hands on the back of his neck, shoving him headfirst into the ice-crusted ramparts. He wouldn't have known who had pushed him, except that he distinctly heard the words *filthy vackie* just before his face was plunged into the snow and everything went silent save for the beating of his own heart in his ears.

Edmund kicked out at Jack and Simon, but one of them held his arms behind him, and he couldn't get enough leverage to extricate himself from the pile of snow. He shook his head wildly, trying to clear a space to breathe, but melting snow filled his nose and mouth. It was just as he began to genuinely panic that his arms were at last released and he was able to raise his head out of the snowbank. He turned, still on hands and knees, to face his attackers.

They were nowhere to be seen. It was only William who stood over him, extending a hand to help him up. Sodden and panting, Edmund took his brother's hand and staggered upright, still looking this way and that, bracing himself for Jack and Simon's next onslaught.

"Where are they?" he asked, coughing.

His question was answered by the boys now gathering round William.

"Well done you," one boy said, clapping William on the back and gesturing toward Edmund. "I thought they were going to drown him."

"Yeah," said another. "Direct hit, that was. Nice punch!"

Edmund's eyes fairly popped out of his head. "You punched them?"

Ernest, the round boy from the ratting, answered for William. "One of them, at least! Right in the jaw, he got him! Right in the jaw! Served them right, I say, going two on one like that!" Ernest pumped William's hand and walked away, shaking his head in admiration.

Edmund stared at his brother. "You? You punched—which one—Jack or Simon?"

"I don't know. They were too bundled up for me to tell. Does it matter?"

"I suppose not." Edmund grinned. "Thanks."

William didn't return the smile. "I thought they were going to murder you."

Edmund shook his head. "I only wish I'd seen it. Direct hit, right in the jaw?"

"I guess it was," William said, trying to camouflage the pride creeping onto his face. He could see Anna approaching with the girls from the other side of the square.

"Don't tell her," he said.

Edmund's eyes went wide. "I won't have to," he said. "By Monday you'll be legendary."

Anna announced that the little ones were soaked to the skin and ready to go home. In fact, they all were. By now it was getting on toward dusk, and the children's clothes and shoes were heavy with melted snow and sweat. On the walk back to Livingston Lane, they all began to notice their stinging toes and fingers. All three wished they were returning to a crackling fire and a cup of cocoa, but they were painfully aware that this was not to be.

Mrs. Griffith greeted them with her hands on her hips. "What have you been at, then, dunking the girls in the river? They're soaked!"

Anna spoke up. "I think they had ever so much fun... they made snow angels and built snowmen, and—"

"And likely ruined their shoes," Mrs. Griffith said, stripping off the girls' coats.

Edmund was cross. "Well, you did say to take them out with us. Did you expect them to come home dry after a day in the snow?"

Mrs. Griffith scowled at him. "None of your cheek. Put these dripping things by the stove—and get the girls some dry clothes before they catch their deaths."

As if on cue, Edmund sneezed. He swiped at his nose with his shirtsleeve, then went to find dry clothes for Penny, Jane, and Helen.

Upstairs in their bedroom that night, the children huddled in their blankets. The magic of the day had faded, and the three were left shivering on their pallets.

"What would you wish for, if someone could magic it for you?" Anna asked.

"There's no such thing as magic," Edmund grumbled. His throat hurt terribly.

Anna clicked her tongue. "It's just a game, Edmund."

Edmund sneezed.

William smiled. "I'd wish for split pea soup with lots of potatoes and ham. The kind of soup that's so thick you can stand your spoon in it."

"And slices of hot buttered bread to dunk in it," Anna added.

William's stomach gave an audible rumble. "And cinnamon buns."

Anna nodded. "Dripping with icing. With a cup of hot, milky tea to wash it down." Her stomach did backflips at the mere thought.

"Not tea," Edmund said. "Cocoa. Gallons of it." He rolled over. "Honestly. If you're going to wish for something, wish big."

Tuesday—Christmas Eve—dawned icy, crisp, and white. The children remained rolled in their blankets as long as they could, loath to leave the meager warmth.

"Do you think Father Christmas will know where to find us?" Anna asked.

Edmund and William exchanged looks. "Ehm . . . sure," William said.

"What about Mrs. Griffith?" Anna said. "Do you think she's gotten us anything?"

Her brothers only stared at her.

Anna remained optimistic. "Well, she might have."

"Mmmm, and I might have grown wings and flown to America," Edmund said. He had a proper cold now, which made him muzzy-headed and irritable.

"Hopefully one of the warm bits of it," William added. "Florida, maybe."

"Perhaps we should have got her something," Anna said.

Edmund coughed. "Like a new personality, maybe?"

"Got her something with what?" William wrapped himself more tightly in his blanket. "It's not as if we've any pocket money."

"I know," Anna said, "but we could . . . I don't know . . . draw her a picture or something."

"I'm sure she'd treasure that," Edmund growled.

William squeezed Anna's fingers. "I think it's a nice idea, Anna. It's Christmas. We should be grateful, right? We're all together, and we're out of harm's way."

They dressed and made their way downstairs. Mrs. Griffith was stirring the porridge.

"Happy Christmas Eve!" Anna chirped.

"Right. Get that table laid and help Penny with the newspapers for the petty."

Anna's Christmas spirit was undaunted. "Will you be coming to the Nativity Play this afternoon, Mrs. Griffith?"

"What Nativity Play?"

"The Christmas Nativity at St. Andrew's. The evacuees

are putting it on. William's a shepherd, Edmund's the star over the stable, and I'm an angel."

Mrs. Griffith rapped the spoon against the rim of the pot. "The baby would never sit through a play." The children knew she made a fair point.

The table set, they joined Penny on the floor, where she was ripping newspapers into ragged squares. William and Edmund began tearing, while Anna set to the admittedly useless task of neatening Penny's haphazard pile. As her fingers blackened with a film of newspaper ink, she was surprised when she came to a series of squares printed, not just with words, but with pictures: a corner of a flower here; what might have been the turret of a castle there; on one, a rather cloudish-looking swirl. The fragmented images were familiar, somehow, and a sort of sick fear was born in the pit of Anna's stomach. She paged through more squares, hoping she was mistaken.

She wasn't. One piece bore the name *Dantès*, another *Sara*. It was when she came to a square bearing the unmistakable image of the head of a bull, surrounded by flowers, that Anna's breath caught.

"Penny?" She turned to the child. "Where did you get these pages?"

Penny only looked at Anna, clearly ignorant of any wrongdoing. Anna stood and surveyed the room in a panic, her eyes landing at last on the evidence. In the corner lay a small pile of what had once been books. On top was *The Story of Ferdinand,* eviscerated.

Anna stood for the longest time, staring at the remains, before turning to her brothers. "She's torn them up," Anna whispered. "She's torn up our books."

The boys looked at the bits of *Ferdinand,* the *Britannica,* the *Count,* Anna's *Princess,* comprehension dawning. They turned to Penny, ready to reprimand her, before recalling that she was practically a baby and couldn't be held responsible. Mrs. Griffith, however, would enjoy no such immunity, if Edmund had anything to say about it.

"Penny's torn up our books!"

Mrs. Griffith only stared at him, irritated. "Well, you've already read them, haven't you?" she said, huffing a sigh. "All the time you spend on it, I should think you'd have finished them by now."

Edmund clapped a hand to his head. "That's not the point, is it? One of them's not even ours. It's the library's, and Penny's torn it up! Did you let her into our room?"

Mrs. Griffith turned on him. "Your room, is it? Last I checked, this is my house."

Edmund stood rigid, his fists clenched and his chest heaving with rage—about the desecrated books, certainly—but about all of it. All the want and cruelty and indignity of the past months threatened the fragile restraints of his heart. "You shouldn't have let her do it!" He was shouting now. "Or at least you should feel sorry about it, now it's happened! If you were a proper mum, that's what you'd do!"

Anna and William agreed with everything Edmund was saying, but both feared the rising heat of the argument and wished he would back down and let it be.

Mrs. Griffith set the spoon in the pot and bent over Edmund, her face menacingly close. "I've let you into my home. I've fed you. I've given you a place to sleep. And you have the nerve to make out I've committed some sort of crime because Penny tore up your stupid books?"

Edmund stood almost on tiptoe, matching Mrs. Griffith's venom with his own. "Apologize, you miserable cow!"

He didn't see the slap coming. Whether it was the force of the blow or simply the shock of it, he stumbled backward and landed in a heap on the kitchen floor, holding his cheek in his hands.

William and Anna both sprang to their brother as if shot from cannons. They hauled Edmund to his feet, then stood staring at one another, all three pairs of eyes brimming with tears, all three pairs of cheeks aflame with fury or fear or both.

An age seemed to pass before William spoke in a voice barely audible.

"Let's go."

Pushing past Mrs. Griffith at the stove, he scooped up their shoes and coats, handing Edmund and Anna theirs, then putting on his own as quickly as he could before helping a shaking Anna with her laces.

Mrs. Griffith's eyes narrowed. "Where do you think you're going?"

William glanced at Edmund, then Anna. He took her hand. None of them spared Mrs. Griffith so much as a backward glance as they slammed the door of number four Livingston Lane behind them.

Chapter Sixteen

Out on the street, the children looked at one another. "Are you all right?" William asked Edmund, who was testing his smarting cheek with the heel of his hand. He only nodded, afraid that if he spoke, he might cry.

Anna swiped at her face with her sleeve. "What are we going to do?" she asked, hugging herself against the soggy chill of the morning.

"I don't know," William said. "Just start walking."

"Start walking where?" Anna asked.

"Anyplace. Just walk."

"But where, William?" Anna's voice was shrill and wild. "We've nowhere to go!"

Bilious panic rose in William's throat. "I don't know! I don't know, Anna!" There was a sort of shrieking sound inside his skull. "I don't have all the answers, you know! I'm only twelve years old!"

Anna stepped back, terrified. Edmund read this in her eyes and felt no small measure of responsibility. His cheek stung awfully, and the icy morning air only made it worse.

The three of them stood in the slushy snow of the lane, shifting from one foot to another to stop their toes from going numb. Edmund and Anna knew their brother was at the end of his tether, but neither of them had any idea as to where they might go. School was closed for Christmas Eve. Anna thought of the library—of course—but knew it would be closed as well. Edmund considered the Forresters', but only for a moment. The memory of Jack and Simon brought him back to reality. He sneezed violently, and this shook William from his fog of panicked thoughts.

"The church will be warm, and we're to be there for the Nativity Play this afternoon anyhow," he said. "Let's go there until things simmer down."

The church was warm indeed. The children inhaled its ancient silence, removed their sodden shoes and socks, and tiptoed down the side aisle to a pew near the front. The sanctuary was greened for the holiday, sprigs of foraged pine and holly tied to the altar railings and the ends of the choir stalls, where costumes and props had already been piled in preparation for the afternoon's event. On their walk to the church, all three had thought perhaps its very *churchness* would bring them at least a small measure of comfort, but as they sat huddled together, a shuddering breath escaping Anna's throat every now and then, none of them felt any better.

"Perhaps we should go back to London," Edmund said.

"London's been bombed nearly every night since September. We don't even know if our house is still standing," William said.

Anna stiffened.

"We can ring Engersoll," Edmund said insistently. "He said we could."

"Ed, it's Christmas Eve. If Engersoll hasn't been blown to bits yet, he'll be out caroling or doing whatever it is people do on Christmas Eve." William leaned his head against the back of the pew, turning over their situation in his mind and feeling crushed by the weight of responsibility.

"We could ask Miss Carr about another billet," Anna said. When she said *we,* she really meant *William.*

William shook his head. "We can ask, but I can't imagine she can come up with one on Christmas."

The children reclined on the narrow church pews and closed their eyes. Anna wanted desperately to ask William, *tell me something,* but a voice in her head said this was not the time. Instead, she offered another suggestion. "What about Mrs. Müller?"

The boys' sighs mirrored each other. William mustered what little reserves he had and answered his sister. "I know you like that idea, Anna. Part of me likes it, too, but we can't. For one thing, it's Christmas. For another, we don't know where she lives. And even if we did, Miss Carr and Mrs. Norton say she's unsuitable."

Anna remained unconvinced. "It's not her that's unsuitable, it's her husband—and we don't even know whether that bit's true, do we?"

Edmund shifted on the uncomfortable pew. "Anna, we can't very well go to stay with someone whose husband may turn up tomorrow in his Nazi uniform, can we?"

William looked at his brother. "I can't imagine anyone just *turning up* here in the village in a Nazi uniform, Ed."

"I didn't mean it literally. That was a—a . . . what do you call it? Meta-something."

"A metaphor."

"Right. It was a metaphor."

"No, it wasn't. A metaphor is when . . ." William faltered. "Never mind. That's not the point, is it?" He turned back to his sister. "The point, Anna, is that we've got to think about what's best for the three of us, and I hardly think the wife of someone who may be a German sympathizer is the guardian Mr. Engersoll was picturing for us, do you?"

Anna returned her brother's stare. "And Mrs. Griffith is?"

William's shoulders sagged. "Fair enough." Of course, Anna was right. "Look—we can't think much beyond tonight just now, can we? And for tonight, at least, we'll probably have to go back to Livingston Lane and hope for the best." Edmund put his hand to his cheek, where he could tell an angry welt was blossoming.

Nothing more was said for a long time, as each of the children got lost in thought. William tried to work out a plan. Anna tried to picture what Mrs. Müller's house might look like. Edmund, feverish, nodded off, drifting into a dream where something wicked was chasing him over a floor of glass. His feet broke through with every step he took, and he had to keep running faster and faster to keep himself from falling through altogether.

He startled awake when the church door opened with a groan. Miss Carr appeared, laden with paper crowns and other accoutrements of the Nativity Play, gone somewhat limp in the afternoon's drizzle. She looked almost pleased to see the three of them. Almost.

"Ah—children," she said, breathing hard. "You're here early. Excellent. You can help me put the manger together."

William stood and looked at Edmund and Anna, who silently encouraged him to plead their case with the teacher.

Miss Carr looked at his feet. "Where are your shoes?"

William approached her with a gulp. "Miss Carr, I'm sorry to trouble you, and on Christmas Eve especially, but I'm wondering if there happen to be any other billets available just now?" His request suddenly sounded comic as it hung in the cavernous silence of the church.

For a long moment, Miss Carr simply stared at him, her eyes narrowed. Then her jaw set and her eyes blazed. She took a deep breath. "That is not a funny joke, children. Now help me with the manger, please, all three of you."

Anna thought an explanation might help. "Mrs. Griffith slapped Edmund."

Miss Carr's nostrils flared. She turned to Edmund. "What did you do?"

Edmund collected himself and looked up at her. "She let one of her girls tear up our books, and she didn't even feel sorry about it." For a passing moment, he thought the desecration of books might stir sympathy in a teacher.

It did not. Miss Carr only glared at him and said again, "What did you do?"

Edmund didn't think his actions were especially pertinent. "We all hate her. She's not equipped to take care of us."

The teacher stood stock-still. Even her mouth hardly moved as she spoke. "Your liking or not liking your foster mother is irrelevant. You *will* go back tonight, and you *will* apologize." She took another long breath. "Have you any idea the trouble you've caused already?" She straightened herself. "A third billet is out of the question. Apologize to Mrs. Griffith and be done with it."

The church door was heaved open just then, admitting the first of the other Christmas players—one of William's fellow shepherds. Facing the approaching Nativity Play, Miss Carr raised her eyebrows at our bedraggled threesome. "Put on your shoes."

* * *

Just now, the idea of performing in a Nativity Play—or any play—seemed ridiculous to the children, but as they didn't fancy returning to Livingston Lane any sooner than was necessary, they began to ready themselves with their classmates.

The newspaper wings of one of the smaller angels fell apart as she put on her costume. Two of the shepherds began dueling with their staffs and had to be separated. The jewels—in truth, painted pebbles—in the kings' paper crowns were coming unglued, and the altar was soon littered with the rubies and emeralds of the wise men. These minor catastrophes notwithstanding, townspeople began to stream in, twining themselves out of scarves and offering hearty greetings of *Happy Christmas*.

The evacuees' Nativity Play was afoot.

Under the circumstances, it went quite well. The setting of the action being more or less the stable, Edmund was onstage nearly the entire time, dangling his star over the cradle where the baby—a doll on loan from a willing parishioner—lay. He felt awful, and he wasn't sure which was the worst bit: that he'd gotten the three of them in trouble again; the welt on his cheek; or that his head felt like it might split open at any moment. He sneezed, and in trying to cover his mouth, lost his grip on the star's anchoring stick, bashing Joseph over the head with it. A chuckle made its way through the congregation, but Edmund recovered the star, and Joseph gave the sign that he was all right.

William's role also involved a good deal of stage time, and a more halfhearted shepherd has never been seen before or since. As he trudged in with his fellow herders, William's mind was anywhere but Bethlehem. He saw Edmund nearly flatten Joseph, but even this roused him only momentarily from the darkness in his head. The thought of returning to Mrs. Griffith's did little for his Christmas spirit.

Anna did her best to flit with the other angels, but even if flitting had come naturally to her, her heart was not in her performance. *If only I hadn't made a fuss about the books,* she thought, *Edmund wouldn't have gotten angry.* The thought of books made her think of Mrs. Müller, and she felt a pang of guilt about *Ferdinand*'s being ruined. She sang along with "Angels We Have Heard on High," offering the bravest *Gloria* she could.

The three wise men made their grand entrance, each singing a verse of "We Three Kings" as he processed down the aisle. The boys carrying gold and frankincense had pleasant voices. The one carrying myrrh was tone-deaf but made up for it with volume. Edmund was to hold the *star of wonder* high during the refrains but, done in with fever, rather forgot and let it sag.

The great story told, the ragtag band of players made their way out, proceeding down the aisle to the back of the church while singing "Away in a Manger." Anna thought her heart would surely shatter at *Bless all the dear children in Thy tender care*... Tears began to make their way down her face as she reached the rear of the church, giving up on the singing as her classmates carried on around her.

The Star was last to make his way down the aisle. He followed the procession to the vestry room, where a small reception was to be held. Edmund brightened. *Something to eat, at least.*

The tray of Christmas cookies had been nearly demolished by the stable animals by the time the children reached it, but Anna and Edmund each got one, and William made do with some broken bits. Their stomachs neglected since the night before, they savored the crumbs.

Licking the last morsels from their fingers, they warmed to a familiar face approaching through the herd of cows and sheep. Excusing herself and moving around the other villagers, Mrs. Müller reached the children. "Well done, all of you. You were excellent!"

All three mustered wan smiles.

"Thanks very much, Mrs. Müller," William replied. "And happy Christmas."

"Happy Christmas to you as well," the librarian echoed, but her greeting drifted away as she took in their faces. She moved a step closer. "What's happened, children?"

Nothing at all. We're fine, thanks, crossed William's mind, but he knew he couldn't make it sound convincing.

"I have a head cold," Edmund muttered.

"I'm sorry to hear that," Mrs. Müller whispered. "But a head cold doesn't leave a great welt on your face. What's happened?" Edmund recoiled involuntarily as she reached for his cheek.

Anna swiped at her eyes and looked at her brothers, then at the librarian, then back at the boys again. It is terribly difficult to think up an on-the-spot story to explain a welt on someone's face. "Mrs. Griffith slapped Edmund."

Edmund swallowed thickly. The librarian reached out again to brush her fingers against his cheek. This time he did not recoil.

"Can we come home with you?" The words surprised even Anna, though it was she who said them.

William laid a hand on his sister's shoulder. "Ehm—Anna's just upset about Edmund, Mrs. Müller. We don't—"

"Of course you're upset about Edmund," the librarian whispered. She knelt in front of Anna. "And of course you can come home with me."

The boys watched as Anna dissolved into tears. They watched as the librarian caught her and gathered her up and let her sob into the shoulder of her coat. They knew the decision was made for the night. And both found they felt relief beyond words.

William gave the briefest of glances at his brother before he met Mrs. Müller's tearful gaze. "Thank you."

"Yeah, thanks, Mrs. Müller," Edmund echoed, then sneezed.

"God bless you, Edmund," Mrs. Müller said. "And no thanks are necessary. I had an inkling things were bad for you. I should have screwed up my courage and done this long ago, and not listened to the voices in the village—or in my own head, come to that—telling me you were better off with someone other than me."

The boys lowered their heads. Anna took the sort of shuddering breath one takes after a great deal too much crying. "Mrs. Griffith's girls tore up our books."

Mrs. Müller brushed a wisp of hair from Anna's face. "Whyever would they do such a thing?"

"For the petty," Anna answered.

"The toilet," Edmund explained.

"Oh, how awful," Mrs. Müller said. "Your special books from home."

"Not just those, Mrs. Müller," Anna continued. "One of the books they tore up was yours—I mean, the library's."

"Darling girl," the librarian said, taking Anna's face in her hands. "I hate to think you spent time worrying I'd be angry about a library book?"

Anna gave another shuddering sigh.

"It was *Ferdinand,*" Edmund said.

"Hmmm," Mrs. Müller hummed. "Poor Ferdinand. But you're not to fret about that, all right?" She glanced around the emptying reception. "I suppose we ought to let the ladies in charge know you'll be coming with me?"

The children nodded. Mrs. Müller squared herself before taking Anna by the hand and shepherding the Shepherd and the Star back into the nave. Miss Carr was on the altar, sweeping up hay. She didn't notice the children's approach until Edmund sneezed.

"God bless you, Edmund," Mrs. Müller whispered.

Miss Carr turned. "Back to your billet now, children. And we'll have no more nonsense, will we?"

Mrs. Müller led the children up the altar steps and extended her hand. "You'll be Miss Carr, then? I'm Nora Müller, and Anna, Edmund, and William won't be returning to Mrs. Griffith's." Her voice cracked a bit. "They'll be coming home with me."

Miss Carr took Mrs. Müller's hand with reluctance. She opened her mouth to speak but was interrupted by another ferocious sneeze from Edmund. Mrs. Müller retrieved a neatly folded handkerchief from her coat pocket and offered it to him, laying a cool hand on his neck. Edmund wiped his streaming nose.

Miss Carr returned her attention to the librarian. "I appreciate your concern, Mrs. Müller, and thank you for your kind offer; however, the children's present billet remains the most suitable."

Edmund could feel Mrs. Müller's hand tremble on his neck.

"I am well aware that I've been designated an unsuitable billet," she said. "I am also well aware, perhaps more than anyone, as to why."

"Yes—well . . ." Miss Carr hesitated. "I have not been—privy—to those conversations directly. I do understand—have heard—that there is some—concern . . ."

"Indeed." The librarian appeared to grow several inches. "I am—again—well aware of Mrs. Norton's *concern,* as you put it, but I think perhaps the more pressing *concern*"—she emphasized the word each time she used it—"is the fact that these children have gone some months now without proper care. I intend to remedy that situation, so you needn't *concern* yourself any further." The children had never heard Mrs. Müller speak so forcefully. The transformation left them spellbound.

While the librarian seemed to have grown several inches, Miss Carr had rather shrunk. "Right." She faltered. "This is the first I've been made aware of any—shortcomings—in the children's care."

The suddenly formidable Mrs. Müller softened just a hairsbreadth. "I recognize, Miss Carr, that you have been handed a Herculean task, supervising so many children.

Under the circumstances, I cannot fault you for any oversights that may have occurred. Now that the facts have been brought to you, however, I expect you to make it right. My home is small, but I can assure you that the children will be well cared for there."

Looking out at the gathering dusk, Miss Carr seemed to resign herself to the blackout regulations and the librarian's will. "Right, then." She gave a weak smile. "Well, Mrs. Müller, your offer is very much appreciated." She raised her eyebrows. "I wish I could offer you some advice on how to manage these three, but it sounds as if you are aware of what you are signing on for?"

All three children bristled. A sneeze menaced Edmund's nose, but he held his breath, not wishing to draw further attention to himself.

Miss Carr gestured toward him. "This one, in particular, thinks himself quite the lord of the manor."

The librarian somehow looked both amused and angry, which is not a combination one finds very frequently in nature. "By *this one,* I assume you mean Edmund." She gathered him, streaming nose and all, to her side. "Frankly, Miss Carr, I rather think we would all do well to have a bit more Edmund in us."

Unused, as he was, to being complimented on his Edmundishness, Edmund only gaped at Mrs. Müller as she turned to the children and continued. "You're all three in need of something hot to drink. So, if that's all, Miss Carr?" When the teacher said nothing, Mrs. Müller offered a perfunctory smile. "Happy Christmas, then." She turned on her heel and bustled the children down the aisle.

"What a dreadful woman," she whispered.

Edmund couldn't help but grin.

Stopping at the ribbon of chill making its way through the closed doors of the church, Mrs. Müller turned to the children. "It's nearly a mile's walk to my house. Can you make it?"

"Yes, ma'am. We'll manage," William said.

The librarian gave him a long look. "I expect you've already done more than your share of managing." She fastened the top button of her coat. "I'll carry Anna, and in two shakes we'll all be warm and dry at home."

The very words were like a blanket wrapped around Anna's heart as they stepped out into the night.

Chapter Seventeen

None of them spoke as they trudged through the snow, crisp with the freezing drizzle that continued to glaze the landscape. Past the library and the village green. Past the graveyard, whose residents no doubt held their own Christmas revels in a manner none of us will know until we join them. On toward the stream that bordered the north side of the village. By now it was nearly dark, and our foursome were spurred on by the encroaching blackness.

On the other side of a hill, Mrs. Müller stopped at the gate of a stone cottage with a tiny front garden, its borders marked by a ramshackle wall of similar stones. She set Anna on her feet to fumble with the gate's latch, then led them to the front door. "It's not fancy." Juddering a key into its lock, she gave the door a push. "But—here we are."

The warmth that greeted them as they crossed the threshold made the children gasp. They blinked when Mrs. Müller switched on a light in the front hall. She steered them into a wide kitchen where embers glowed in a fireplace nearly as tall as Anna. Pulling logs from a bin and stacking them in the grate, Mrs. Müller poked at the wood, then turned to the children and arranged each of them, like overgrown porcelain dolls, on the hearth.

"Warm yourselves." She offered a small smile. "Take off your wet things while I fetch you some blankets. All right?"

Mrs. Müller disappeared down a hall on the other side of the room, leaving the children to take in their surroundings. The kitchen was quite large for a cottage so tiny. A long wooden countertop flanked a range and a great porcelain sink. A bank of windows must have provided a view into the back garden if the blackout curtains had been opened. The children thought they heard a chicken protesting some injustice in the garden, but, having limited experience with poultry—other than the eating of it—none of them could be sure. On the far side of the kitchen, a wooden icebox stood under a rack of hanging pots and pans, while the wall to the left boasted a cupboard and a great hutch filled with tottering piles of crockery, its top shelf thickly hung with drying herbs gone crisp in the heat of the winter kitchen. In the middle of the room stood a wide-planked table with four mismatched chairs. *Four,* Anna thought. *Just right.*

Edmund sneezed.

"Take off the wet coats, both of you," William advised, removing his own and draping all three of them over kitchen chairs.

As the children sat down on the hearth to take off their

shoes, Mrs. Müller returned with woolen blankets. "Here you are," she said, wrapping one round each child's shoulders. "The three of you look half frozen. Shall our first order of business be to get something hot in your tummies?"

"Thank you," William answered.

The librarian retrieved a bottle of milk from the icebox. Pouring a generous measure into a copper pot and bringing one of the stovetop burners to life, she went to the cupboard and withdrew a sugar bowl and a block of something wrapped in brown paper. The children's eyes went wide. Surely, it couldn't be chocolate.

And yet it was. Anna nearly wept as Mrs. Müller spooned sugar into the milk, then shaved bits of chocolate off the block with a paring knife and added those. She stirred the potion with a wooden spoon. "What time did you leave your billet this morning, children?"

"Around nine or ten," William answered.

"Then you've had nothing to eat since breakfast?"

William hesitated. "Actually, we sort of missed that as well."

"Tsk, children." Mrs. Müller went to a bread box on the counter and extracted a great, crusty loaf. From this she sawed three thick slices, which she laid in the oven. "Let's get some food in you, and then we'll find you some dry things to sleep in, all right?"

The blankets and fire, coupled with the promise of hot

chocolate and toast, had begun to take the edge off the chill in their bones. William drew his blanket tighter. "Thank you ever so much, Mrs. Müller."

She surveyed the three of them. "You're welcome at the table, but under the circumstances, a picnic by the fire seems wise."

The children accepted steaming cups of chocolate from their huddled heap of blankets by the kitchen fire. All three burned their tongues, but this didn't lessen the relief as the brew made its way to their groaning stomachs. Mrs. Müller delivered the toast, hot and sopping with melting butter. The children ate in silence, spent with cold and with the consuming fear of the day

The librarian took this all in, standing by the fire and observing the children for a while, letting the silence be. Somehow, it didn't feel awkward, the way silences often do. Perhaps librarians are more used to quiet than most.

The children finished their toast and drained the last of their hot chocolates. Anna thought to send her tongue round the inside of the cup but remembered her manners. She was certain she could put her head down on the floor and find sleep in moments. Edmund appeared to be at risk of actually doing so.

Mrs. Müller laid a hand on his forehead. "You *are* in a bad way, aren't you?"

Unused to much in the way of tenderness, Edmund

pulled away from the librarian's touch. "I'm all right," he said as a shiver made its way from his insides out.

Mrs. Müller folded her arms across her chest. "I've a notion you'd be all right-er in bed?" Edmund raised his eyes to meet hers in wordless surrender. "Right, then. Upstairs we go," she said.

William began to gather the dishes from the hearth, but Mrs. Müller stopped him. "Leave all of that. You've had quite enough activity. I'll clear it away after you're safely tucked upstairs." She held out her hand to Anna, whose heart swelled as warm fingers enclosed hers and guided her gently from the kitchen. Her brothers followed.

Through the kitchen's back door, a narrow hallway led to an even narrower staircase. At the top, a landing opened onto two bedrooms. Mrs. Müller steered the children to the smaller of these, where a single bed was dwarfed by a simply carved wardrobe. Opening its massive doors, she withdrew a white garment. She handed it to Anna, who unfolded it to find that it was a nightdress of the heaviest flannel.

"It was meant for my niece in Belfast," Mrs. Müller explained. "Her birthday is next month, but it seems it's needed here sooner." She smiled. "It's about the right size, don't you think?"

Anna clutched the nightdress in her hands, shaking her head ever so slightly. "I can't take it if it's meant for your niece."

"Nonsense," the librarian said, then lowered her voice. "Never really cared for my sister's daughter," she confessed. "Besides which, I really ought to send her a book instead. Though she's not much of a reader." She paused. "Evidence as to her character."

Anna smiled. "Thank you."

Mrs. Müller touched Anna's chin tenderly. "Now—" She turned to Edmund and William. "I think there'll be something for each of you in here as well." She rummaged through a low shelf, where the boys could see what was unmistakably a man's clothing, neatly folded and stacked. Mrs. Müller emerged with two pairs of pajamas in plaid flannel. "These will be big on you." She held the nightclothes out to the boys. "But we can take them up. They're Martin's."

"We're to wear a Nazi's pajamas?" Edmund said.

He hadn't meant for it to come out as stark as it did, but one doesn't measure one's words when one is ill. To be fair, however, Edmund rarely measured his words when he was well.

William's breath caught. "Edmund!"

Mrs. Müller faltered. "It's not a perfect solution, is it?" She grew suddenly quite intent on her own hands. "I—I wish I had something else to offer, but short of wrapping yourself in a bedsheet or wearing one of my nightdresses, I'm afraid I'm at a bit of a loss for tonight."

Edmund only briefly considered the possibility of donning a lady's nightdress.

He took Martin's pajamas.

Clearly keen to leave the subject, Mrs. Müller led the threesome to the bedroom on the other side of the stairs. An enormous bed stood against the far wall, swathed all in white but for a dove-gray woolen blanket folded at the foot of it. The tables on either side of the bed each bore a lamp, a tiny vase of holly, and a pile of books. A small fireplace filled the space between two windows, whose cheerful white curtains did their best to hide the blackout shades behind them.

"Right," Mrs. Müller said, choosing bits of wood from a metal pail on the hearth and stacking them deftly in the fireplace before striking a match on the stones and holding it to the kindling. "I haven't had a fire in here in a good while, but tonight seems the night for it. Change into the dry things, and I'll fetch some fresh linens."

William looked around. "Isn't this your bedroom, though, Mrs. Müller?"

She gave a twitch of a smile. "I'll be perfectly cozy in the spare room. This will be a bit snug for the three of you, but until we can figure out a better arrangement—"

"Honestly, it's fine for us," William said. "We just don't want to put you out."

The fleeting smile again. She closed the door behind her.

All thoughts of modesty shelved for the moment, the children each took a spot by the growing fire and changed into the dry nightclothes. William bent to help Anna with the button at the back of her neck.

She turned to face her brothers, eyes shining. "This is where I want to stay forever."

"I know, Anna." William hugged himself. "Let's just be glad we're here for now and not think about the future, all right?"

Anna nodded, her cheeks now flushed from the fire.

"And Edmund"—William turned to his brother—"please just—you know—just . . . hold your tongue."

Edmund wasn't in any mood for a lecture. "I know I shouldn't have said that thing about the pajamas, but we were all thinking it, weren't we?"

"I wasn't," Anna said.

William sighed, exhausted. "It's just—if you could only mind what you say."

Edmund scowled at him. "Right. Best behavior."

"Ed, please . . . ," William began.

"I know, Will," Edmund said. "You needn't worry. I won't muck anything up." He peeled back the duvet, climbed into the bed, and curled himself into a ball.

At this, Mrs. Müller appeared in the doorway bearing a load of crisp white linens, patchwork quilts, and hot-water bottles wrapped in knitted cases the same dove gray as the blanket. On top of the teetering pile was a book. As she set her load down on the dressing table, she looked at Edmund.

"Lord love you, child." She went to the bedside, lifted

the duvet, and tucked a hot-water bottle at Edmund's feet. She tested his forehead once again with the palm of her hand. "Perhaps we'll forgo the clean linens, just for tonight," she said. "I hate to extract you, Edmund."

"Yes. I mean—thank you," he murmured.

The librarian smiled and looked at William and Anna. "If I had someplace else to put you two, I'd keep you out of the sick room, but short of making up beds on the floor somewhere . . ." She trailed off.

"We'll be fine," William said. "Honestly."

Anna nodded in agreement. None of them wanted to be separated, anyhow.

"In bed, then," Mrs. Müller said. "All three of you." She pulled back the duvet on the other side of the bed and laid down another hot-water bottle. Anna climbed into the middle, and William took his place beside her. The librarian tucked the duvet around the three of them and brushed each one's cheek with a tenderness that even Edmund found acceptable. She retrieved the book she'd carried in with the linens and handed it to William. "Perhaps you're all too old for bedtime stories, but what sort of librarian would I be if I didn't provide you with some reading material?"

For a long moment, the children only looked at one another. Mrs. Müller drew the wrong conclusion from their silence. "Oh, dear. You are entirely too old for bedtime stories, aren't you?" She took a step back. "Not having children of my own, I'm sure to make a mess of these things—"

"No," Anna whispered. "We're not too old."

Mrs. Müller looked at the boys.

"We're not too old," William agreed.

"Definitely not," Edmund said, his voice cracking. Perhaps it was his head cold. But probably not.

"Well"—the librarian gestured toward the book in William's hands—"I hope that one will suit you."

"It will," Anna said.

"Good night, then," the librarian whispered.

As she headed for the door, all three children had the same wish. All three children were surprised that it was William who voiced it. "Would *you* read it to us?"

Mrs. Müller smiled a sort of smile they hadn't seen before. A smile that showed something like joy. Something like sorrow. Something like gratitude. "I'd be glad to."

The children stretched their toes to the hot-water bottles. Mrs. Müller took the book and arranged herself on the bench at the foot of the bed. She opened to the first page, turned it sidewise the way proper readers do when there are pictures involved, and began.

'Twas the night before Christmas . . .

You've experienced a variety of bedtime stories, I'm certain. You know their magic. A well-chosen bedtime story sets you on the path to the dream you most need to have. Some speak of adventure—but our threesome had had quite enough of that already. Some frighten you deliciously enough to look under your bed before nodding off, just in case... well, no more need be said about that sort of story. This story, this night, was unlike any other. As the children sank into sleep, the words of the familiar rhyming tale were comfort and tenderness, ritual and home. A sort of prayer. A sort of lullaby. It set them on the path to dreams that felt rather like hope.

Chapter Eighteen

None of them had the slightest idea what time it was when they woke the next day. The blackout curtains sealed the room in a timeless dark, and when at last William opened his eyes, he lay on his back, savoring the occasional pop from the fireplace and listening to the rasp of Edmund's breathing on the other side of the bed. The wind outside howled, but its tune was almost pleasant now that it wasn't making its way between cracks in windows. Anna woke next and, when she saw William's eyes open, placed her hand in his. There they lay, mismatched cutlery in a drawer. Edmund slept on. There was something glorious about staying there, not because they dreaded what lay in wait for them when they rose, but because it all felt so lovely.

A long while passed in blanketed silence before William whispered, "Quite a difference from yesterday morning, isn't it?"

Anna squeezed his fingers. "Mmmm."

"Warm," he said.

"Mmmm."

"First I've been warm since November, I think."

Anna stretched. "Me as well," she said.

"First hot chocolate since . . . since . . . I can't remember."

"It was perfect."

"First proper bedtime story, too," he whispered. "I mean, a grown-up doing it."

Anna propped herself on her elbows, reminded suddenly. "It's Christmas!"

William, too, had forgotten.

"Do you think Father Christmas knew where to find us?" Anna asked.

William offered his sister a rueful smile. "I think maybe we already got our present from Father Christmas last night."

Anna's face betrayed only a glimmer of disappointment. She sat up and looked at the clock on the dressing table. "Eleven-thirty! That can't be right!"

William glanced at the clock himself, then reached over to shake Edmund's shoulder. "Ed! Wake up. It's eleven-thirty."

Edmund groaned and pulled the duvet over his head. "I don't feel well."

"It's Christmas," Anna said. "And maybe Father Christmas found us."

Edmund rolled away from his sister. "Don't be daft."

There was a soft rap on the bedroom door, whereupon

Mrs. Müller appeared. "I'm so glad you slept so long," she said. "I expect you needed it. Happy Christmas, all of you!"

The children chorused Christmas greetings in return as Mrs. Müller approached Edmund and laid a hand on his forehead. "Would you like to go back to sleep, or would you prefer a bit of breakfast?"

Edmund weighed the need for sleep against the need of a stomach that had seen far too much emptiness of late. "Breakfast?"

The librarian grinned. "I thought that might be your decision." She disappeared into the hall for a moment, returning with a wooden tray laden with food. It smelled of all that is best in the world.

"Here? In bed?" William gasped. "Mrs. Müller . . . thanks ever so much, but you needn't have—"

"I know I needn't have. I wanted to." The librarian passed plates to each of them.

"But you've already done so much for us." William squinted at her. "Just letting us come here last night, it's . . . it's enough."

Mrs. Müller looked at the children, then at the floor. "You seem to be under the impression that I am doing you a kindness." She knitted her fingers in and out of one another. "The fact is, children, that I have wished for a Christmas morning in a house that wasn't empty for too many Christmases now. It is therefore you three who are doing a kindness for me, reminding me that I'm not *entirely* unsuitable." She sniffed. Edmund and William couldn't manage to look at her.

"Now then—don't let's wait any longer, or your breakfast will be cold. Tuck in, all of you." Mrs. Müller began filling their plates with all manner of goodness. Sausages glistening brown at the edges, slices of warm bread flecked with currants and slathered in butter, boiled eggs, and cups of hot, milky tea.

"How did you do all this?" Edmund took an enormous bite of sausage. His head cold was evidently having little effect on his appetite. "With the rationing?"

"Making do," the librarian said with a shrug. "I did the shopping day before yesterday, so I was as well stocked as a body can be. My back garden keeps me in good form if I'm willing to be creative, especially as it's just me." She lowered her gaze. "Martin was always bent on self-sufficiency. I suppose that's one thing he left for which I'm rather grateful now. When you feel up to peeking outside, you'll see my girls."

"Are they chickens?" Anna asked. "I thought I heard a chicken!"

"Yes. They're named for the Brontë sisters. There is also a goat named Jane. Though you'd think she was a herd of elephants, for all she tears things up in the garden. I don't name the rabbits," Mrs. Müller said, "as they're rather... temporary."

Edmund nodded in dark understanding. He turned to Anna. "She means she eats them."

"Oh," Anna said, and swallowed hard.

The librarian grimaced. "Rather a wicked business, isn't it?"

Anna sipped her tea. "Let's don't think about it."

They chatted on as they ate. It seemed all the stories that had sat so long in Mrs. Müller's head, just waiting for someone to know them, came pouring out. Nothing scandalous, mind you only the everyday things that don't find ears when one lives alone. She told them about Jane the goat, and how she had once eaten a three-foot length of garden hose. She told them about the Brontë sisters and their characters: Charlotte jealous; Emily fastidious; Anne quick-tempered. This was rather a revelation for the children, who hadn't realized chickens had characters.

In this way, afternoon arrived, and not a morsel was left on any of their plates. "Goodness, I've been nattering on forever and a day now," the librarian said. "It's your turn. I don't know anything about your lives in London... tell me about your parents."

Agh, William thought. *I forgot... we haven't done this yet.*

Anna and Edmund both found the duvet of intense interest all of a sudden.

William took a deep breath. "It's just our grandmother, actually."

"Oh." The eager light in Mrs. Müller's eyes went out. "Oh, dear. I'm so terribly sorry. I never asked—"

"It's been a long time," William said.

"Oh." The children saw the librarian rearranging the picture she had made of them in her mind. "I'm so sorry, children. Tell me about your grandmother."

Mrs. Forrester had made things simple by assuming the grandmother was lovely. *A blessing* was how she'd put it. Mrs. Griffith had made things simple by not giving a fig one way or the other. Mrs. Müller was more difficult to answer.

"Ehm—well, she's j-just—our grandmother," William stammered. "I'm not sure how to describe her."

Cold, thought Edmund. *Cold would describe her, both literally and—what's that word again? Metaphorically.*

"Her name is Eleanor," William said.

Mrs. Müller looked at the three of them, waiting for more, then realized that nothing further was forthcoming. "Right, then." She stacked the empty dishes. "Are the three of you in need of more rest, or would you like to come downstairs to the snug?"

"What's a snug?" Edmund asked.

"Like a parlor, only friendlier, I hope." Crinkles appeared at the corners of her eyes. "That's where Father Christmas has left your things."

Anna gasped. "I knew he'd find us."

William cast a questioning glance at the librarian. "How could—"

Mrs. Müller's eyes sparkled. "I believe it was the poet, Mr. Yeats, who said that the world is full of magic things, patiently waiting for our senses to grow sharper?"

Edmund swiped at his nose with the sleeve of his pajamas. "Let's go."

The name *snug* was fitting. Two chairs and a sofa, a faded ottoman bearing a knitted blanket, a glowing fireplace. Aside from these, it was all books. Shelves lined every available bit of wall, and more books made themselves comfortable on the floor, stacked on side tables, lined up between bookends on the mantel. What could have felt untidy felt instead as Mrs. Müller had said. Friendly.

Candles glowed on windowsills and glass balls hung from lampshades. There was no Christmas tree, of course—timber was needed elsewhere this holiday. Somehow, this did little to dampen the spirit of the place. A jug of holly branches bearing mismatched ornaments stood in as a Christmas tree.

The children's eyes lit up as they approached and saw the labeled items laid out in front of it.

For Anna, from Father Christmas: three crisp white handkerchiefs, each with a spray of tiny shamrocks embroidered at the corner.

For Edmund, from Father Christmas: a bundle of only-slightly-used colored pencils tied with red twine.

For William, from Father Christmas: a jigsaw puzzle of the RMS *Mauretania.*

Just next to these was a stack of three books—not new, but in fine condition. They bore no tags, but no tags were required. The children needed only to read the spines.

The Count of Monte Cristo.

A Little Princess.

The Encyclopaedia Britannica, HER-ITA.

"It's our books," Edmund whispered. "I mean—not ours, but . . ."

William stared at Mrs. Müller, his eyes asking questions for which there were no answers. Clearly, a librarian would have a fair supply of books about, but all three?

She laid a hand on his shoulder. "Magic," she whispered, nudging him toward the gifts.

A mist of wonder hung in the air as the children paged through the books that had somehow been spirited back to them after yesterday's tragedy. Had it only been yesterday?

The reverent silence was broken when Edmund sneezed.

"Bless you, Edmund," Mrs. Müller said. "Closer to the fire, all of you, in your bare feet. Which reminds me . . ." She paused, retreating to the front hall and returning with her arms full of packages wrapped in brown paper and tied with knitting wool. To each of the children, she gave a tiny parcel whose insides crackled, and a slightly larger one, lumpy and soft.

William bit his lower lip. "We can't, Mrs. Müller. We just can't. You've been extraordinary to us. Really, you have. And we can't accept any more—"

"Nonsense."

Inside the crackling packages were peppermints—bright, spiral reminders of a sweeter time. Edmund unwrapped one and popped it into his mouth with a grin. The lumpy packages each contained a pair of dove-gray socks.

Now, you may think that socks are a dreadfully dull gift. Perhaps, in times of abundance, you would have a fair point. To Edmund, Anna, and William, however, socks were evidence that Mrs. Müller had been thinking of them for quite a long time indeed. Hand-knitted socks don't materialize overnight, after all, no matter the magic.

Anna rose and wrapped her arms about Mrs. Müller. "Thank you."

Whether the librarian knew it or not, she wasn't really talking about the socks.

* * *

In the midafternoon, Mrs. Müller turned on the radio for the king's Christmas broadcast. Having got used to doing without a radio at Mrs. Griffith's, the children found the machine almost otherworldly.

"God Save the King," somehow more significant in those dark days, played first. Then the king began, measuring each word as he might have done with sugar in a cake, if kings baked cakes.

In days of peace, the feast of Christmas is a time when we all are gathered together in our homes, the young and old, to enjoy the happy festivity and good will which the Christmas message brings. It is, above all, a children's day, and I am sure that we shall all do our best to make it a happy one for them, wherever they may be.

Mrs. Müller dabbed at her nose with a handkerchief. "No doubt your grandmother will be anxious to hear from you, children. We can go into town tomorrow if you'd like to telephone her?"

William hesitated. "A letter would be fine, I think," he said.

Mrs. Müller nodded. "I'll fetch you some paper."

The children retreated to the bedroom to write. This

time, it was Anna who composed the letter. The boys read over her shoulder as she checked her spelling.

Edmund sniffled. "You don't need to put our last name, you know. How many children do you think she knows named Anna, Edmund, and William?"

Anna shrugged. William sighed as he read the letter.

Dear Miss Collins,

Happy Christmas! It is Christmas night here and we are at a new billet. We left our old one because it was dreadful but now we're with the librarian and it's perfect. I've told William and Edmund this is the place for us, but they don't believe me because Mrs. Müller's husband might be a Nazi but I don't think so. Edmund has a cold. I hope you are having a happy Christmas with your sister.

Yours sincerely,
Anna and Edmund and William Pearce
P.S. Mrs. Müller has a goat called Jane.

"Anna," William began, "I understand. Really, I do. You want to stay here forever. It's just—"

"I know, William." Anna stopped him. "You don't have to explain it to me again."

"Yes, please don't, Will," said Edmund. He found

himself quite content and thought it rather a shame to spoil Christmas with talk of dark things.

The sun was hardly behind the trees when the children began yawning. After sleeping so long the night before, it seemed impossible that anyone should be ready for bed; however, there was much sleep to be made up from the months before. They ate an early supper—steaming bowls of soup, thick with potatoes and turnips, carrots and parsnips. None of them had got out of their nightclothes the whole day long.

Mrs. Müller read to them again that night.

This time, it was *The Hobbit.*

This time, they didn't have to ask her to.

Boxing Day and the beginning of the week leading up to 1941 passed in a soft haze. The library and school were closed for the week, leaving Mrs. Müller and the children to settle in with one another. A folding table was set up by the fire in the snug, and William and Anna got lost in the *Mauretania* puzzle. Mrs. Müller fussed over Edmund, who continued to sniffle for some days. She provided a steady supply of clean handkerchiefs and endless cups of tea sweetened with honey. Edmund grumbled at the weight of the blankets she wrapped about him as he dozed by the fire. "I feel like Tutankhamun," he said. In his secret heart, however, he found the unfamiliar kindness rather delightful.

They read for as long as they liked. And as it turned out,

they liked to do so for a very long time indeed. Mrs. Müller's bookcases overflowed with enough stories to last them all their lives. Fingering an ancient set of *The Arabian Nights,* William remarked that the pages of one volume had gone all wibbly. "As if it had been dropped in the bath."

Mrs. Müller looked up from her knitting. "Mmmm... the Thames, actually. I was reading that one at Tower Beach."

"We went to Tower Beach once!" Anna exclaimed.

"Only once?" the librarian asked. "Growing up in London, I should think you would have spent oodles of time there."

"Only just the one time," Anna said, remembering the toffee apples they had devoured that afternoon. "Our housekeeper, Miss Collins, took us once on her day off. We never went again, though. I don't think the grandmother approved."

Mrs. Müller chuckled. "*The* grandmother?"

"I m-mean... *our* grandmother," Anna stammered, glancing at her brothers.

Mrs. Müller cocked her head. "Your grandmother sounds an interesting sort."

"She certainly is," Edmund agreed. *You don't know the half of it,* he thought.

Winter left little work in the garden, but spinach did have to be harvested from the cold frame, and the animals needed tending. Each morning after breakfast, Mrs. Müller carried a wide metal dish of mash to the demanding chickens, then a bucket to Jane, and another to the rabbit hutch at the back of the garden. While the animals were thus occupied, she collected whatever eggs might have been produced the day before. A stool and pail were then brought to Jane for milking time.

The children positively ached to help, but for the time being, Mrs. Müller would have none of it. "It's dreadful out, and your cold, Edmund—you'll stay right where you are, tucked up by the fire." And that was the end of that. The children had to be content watching out the kitchen window as Mrs. Müller went about her tasks.

Anna eyed the rabbit hutch, thinking of the velveteen one from the story.

"Do you think she kills them herself?" Edmund asked.

Anna went a bit pale. "Ugh."

"I'll bet she does." Edmund craned his neck to see what Mrs. Müller was doing. "She'd have to, wouldn't she?"

"Honestly," William said.

"Not as if you can cart them off to the town rabbit killer or something, can you?" Edmund sniffled. "How d'you think she does it? She must bash it with something."

"Stop it, Edmund," William said.

Anna wrinkled her nose in disgust.

"Or maybe wring their necks, like chickens."

"Please stop, Edmund," Anna pleaded.

"And don't you dare say anything to her about it," William warned, looking out the window at Mrs. Müller.

"Don't worry," Edmund said. "I don't want any part of it." He grinned. "Except maybe rabbit sausages. I'll bet those are all right."

Anna jumped down from her perch on the counter and left the kitchen in a hurry.

Chapter Nineteen

As January neared, the thought occurred to the children that they might one day need to venture out of the cottage. Before bedtime one night, William approached Mrs. Müller. "I suppose we ought to retrieve our things from Mrs. Griffith's."

Mrs. Müller seemed to see into his heart. "I've been thinking the same thing, but you children will have nothing whatever to do with it. You won't be going back there."

William looked at the floor. "It's all right. We can manage it."

Mrs. Müller raised his chin with two fingers. "I believe there is little you can't manage, William." She held his gaze. "I also believe that all three of you—but you especially—have managed far more than anyone ought to, these past few months. I hope that while you are in my care you will allow yourself a rest from . . . from managing."

William had wanted to hear these words for so long, he couldn't remember a time of not wanting to hear them. He stared back at Mrs. Müller as a flush rose to his cheeks.

This seemed answer enough for the librarian. She pinched his chin gently. "It's decided, then. I shall pay a call on Mrs. Griffith tomorrow."

Edmund, for obvious reasons, was delighted at the prospect of never seeing Mrs. Griffith again. He was, however, concerned for the librarian. "You've got to be careful, Mrs. Müller. She's a bad egg."

"Mmmm. So I understand," Mrs. Müller said, buttoning her coat. "Shall I bring my pistol?"

Edmund marveled. "You've got a pistol?" *So that's how she does in the rabbits,* he thought.

Mrs. Müller grinned. "I was speaking metaphorically."

"What's *metaphorically,* again?" Anna asked. "I always forget that one."

"Comparing one thing to another in a way that isn't literal," the librarian explained.

Anna didn't blink. "So . . . do you have a pistol?"

Mrs. Müller laughed outright. "I don't, Anna. Do you think I'll be sorry of that, once I've arrived at Livingston Lane?"

Anna looked worried. "I hope not."

The children spent that morning much as they had every other since their arrival at the cottage. They worked on the *Mauretania.* They sat by the fire with their noses in books and continued a game of Monopoly that had gone on for three days now. With both Mayfair and Park Lane, William had built up an expensive real estate empire. Edmund, nearing this section of the board, suggested they take a break.

It was then that Mrs. Müller returned, looking rather like a pack mule, wearing three gas masks round her neck and carrying two of their suitcases. "I stuffed as much as I could into these," she said, her cheeks pink. "It was all I could carry in one go." She deposited the children's belongings in the hall and joined them in the snug, her eyes brimming.

"Was she awful to you?" Anna asked.

"No, Anna, she wasn't. Well—I suppose she was, but that's not what's making me misty." Mrs. Müller laid a hand on Anna's head. "It's just that it's dreadful to think of the three of you in that house."

Edmund nodded. "Was it the smell?"

Mrs. Müller grimaced. "There was rather an odor, Edmund. But more than that, it was the funk of sadness about the place." She took Anna's hand. "Can you children ever forgive me for not stepping in sooner?"

"How could you have, Mrs. Müller?" William asked. "We didn't say anything."

"You shouldn't have had to. I ought to have noticed."

"Did she give you trouble about our things?" Edmund asked.

Mrs. Müller unwound her scarf. "She was none too

pleased to see me, I can tell you that. I think she intended to use your belongings herself. And perhaps we ought to let her—just leave the rest of it there. I can get you new things, and she could use your old, by the looks of that place." She heaved a sigh.

She unbuttoned her coat, retrieving a copy of the *Daily Mail* from her pocket. "I stopped at the newsagent on my way through town." She laid the paper on the ottoman. The front page bore a photograph of St. Paul's Cathedral, shrouded in smoke and fire.

William picked it up. "They've hit St. Paul's?" he whispered.

"No, I don't believe they have." Mrs. Müller began extricating herself from her coat. "I hadn't time to read all of it, but I skimmed it in the newsagent. Look at the headline. *St. Paul's Stands Unharmed in the Midst of the Burning City.* The fire brigade saved it."

This was certainly good news, but William took in the hellish scene in the photo, the words *burning city,* and felt an unexpected heave of panic in his stomach. "Ehm—if you'll excuse me for just a moment, I just need to—ehm..." His sentence trailed off as he retreated upstairs to the bedroom. There, he lowered himself onto the bed, closed his eyes, and took deep breaths, trying to settle his nerves.

It wasn't long before he heard a soft rap at the door.

"Will? You all right?" It was Edmund.

William sighed. "I'm fine, Ed. Down in a minute."

"Can I come in?"

"Not just now, Edmund. I'll be down soon, all right? Just give me a second."

Never one for heeding commands, Edmund opened the door. William raised himself on his elbows and narrowed his eyes at his brother as he made his way to the side of the bed and took a seat. Edmund didn't say a word—only sat there. William found that Edmund's uncharacteristically quiet presence was calming, actually. This was a surprise.

It was a long while before William broke the silence. "Seeing that photo just made me panic."

"Mmmm," Edmund murmured.

"The direness of things, I mean."

"Of the war."

"Of the war, sure, but of the three of us, more than that. Sometimes I just feel punched in the gut with the weight of it all . . . figuring out how to keep us together."

"But we *are* together."

"I know." William rolled to his side. "It's just—seeing London in flames like that made Engersoll's plan feel a great deal more . . . necessary."

"Mmmm," Edmund hummed again. He drew his knees to his chest and hugged them.

"But it's an awfully big thing, choosing a family, isn't it? It seems terribly important to get it right," William said.

Edmund was quiet for a moment. "How d'you think you know you've got it right?"

William shook his head. "I don't know. Not a lot of experience in the mum-and-dad-choosing department."

"You do have, though, Will. You've been choosing our Mum and Dad—the dead ones, I mean—for ages now. Making up those stories every time Anna asks you to tell her something? You've been choosing bits and pieces of them all along."

William stared at his brother. "You knew I was making that stuff up?"

"Of course I did. Honestly, that one about Mum wanting to be a cabbie? Ridiculous."

"Well, why've you played along, then?"

Edmund shrugged. "Just because I don't believe it doesn't mean I don't like it."

William lay back on the bed. "I didn't make up the bit about her thinking her children hung the moon." *At least, I don't think I did,* he added, but not out loud.

"I know you didn't," Edmund whispered. He thought a long time before he spoke again. "Maybe that's how you know."

William squinted at him. "What do you mean?"

"I mean, maybe you know you've got the right mum when you find one that thinks you hung the moon."

William grinned. "Thanks for coming up here to check on me."

"Mrs. Müller wanted to, but I stopped her. I told her we both had a soft spot for St. Paul's, because of all the special times we'd spent there with Gran."

"Gran?" William chuckled in spite of himself.

"Yeah. Mrs. Müller offered again to take us to town to telephone her and make sure she's all right."

"Did you really say *special times*?"

"I did. I thought it was rather inspired. Better than telling her that dear old Gran is actually six feet under. And I told her the phones would probably be down in London, so we'd just write her another letter."

"You're brilliant, Ed. Thanks for taking care of that."

"No problem. Thanks to you for taking care of . . . well . . . everything else."

The turning of the year meant the return to school and work. The children were loath to leave the warmth of the stone cottage.

Mrs. Müller clearly felt the same. "Perhaps I ought to keep you home a bit longer." She felt Edmund's forehead. "I wonder if you're really over your cold."

Edmund, who hadn't so much as sniffled in two days, was tempted to feign feverishness and buy himself another day by the fire. He had nearly finished all nearly-a-thousand pages of the *Count* and would have liked nothing better than to read the last few at his leisure.

"He's fine. Really, Mrs. Müller. We're all fine," William said.

Mrs. Müller crossed her arms over her chest, resigned. "Well, at the very least, we'll walk to town together. It won't hurt me to get in early this morning, having been on holiday so long now."

The children donned their coats, as well as hats and mittens from Mrs. Müller's closet, and made their way into the frosty January morning. They walked Mrs. Müller to the door of the library, where they agreed to return after their lunches in the village hall.

Fortified as they were by their week in their new billet, even the prospect of seeing Miss Carr couldn't darken the children's spirits that morning. The whole class hummed with excitement as children told tales of their holiday weeks.

A pink-cheeked Frances approached William. "My mum came to visit for Christmas and gave me this." She smoothed the pleats of her dress. "How do I look?"

Edmund was more than happy to play along. "Yeah, Will, how does she look?"

William could think of nothing to say. *You look lovely,* while polite, would almost certainly give Frances the wrong idea. *You look the same as you did last week* felt unkind, as did *Please, won't you just leave me alone?*

Anna came to her brother's rescue. "That's beautiful, Frances. I wish I had a dress like that."

As the children took their seats, young Hugh, who looked ever so much rosier than he had on their arrival in the village last summer, surprised Edmund by presenting him with a square of chocolate. "My foster mum gave me a whole bar on Christmas. I always remember you giving me yours the day we got here, and I meant to pay you back." Unwrapped as it was, the chocolate had gone soft around the edges and bore traces of lint from Hugh's pocket. Edmund ate it on the spot.

"Thanks." He smiled, his teeth streaked in Dairy Milk bar. "This makes coming back to school almost bearable, even with a teacher like Carr-buncle."

And there she was, standing over him.

Miss Carr smiled the sort of smile that is not really a smile at all. "I trust," she said, "that you have managed to last the whole of the week in the same billet?"

Edmund's cheeks burned. "Yes, ma'am."

"Mmmm. Will wonders never cease?" She cleared her throat. "I couldn't help overhearing your last few words just now. Do you know what a *carbuncle* is?"

Edmund sank deeper in his seat. By now, the whole class was listening.

"Yes, ma'am."

"Would you please enlighten us all?"

He took a deep breath. "It's a sort of a pus-filled boil, I think."

A few of the children giggled.

"Indeed," said Miss Carr. "Did you also know . . . that a *carbuncle* is a sort of a brilliant red gem?"

Is it really? Edmund sighed. "I didn't, ma'am."

"Hmmm." Miss Carr folded her hands. "I see this as a fine opportunity to educate you. You shall enjoy a special assignment this evening: writing the definition of *carbuncle*—*my* definition—five hundred times."

Edmund gasped. "Five hundred times? That'll take hours!"

"That will no doubt make the lesson memorable," the teacher replied.

And with that, the new year in the classroom began.

Edmund put off doing his lines as long as he could that night. Truth be told, he was ashamed of himself. His brother's repeated eyebrow-raisings were little help.

"You might as well get started, Ed—you're going to be up half the night," William said as the children cleared the supper table.

"Whyever are you going to be up half the night, Edmund?" Mrs. Müller asked.

"I'm to write lines," Edmund said, downcast.

Mrs. Müller grimaced. "What are you to write?"

"The definition of *carbuncle*."

"Oh, dear." Mrs. Müller's chuckle was only just contained. "I can only imagine why that assignment might have been given. How many times?"

"Five hundred."

"Heavens. You *will* be up half the night." She mussed his hair. "Perhaps I ought to make some cocoa?"

William and Anna retired to bed while Mrs. Müller sat at the kitchen table with her knitting, keeping Edmund company as he wrote.

"That woman really has it in for you, hasn't she?" the librarian said.

Edmund nodded. "She's hated me from the start." The cocoa tasted sweet against the bitter tang of anger.

Mrs. Müller sighed. "I'm awfully sorry, Edmund. A person must have the darkest of souls to hate someone as dear as you."

Edmund wasn't used to being characterized as *dear.* He sat with the idea for a moment, turning it over in his mind and finding he had no objections to the notion. In fact, he found it rather delightful. "Thanks," he said.

"I suppose the only reasonable course of action, under the circumstances, is to keep your head down. What did Mr. Tolkien say in *The Hobbit* the other night? *It does not do to leave a live dragon out of your calculations, if you live near him?*"

Edmund smiled. "I know you're right about keeping my

head down, and I try to. I really do. But I seem to keep lifting it up again."

Mrs. Müller studied him. "Perhaps I'm the wrong one to give advice. I keep my head down quite a bit more than necessary, I suppose."

Now it was Edmund's turn to study the librarian. "You do," he said. "You ought not to let Mrs. Norton and her lot treat you the way they do. You've done nothing wrong and you should let everyone know it. It's not as if you've put a snake in someone's bed." He grinned.

Mrs. Müller gave a soft chuckle. "I haven't." She paused. "Though there are a couple of people I might like to . . ."

Edmund wrote in silence for a long while. The only sounds were the occasional hiss from the fire and the rhythmic clicking of Mrs. Müller's needles. By the time he got to five hundred lines, the clock in the hall was about to strike midnight. His pencil had long ago gone blunt. He cracked his knuckles, stretched his neck this way and that, and tipped back his empty cup to gather up every last drop of sweetness.

"Thanks, Mrs. Müller."

She took the cup, setting it in the basin. "I always find that a cup of chocolate makes an unpleasant task a bit more bearable."

"I didn't just mean about the chocolate. For sitting with me, too."

"I'm glad to," she said.

She reached out to muss his hair again, but he misread the gesture and found himself opening his arms for a hug. It might have been a terribly awkward moment, had it not felt—to Edmund's very great surprise—entirely right. As if this sort of thing—this *hugging* sort of thing—happened all the time.

After a moment, they released each other. Edmund smiled up at the librarian. "And thanks for the advice about dragons." He stifled a yawn. "I'll try to be more mindful of them."

"Right," she said. "And I'll try to be less."

CHAPTER TWENTY

On a gray February Friday, Mrs. Müller and the children arrived home later than usual, having got engrossed in their books by the library fire. They hung their coats and Mrs. Müller picked up a letter that had been dropped through the mail slot. She remarked on its postmark with some curiosity. "I don't know anybody in Switzerland." She slid her finger under the flap as they went to the kitchen to set the table for supper.

The children washed their hands and began retrieving dishes from the shelves. All three were startled to attention at a soft cry from Mrs. Müller.

They turned to see that her face had gone quite pale. "Excuse me, please, children," she said, dropping the letter on the table and disappearing up the stairs.

The children gaped at one another.

"Do you think she's ill?" Anna ventured.

William shook his head.

Edmund grabbed the letter.

"Edmund!" William whispered. "You ought not to read other people's—"

The look on Edmund's face stopped him cold.

"He's dead," Edmund said. "Martin. Her husband." He offered William the letter.

William took it, skimming it silently. The three of them stood there, their hearts hurting for Mrs. Müller.

"I'll go up," William said.

"And do what?" Edmund asked.

"And—I don't know—tell her we're sorry."

"We should all go," Edmund said.

"Maybe she doesn't want all of us up there."

"Maybe she doesn't." Edmund shrugged. "And maybe she does."

William gave his brother a long look. "All right. All of us, then."

"I don't know what to say to her," Anna whispered.

William looked at his sister. "Do you want to stay down here?"

"No."

The children went on tiptoe. When they reached the spare bedroom, William started to knock, then thought better of it. "Mrs. Müller?" he called.

"Come in."

They found the librarian perched on the end of the bed. "Ah, children." Her voice was thick. "I just—"

"We're ever so sorry, Mrs. Müller," William whispered.

The librarian looked up at them, an involuntary shudder making its way through her thin frame.

"I read your letter," Edmund confessed. "I know I shouldn't have, but it was right there, and we—"

Anna interrupted her brother, not with words, but by lurching forward and wrapping her arms about the librarian as tightly as she knew how. A sob escaped Mrs. Müller's throat as she returned Anna's embrace with fierce desperation. The boys said nothing, only looked at their feet as their sister offered comfort from all of them. Anna might not have known what to say, but she knew what to do.

Which is often the more important thing, as it turns out.

It seemed an age before Mrs. Müller released Anna. She ferreted in her pocket for a handkerchief. When she found none, Anna produced one of hers from Christmas. Mrs. Müller mopped her eyes and drew another shuddering breath. "I'm terribly sorry, children, putting this on you."

"We understand," William whispered. "Really, we do."

Mrs. Müller surveyed the three of them for a long moment. "I suppose you do, don't you? But that doesn't mean you're keen on listening to my blubbering. I'll be all right shortly. Really. I'll be down in just a minute, and—"

"No," said Edmund.

Mrs. Müller looked at him. So did Anna and William, come to that.

"I mean," he continued, "that you're not to worry about

coming down. We can make supper and . . . and do whatever else needs to be done."

The librarian wiped her eyes again. "You're awfully kind, Edmund, but really—"

"Please," Edmund said. "Let us do this for you."

Alone in the kitchen, the children realized that they didn't actually know how to make a proper supper. In the end, they decided on the offering that had so comforted them on Christmas Eve: thick slices of buttered toast and steaming cups of dark, sugary chocolate. Mrs. Müller's chocolate supply was dwindling, but tonight hardly seemed the time to worry about such things.

Anna sliced the bread. "Did he die in Switzerland?"

"What?" William asked.

"Switzerland. Mrs. Müller said the letter was from Switzerland," she said in a small voice.

"Oh. Right." William shook his head. "No. The letter was from someone named Müller, so it must have been her husband's family. It's just—you can't post a letter here from Germany because of the war. It's got to go through someplace else. Like Switzerland. They must have mailed it through someone there. A friend, maybe."

"He died in Berlin, it said," Edmund added. "In the raids in August."

Anna turned from the counter. "It's awful, but—doesn't this mean we can stay?"

William put down the knife he was using to chop chocolate. "What?"

"Well . . ." Anna gulped, knowing how selfish she sounded. "I just mean . . . now we know we're not to be living with *him,* can't we stay forever?"

Edmund snorted. Truth be told, he'd had the same thought himself, but he hadn't quite turned it over in his brain enough to say it out loud. Besides which, even Edmund knew the moment was terribly inappropriate. And that was saying something. "Sure, Anna. Why don't we ask her when we go upstairs? 'Here's your toast, Mrs. Müller. Now that we don't have to worry about your husband one way or the other, how'd you like to be our mum?' "

William looked at Anna. "Edmund's right. It's probably not the best time."

"I know that." Anna huffed. "I just—"

"And besides," William continued, "even though that letter may make things less . . . complicated . . . it's still important to think about it, the choosing."

"I've thought about it. And I've chosen," Anna said. "I chose ages ago."

"I know." William gave a winsome grin. "I just want us all to be sure."

"I am sure. When will you be sure?" Anna crossed her arms and looked from one to the other of them.

William looked at Edmund, who avoided his gaze, staring resolutely into the pot of chocolate. "Ed says we'll know when we find someone who thinks we hung the moon," William said.

Anna smiled, entirely satisfied.

Despite Mrs. Müller's protests, the children insisted on taking care of her for the remainder of the weekend. They fed the animals and gathered the eggs. Edmund tried to milk the goat, but Mrs. Müller eventually had to take over when it became apparent that—having little in the way of training—Edmund was only making the poor creature cross and nippy.

Mrs. Müller spent a great deal of time in her bed, reading and sleeping, sleeping and reading. On Sunday afternoon, she accepted the children's offer of a game of Monopoly. Anna made tea, which they savored while the librarian proceeded to bankrupt the three of them, despite the fact that they were all actually trying. Only William briefly considered letting Mrs. Müller win out of pity, but he soon found this both unnecessary and irrelevant.

The librarian offered the first genuine smile the children had seen from her since Friday's news. "After all you three have done for me, fancy my trouncing you so shamelessly."

Edmund sorted his pathetic pile of money and put it away. "That's all right. You can always tell when someone's letting you win, and it's never fun that way."

"Indeed." The librarian nodded. "Thank you ever so much, children."

"We're glad to, Mrs. Müller," William said.

Anna and Edmund set to clearing away the teacups.

"I know I lost Martin years ago, really . . . when his letters stopped, I suppose," Mrs. Müller said. "But somehow seeing it there, in writing . . . made that loss real."

William nodded.

Mrs. Müller sniffed. "Not only the loss of him, I mean, but the loss of . . . whatever hope remained of understanding why he disappeared in the first place."

William nodded again. "I understand," he said.

She met his gaze. "You do, William, don't you?" She laid a hand on his. "You've taken care of me as you only could have done if you knew what I was feeling." She paused. "That's an awful lot to know, as a boy of only twelve."

William looked down at the table. "Actually, I'm thirteen."

"I thought you were twelve." Mrs. Müller's brow creased.

"I was." William smiled. "And now I'm thirteen. My birthday was last month."

Mrs. Müller stood abruptly. "While you were here with me? Why didn't you say anything?"

He shrugged. "You . . . had already done so much for us,

I didn't want to ask for more. And really, it's not important. Even back in London, I never—"

Mrs. Müller went fiery in the eyes. "Not important? A boy turning thirteen? Gracious, William." Anna and Edmund returned from the kitchen. "Children," the librarian asked, "did you know your brother had a birthday last month?"

Anna bit her lower lip. "January eleventh."

"Cripes, Will," Edmund said. "I'm really sorry."

By now, William felt rather guilty about the whole affair. "Honestly—we'd only been here a couple of weeks or so at that point, and everything was such a muddle, I hardly thought about it myself."

Mrs. Müller took William's face in her hands and kissed the top of his head. His cheeks went pink. "Upstairs," she commanded. "You're to occupy yourself with something pleasant until your brother and sister and I tell you to come back down. Isn't that right, Anna, Edmund?" She stopped, studying the two of them. "Heavens, when are *your* birthdays?"

"Both of us are May," Edmund answered.

"So we haven't missed any others." Mrs. Müller sighed. "Upstairs," she repeated, shooing William toward the staircase. "We've a celebration to plan."

William started to protest again, but she would have none of it. "Go!"

So, at last, he went.

Anna and Edmund thought they had never had so much fun as they did in the preparations for their brother's belated birthday party. Mrs. Müller started on a cream sponge cake with what ingredients she had on hand. She set Edmund the task of rummaging through drawers and cupboards to unearth whatever birthday candles he might find. Anna set to decorations with great enthusiasm once Mrs. Müller told her that *paper rationing can go to the devil* for today. After his candle mission, Edmund gathered his colored pencils and joined her, and the two quickly filled the table with brightly penciled paper crowns, bunting, and cards offering heartfelt birthday greetings.

"This is going to be the best birthday William's ever had," Anna chirped.

Mrs. Müller peeked at the cake in the oven. "I should hope not," she said. "Fancy a birthday party pulled together in two hours' time—and a month late, at that!"

Edmund fastened bunting to the kitchen wall with bits of tape. "No, really—he'll love it. This is loads better than anything we'd have done back in London."

The librarian studied Anna and Edmund the way she had so often—as if she had been painting their portraits and suddenly realized she had got the colors all wrong. "Does your gran not go in for birthdays much?"

Edmund shrugged. "Not anymore."

"Mmmm." Mrs. Müller nodded. "Quite a character, your gran."

"Yep," Edmund sighed. "*Character* is a good word for the—for Gran."

Anna gave him a covert scowl.

Mrs. Müller took another look at the cake, then excused herself to the garden for several minutes. She returned bright-cheeked. "Right, then," she said, retrieving the cake from the oven and testing it with a broomstraw. "That's done. We'll just wait for it to cool enough that it will take the icing. Oh, children—what a lovely job on the bunting. And the crowns are perfect. Well done, both of you!"

"Thanks for doing this, Mrs. Müller," Edmund said. "Especially with you just—you know..."

"I couldn't think of a better time to occupy myself with celebrating," Mrs. Müller said. "I've had myself a wallow, and now it's time for a proper *do*."

When the cake was covered in a layer of pillowy whipped cream, Mrs. Müller sent Edmund to fetch the birthday boy. This he did, nudging William down the stairs to the kitchen doorway, where he put his hands over his brother's eyes so as not to reveal the party too soon.

Having never been a guest of honor before, William found himself in a curious state of mingled discomfort and delight. The delight quickly won out, however, as he took in the shining faces of his brother and sister—more gleeful, he thought, than he had ever seen them.

Mrs. Müller wrapped her arms about him. "Happiest of birthdays, William." She planted another kiss on the top of his head.

It occurred to William that the two such kisses he had received that day were, in fact, the only ones he could remember. He felt a sort of a jolt in his stomach at this realization. "Thank you. You really oughtn't—"

"Hush," the librarian replied. "You're only thirteen once in this life."

"Or twice, in this case," said Edmund, "I s'pose."

There followed a rowdy chorus of "Happy Birthday to You." William stood with his hands in his trouser pockets, shifting from one foot to the other.

"Blow out the candles, William!" Anna squealed.

"Make a wish first," Edmund said. "And make it a good one. Don't wish for nonsense."

"What sort of wish would be nonsense, in your esteemed opinion, Edmund?" Mrs. Müller asked.

"I'm sure I don't know, but William is generally far more sensible than is sensible, so I just want him to think carefully. Don't wish for something daft, Will."

"Mmmm." Mrs. Müller turned her attention to the guest of honor.

William smiled at each of them in turn, took a long breath, and blew out the candles in one go.

"That means you're sure to have your wish!" Anna clasped her hands in delight. "What did you wish for?"

William raised his eyebrows at his sister. "You know you're not supposed to tell."

Anna knew what her own wish would have been, and hoped, like Edmund, that William had chosen wisely.

The foursome ate cake until they all felt they would burst wide open. William pushed back from his plate and offered heartfelt thanks for the celebration.

"Not done yet," Mrs. Müller said. "Close your eyes again." William did as he was told. She retreated into the garden, returning momentarily with a bit of bumping and thumping, then telling William to open his eyes. This he did, ever so slowly.

Right there in the kitchen was a bicycle. Not a new one, to be sure, for such things rarely materialize in the space of two hours, but a bicycle nonetheless. It was red, mostly—only rusted in a few spots—and with a bow of dove-gray yarn tied around the center of its handlebars.

"It's a bicycle," William said, breathless.

Mrs. Müller smiled. "It's a bit cold for it now, but once spring arrives, I thought you might fancy a bit of freedom."

William ran a hand through his hair.

"I think it'll work nicely," Mrs. Müller continued, "if we lower the seat just a hair . . . it was Martin's, but he wasn't so tall."

"Thank you," William said, his voice gone thin. "Thank you ever so much."

"You're very welcome. Happiest of birthdays to you, and I shan't miss another one! Even when you've gone back to London, I shall have all your birthdays in my daybook and I shall send you birthday greetings from afar!"

William swallowed thickly. A thought entered his mind—a wish, you might even say—but somehow Edmund's voice rang in his head. *Now that you've got me a bicycle, I wonder if you'd also fancy being my mum?*

"Thank you ever so much," he said again.

"Why don't you take it for a ride?" Mrs. Müller asked. "It isn't quite dark out yet, and it's cold, but if you put on a coat—"

Edmund interrupted her. "He doesn't know how."

The librarian seemed certain she hadn't heard right. "I beg your pardon?"

"He doesn't know how to ride—do you, Will?" Edmund didn't mean to embarrass his brother, least of all at his birthday celebration. He was only stating a fact.

William gave a sheepish grin. "I don't."

"You don't know how to ride a bicycle?" Mrs. Müller asked.

"No," William answered. "None of us do." He looked at Edmund and Anna. "You should both have a go on it as well."

"Yes!" said Edmund.

Anna cocked her head at the size of the bicycle and reserved judgment.

Mrs. Müller hadn't yet come to terms with this latest revelation. "Whyever not?"

William shrugged. "I don't know. It just—there just—wasn't the time, I suppose."

"Wasn't the time? For a child to learn to ride a bicycle?" She looked from one to the next of them. "Didn't your gran ever . . ." The silence hung there, amid the bunting.

"She didn't," Edmund answered.

Mrs. Müller swallowed. "Well. It's high time you all learned." She grabbed her coat and wheeled the bicycle back out into the garden. The children put on their own coats and followed.

The encroaching darkness made the rocky terrain around the cottage a less-than-perfect training ground, so Edmund ran alongside the wobbling bicycle, holding on until William picked up speed enough to leave him behind. Anna stood with Mrs. Müller in the front garden, cheering for every moment he remained upright and covering her eyes each time he didn't. William skinned the palm of one hand in his first attempt, and grazed a knee in his second, but the sting was delicious. The icy wind on his face smelled clean and wild, and the gleeful shouts of his audience were nearly drowned by the thrum of his own heart. It felt like flying.

Still sated with sponge cake, the foursome enjoyed cups of tea by the fire, but nothing more, for dinner that night.

"Thank you, Mrs. Müller," William said. "This has been the best birthday I've ever had."

She met his gaze. "You're very welcome." She cleared her throat. "And I should think it's high time you all three started calling me Nora."

Chapter Twenty-One

As spring began to creep out of cracks in the icy ground, Mrs. Müller greeted the season with the energy that comes from months away from the out-of-doors, and the children couldn't help but be caught up in her garden enthusiasm. She was glad of their help. The few fine days of late February meant the raking of seedbeds and the turning of soil; the grim days were spent organizing seeds and drawing up plans to use every bit of fertile ground in the garden.

It was while counting out peas for planting that Edmund hit upon his grand plan to restore the librarian to village society.

"We should plant a garden at school."

William looked sideways at his brother. "Why would you, of all people, want to do anything that involved spending more time at school?"

Edmund sighed. "I don't want to spend more time at school, but wouldn't it be a perfect way for you to—to . . . I don't know, make friends, Mrs. Müller?"

"Nora."

"Right. Nora."

It didn't take long for Anna to join in. "It would be *digging for victory* and such! There's a sunny patch by the school's side door, and I don't think there's much growing there but dirt just now."

"Dirt doesn't grow," said Edmund.

"I know dirt doesn't grow." Anna rolled her eyes. "That's the point, isn't it? Don't you think it's a good idea, William?"

William cast a glance at the librarian. "I think it's not up to me whether it's a good idea or not."

Mrs. Müller laid her knitting in her lap and looked up at the children. They were surprised to see her eyes shining.

"Oh," Edmund said. "I'm sorry, Nora—I didn't mean—I shouldn't have said that bit about making friends. I only just meant—"

Mrs. Müller reached out and stroked the top of his head. "I'm not getting weepy because you've hurt my feelings, Edmund. Just the opposite. I'm touched that you're devising clever plans to bring me back to the world, is all."

Edmund grinned. "So, *do* you think it's a good idea?"

"I do, actually. If not for my sake, then for the village. I've loads of seeds set by—if we planted them about the school, the extra vegetables might come in useful to folks like your Mrs. Griffith."

Edmund was mildly outraged. "She's not *my* Mrs. Griffith."

"Right," Mrs. Müller said. "Of course she's not. But you know what I mean."

William was enthusiastic now. "And what about the old couple Mrs. Warren was billeted with before her husband... before she—you know—had to leave?"

"Honestly, children, I think it's a smashing idea," Mrs. Müller said. "You'll need to get permission, I suppose, from the village council, or at least the school?"

Edmund raised his eyebrows. "Not us, Nora. You. That's the point, isn't it? Reminding people that you're... *suitable*?"

"Honestly, Edmund," Anna said.

Mrs. Müller only chuckled. "Thank you, Edmund, for your kind words."

"I don't mean you're only suitable, Nora," Edmund said. "You know I think you're a brick. It's just—you need to show the rest of the village. And you can't do that if you're only ever at home and the library. Remember what you said about spending less time minding dragons?" Anna and William hadn't the foggiest idea what Edmund meant, but they nodded approvingly nonetheless.

Mrs. Müller directed a piercing look at Edmund. "I'll make you a bargain," she said. "I'll go to the council. You, darling boy, will go to Miss Carr."

Edmund was horrified. "Miss Carr? She hates me."

"My point exactly." Mrs. Müller's smile held just a bit

of mischief. "Perhaps your evacuee victory garden will show her just how suitable *you* are."

Plans were drawn up, plots outlined, yields estimated, and Mrs. Müller and Edmund steeled themselves for their respective assignments. March was fast approaching, after all, and the earth does not wait for dawdlers.

Edmund rehearsed what he planned to say to Miss Carr over and over in his head as the children walked to school that Thursday morning, grumbling the words under his breath and wishing the librarian hadn't named him to the task.

"It's your own fault," William said in response to his brother's scowl. "You're the one brought up the stuff about dragons. What was that, anyway?"

"That bit from *The Hobbit* about making sure you're mindful of dragons that live round about you. I wish I hadn't brought it up, now it's me minding the dragon."

The dragon, as it turned out, was in a particularly foul temper that morning. She was short with Anna when she couldn't recall the capital of Denmark, and she sentenced Alfie to clapping erasers because he made a rude noise during the mathematics lesson.

It was therefore with some trepidation that Edmund approached the teacher as his classmates filed out toward the noon meal. Anna and William stood close by for moral support, but both were glad that the job had been assigned to Edmund.

He cleared his throat. "Ma'am?"

The frown creasing the teacher's face only deepened as she turned and saw him.

"I was wondering, Miss Carr, if—well, we—that is, my sister and brother and I were wondering if—"

Miss Carr sighed. "I do hope you're not about to request a change of billet, because there aren't any left. That was the only reason Mrs. Norton agreed to the arrangement with Mrs. Müller."

"No, ma'am," Edmund said. "It's not that at all. It's only just that, well, we've had an idea about something we could do as a sort of a . . . a class project, I suppose."

"A class project?" Miss Carr scoffed. "Are you not satisfied with the assignments you've already been given?"

"No—it's not that." Edmund faltered. This was not going well at all. "I'm very satisfied by the assignments—I mean—they're fine . . . not just fine—I mean—they're great. Well, as great as schoolwork can be, mind you—"

"Ed," William whispered. "Get on with it."

Edmund got on with it. "Nora—Mrs. Müller—the lady from our billet—"

"Yes?" Miss Carr looked down her nose at him.

"Well, she's got a garden at her cottage, and we've helped her with it a bit, and we thought that if the evacuees got together and planted a garden here at the school, we could give the vegetables to the mums and dads from our billets, and to other people that might need them, here in the village."

Miss Carr stared at Edmund for a long moment, studying him in a way that was unfamiliar. "Go on."

Edmund thought he'd heard her tell him to *go on.* This was unexpected. His mind raced. "It wouldn't be any more work for you, ma'am. You wouldn't need to spend any more time with us."

The barest shadow of a laugh escaped the teacher's throat. "Small mercies."

"Yes, ma'am," Edmund agreed rather too enthusiastically. "I mean—uh—I'm not sure what you mean, but Mrs. Müller can provide the seeds and most of the supplies, and she's willing to supervise us all."

The furrow in the teacher's brow seemed shallower. "This will no doubt come as a surprise to you, as it does me." She put her hands on her hips. "I like your idea."

"You do? Really? I mean—thank you. Thank you very much."

The teacher nodded. "Yes. I think this could be good for the war effort in general, and our relationship with the village more specifically. But don't get ahead of yourself, young man. The decision isn't mine to make alone. It would be up to the village council."

"Right," Edmund replied. "We know that—I mean, thank you for telling us, but Mrs. Müller is going to speak with the people from the village."

"Mmmm. And you were tasked with speaking to me?"

"Ehm—Yes."

"I see."

Was that a smile on the wicked old witch's face?

"Well," she said, "should the council agree, I am indeed in favor of an evacuee victory garden. In fact, while I appreciate Mrs. Müller's willingness to take charge, I might just pitch in and get my hands dirty."

Edmund had no reply for this. Given Miss Carr's unexpectedly positive response to the idea, *I really wish you wouldn't hang about* seemed rude. Even worse would be *That's the last thing I'd want—to have to see more of you.* In the end, Edmund took a page from his brother's book of diplomacy.

"Excellent."

The children ran to the library as fast as their legs could carry them.

But Miss Carr's approval, while encouraging, was only half the battle. The next evening, the children waited eagerly for Mrs. Müller to return home from her encounter with the powers-that-be at the village council. She arrived just past dusk, her cheeks bright from the cold.

"Did they say yes?" William asked.

Mrs. Müller unwrapped herself from her coat and scarf and joined the children by the kitchen fire. "They did. Eventually."

"Eventually?" Anna asked.

"Mmmm. Evelyn Norton objected straightaway, and when Evelyn Norton speaks, her gaggle listens. She said she didn't think I was *suitable* for supervising such a project."

"She quite likes that word, doesn't she?" Edmund said.

"Indeed." Mrs. Müller nodded. "Her cronies joined in, concerned it would be *tearing up village property* and the like."

Edmund was outraged. "But it's just the opposite!"

Mrs. Müller smiled. "So said Betty Baxter."

"Who's Betty Baxter?" Anna asked.

"She's a retired schoolteacher. And evidently a gardener. She went on and on about how much the school grounds could yield, if we planned it out properly."

"So she convinced them?" William asked.

Mrs. Müller took a seat at the kitchen table. "She got them talking. Evelyn Norton started in on the expense and the demands on your teachers, but when I told them your Miss Carr had agreed, and that I'd provide the supplies free of charge and the vegetables to anyone in need, the council saw reason."

"So they voted?" William asked.

Mrs. Müller nodded. "Seven to three."

Edmund grinned at her. "Seven yeses?"

"Seven yeses," Mrs. Müller said. "Betty Baxter actually hugged me after."

Edmund wrinkled his nose. "Did you want to be hugged by Betty Baxter?"

Mrs. Müller chuckled. "I can't say I've been pining for a hug from Mrs. Baxter, specifically, Edmund, but when the meeting was over, we got to talking and I told her about Martin, and suddenly there she was, hugging me, telling me she's sorry."

Anna grinned. Edmund's plan would work. She knew it would.

And so it was that, on the first fine Saturday in March, Anna, William, and Edmund, accompanied by most of the other evacuees, put spades, picks, and forks to the earth and began turning the soil around the school building. Tools were brought from billets all around the village, and in a few hours' time the scruffy grass and anemic boxwoods gave way to dark, fertile soil. Mrs. Müller supervised and helped the older boys with the heavier tasks of digging out stones and shrubs. Anna and some of the younger children got down on hands and knees to press dampened peas into the cool, rich earth. Edmund and a smattering of others sowed row upon row of radish and lettuce seeds, carrot and beet, seed potato and kale.

William worked on engineering a trellis by the south wall of the school. Kneeling in the damp loam, he felt an unpleasant twinge in his gut when a pair of feet appeared before him and he realized they were attached to the legs of Frances.

"Hullo." She tilted her head just so. "Your brother sent me to help you."

William glanced sidelong at Edmund, who returned his gaze with glee.

"Ehm." William cleared his throat. "Hello, Frances. Ehm . . . perhaps you could work on the other end of the trellis? Dig some holes . . ." He pointed. "Way over there?"

Frances crouched by William's side, far closer than was necessary, in his view. "Why don't I just stay here and keep you company while you work?" she said, smiling. "Isn't that a better idea?"

It's the worst idea I can imagine, William thought. *In the history of worst ideas, it's the worst idea that's ever been.* "Ehm . . . well, you see, Frances—"

She held out a handful of dried peas. "Did you know that if a girl finds nine peas in a pod, the next boy she sees will be her husband?"

William's mouth tasted sour. "No," he squeaked.

"It's true," Frances said. "My auntie told me."

William could see no reasonable means of escape. *A sudden need to visit the toilet?* He was pretty sure he'd used that one fairly recently.

"You'll be Frances, then?"

William exhaled audibly at the sight of Mrs. Müller.

"Yes, ma'am." Frances straightened herself.

"Aren't you lovely?" Mrs. Müller said, offering William the most imperceptible of winks. "It would be a shame to dirty such a pretty dress, wouldn't it?"

"Yes, ma'am." Much as Frances hated to be torn from William, she was glad to be in the company of a woman who understood the importance of not mussing dresses.

"Do you know what we could use?" Mrs. Müller continued. "We could use someone to draw up a map of the garden. You strike me as an artistic girl, Frances. Are you up for it?"

Frances nodded as she was herded off. Mrs. Müller glanced backward only once to throw William a smile.

William sighed. *God bless her.*

A letter arrived for the children that afternoon. "From your grandmother, yes?" Mrs. Müller handed it to William.

William recognized Miss Collins's neat scrawl on the envelope. "Yes."

"I hope she's keeping well, children," Mrs. Müller said. "Why don't you take your letter upstairs while I set to preparing supper?"

The children did just so, lying on their stomachs on the big bed as William read aloud for all of them to hear.

Dear Children,

Your last letter took some time in its travels, by the looks of it. You said you wrote it on Christmas night, but it only just arrived with yesterday's post, on the last day of February. I suppose the mails are hardly the most important thing the war has mucked about with.

I must say, I'm not sure what to make of your new lodgings. I can't imagine the government is billeting children with Nazi sympathizers, are they? Perhaps you're mistaken? I daresay, I hope so. In any case, I have every faith that you children will know what is right and what is wrong when it comes to the preposterous plan.

I hope this reaches you more quickly than yours did me. Please do write again when you can. I think of you often and pray that this cruel time will end well, and soon, for us all.

Yours,
Kezia Collins

William looked up from the letter and was not surprised to find Anna smirking at him. What did surprise him was that Edmund had rather a smirk on his face as well.

"She has every faith that we'll know what's right and what's wrong," Edmund said.

William looked from his brother to his sister, a sort of warmth suffusing his chest. "I do, too," he said.

Anna wrapped her arms about his neck and squeezed him tight.

Just as a watched pot never boils, a watched carrot never sprouts. But in a matter of days the emerging green of radish and kale could be seen in the evacuees' victory garden. There was great excitement in the classroom at the first glimmer of sprouts. Even Miss Carr seemed to understand. She only put a stop to it all when Hugh asked to check on the garden for the fourth time that morning.

"I realize it's all terribly exciting, Hugh, but I expect the radishes won't be quite ready to eat just yet."

"Oh, I know, ma'am. I don't even like radishes." Anna nodded in understanding. "I just want to be sure they're all right."

"You may check on them again after class, Hugh. Back to your work, please."

Hugh sighed and returned to the subject of fractions, which, as it turns out, holds less interest to a nine-year-old boy than does the subject of radishes.

As the garden took flight, so too did the interest of the village. People could be seen smiling warmly as they read the wobbly, hand-lettered sign announcing the EVACUEES' VICTORY GARDEN.

Watering the lettuce sprouts one morning, Anna was met by a familiar and not entirely welcome face.

"What's this?" Mrs. Griffith asked. Penny, Helen, and Jane peeked out from behind her. Robert was in his pram, uncharacteristically quiet.

Anna straightened herself. "The evacuees have planted a victory garden," she said, thinking this really should have been obvious from the sign.

Mrs. Griffith nodded as Jane launched into a fit of coughing. Anna felt a sad sort of ache as she watched the wretched child wipe her mouth on her mother's skirt.

"Jane doesn't sound well," she said.

Mrs. Griffith gave a dismissive wave. "She's fine."

"Have you had word from your husband, Mrs. Griffith?"

"Not since the new year." Mrs. Griffith grew suddenly intent on a worn patch on her shoe. "Still in the north of Africa, far as I know."

Anna swallowed and took a deep breath. "Once the vegetables are ready to pick, we can bring some over for you, Mrs. Griffith."

The woman narrowed her eyes at Anna. "How much are you going to charge?"

"Oh, nothing—that is, the evacuees are growing the vegetables for their billets, and—seeing as how Edmund and William and I were billeted with you last fall—"

Mrs. Griffith brightened. "That's right."

"You're welcome to some," Anna said. "When it's ready, William and Edmund and I will be glad to bring over a parcel."

She felt a sort of glow as she realized that she really would be glad to do just that.

Edmund also found himself facing his past one afternoon that week, as he trained baby pea shoots to grow up the trellis. Threading a delicate green tendril through one of the slats, he recognized Jack Forrester's voice—somehow a growl and a whine at once—before he turned around.

"Who told you it was all right to tear up the ground around our school?"

"Yeah," echoed Simon. "Who said you could do this?"

Edmund centered himself. "Actually," he said, "everyone seems to think it's a grand idea." He made no effort to hide just how smug he felt.

Simon glared at him. "Tell your brother we haven't forgotten about that day on the green."

Edmund grinned. "Oh, believe me, he hasn't forgotten about it, either."

Simon clenched his fists. "We'll get him back, you know," he said, eyeing the plot behind Edmund.

His menacing glance did not go unnoticed. Edmund's fists clenched as well. "If you even think about doing anything to this garden, I'll make certain the whole of the village knows who did it."

"Like anyone'd listen," Jack growled. "Who do you think you are, anyway?"

Edmund looked down at himself—his shoes, crusted with mud from the pea patch, his trouser legs, flecked brown, his fingernails blackened with earth. He suddenly found himself giggling . . . then laughing . . . louder and harder than he had in ages.

"Who do I think I am?" he said, fairly shaking with the hilarity of it all. "I think you two were right all along. I am a filthy vackie!"

The evacuees' victory garden was a success.

Even Miss Carr said so one afternoon as she worked alongside Mrs. Müller, sowing a second crop of lettuces. "You know, your garden has proved a triumph."

"I'm glad you think so," Mrs. Müller replied. "But it's the children's garden, truly. It was their idea."

"Hmmm." The teacher wiped her hands on her apron. "I must say, it's rather changed my opinion of your three wards. Truth be told, I found them quite a cross to bear before this. Especially the middle one. Awful thorn in my side."

Anna, Edmund, and William, tending the spinach patch around the corner of the schoolhouse, could hear every word. Edmund scowled at this last. Which was certainly understandable.

Mrs. Müller wiped her brow with the back of her sleeve. "I know you felt that way, Judith, and I'm awfully glad you've changed your mind. They're very dear to me, you know. It sounds dreadful to say it, but I'm almost grateful for the war. I can't imagine what I'll do without them when they go back to their grandmother in London."

The children paused in their weeding and looked at one another.

Miss Carr brushed earth over the tiny lettuce seeds. "You're not just doing your bit, then, are you?"

"On the contrary. The fact is, they're just the most extraordinary children. I'm quite certain they can do anything they set their minds to . . . read the *Britannica,* end to end . . . help me find my life again . . ."

Mrs. Müller stood, stretching.

"If they wanted to, I'm certain they could hang the moon in the very heavens."

CHAPTER TWENTY-TWO

How funny that she'd said the precise thing.

The children were silent. They all simply knew, as one knows the saltiness of butter, the perfect warmth of the first fine day of spring, the smell of rain.

Of course it was Nora. For heaven's sake, of course it was.

Anna thought of offering up a hearty platter of *I told you so*, but she didn't. Why foul perfection with such a sharp thing as bitterness? It was enough to know that they'd found the place—the person—they'd been so long in seeking.

But knowing this and knowing how to proceed . . . those were two very different animals. After so many months, all the things they hadn't said felt suddenly like treachery. Even Edmund, who had always made a game of the preposterous plan, choosing the most absurd times to wrap his mouth around the words *Will you be our mum*, felt the weight of it, now it had become real. The unspeakable deliciousness of knowing they were beloved had a sort of tarnish around its edges now that it meant they had to come out with—well, with everything.

Not surprisingly, William was elected as their spokesperson. Having at last found the person he knew was meant to remove the mantle of responsibility from his shoulders, he felt the burden of this last task keenly.

At supper that night, he found Anna's eyebrows raised expectantly every time he glanced at her. Edmund kept prodding him with a toe under the table.

"You lot are especially quiet this evening," Mrs. Müller said, eyeing the children's plates. "Edmund, you haven't touched your food. Are you feeling all right?"

"I'm fine, thanks," Edmund answered, nudging William again.

William cleared his throat. "Nora—we need to—ehm . . . that is, we all three—Edmund and Anna and I—we've got—we need to talk to you about something." He took a tremulous breath.

Mrs. Müller set her fork on her plate. She felt the weight of the children's hearts. "What's the matter, children?"

"Nothing's the matter," William was quick to reply. "I mean—we're all fine. It's only just . . ." *We haven't been honest with you* seemed to get things off on the wrong foot. *Our grandmother is dead* would be a rather jarring way to begin.

He started again. "First of all," he said, "we want you to know how grateful we are for everything you've done for us these past months. Not just letting us stay here and feeding us. It's much more than that. You've been kinder to us than anybody ever has, our whole lives."

Anna suddenly possessed a keen understanding of how a moment could become *momentous*.

Mrs. Müller felt it, too, but drew the wrong conclusion. "Your grandmother's summoning you home, isn't she?" Her face had gone pallid. "Oh—children—I knew this day would come, but I didn't expect it to come quite so—"

"No!" William exclaimed. "It's not that." The librarian exhaled audibly, but the panic remained in her eyes as William continued. "It's not that at all. Just the opposite, actually."

A bit of the blood returned to Mrs. Müller's cheeks.

"We've told you we were raised by our grandmother," William said. "And we were. At least . . . she was officially in charge of us. Though the truth is, she was never really . . . well . . . there."

"Mmmm," Mrs. Müller murmured. "You never learned to ride a bicycle."

"Right," William said. "The thing is, when we came here, to the village, she wasn't—ehm . . . That is—she hadn't . . ." He fumbled again, chewing his lower lip. "Well, you see . . ."

Edmund could stand it no longer.

"Our grandmother died last summer and we were sent here to find a family and we did and . . ." He realized that two fat tears—only two—had somehow wound up on his cheeks. "And it's you."

Anna grabbed William's hand under the table as the four of them sat in the silence of the kitchen. None of them heard silence, though, for the thrumming of their hearts in their ears.

Mrs. Müller was slack-jawed in dawning comprehension. She reached across the table and took Anna's other hand, pulling her from her seat, drawing her close, cradling her in one arm as the other reached out to grasp William's and Edmund's hands. Their jumble of fingers was a lock.

"You mean, children," Mrs. Müller whispered, "that you haven't had a grandmother all this time?"

The children shook their heads almost imperceptibly.

"You've had no one?" She made no move to stop the tears from spilling.

Again, the children's heads shook only the tiniest bit.

"No one," Mrs. Müller said, taking it in.

"Nope," Edmund said, only now swiping the tears from his cheeks.

"And now you want to stay?"

All three nodded.

"Here. With me."

"Ever so much," Anna whispered.

"If you'll have us," William said.

Mrs. Müller made a sound like choking. "If I'll have you?"

William faltered. "I know it's a lot to ask. It's three of us, after all, and I'm sure you only planned on us being temporary, and I know we aren't always easy to manage—" William stole only the tiniest of glances at his brother. "But if you'll have us, we promise, all of us, to be good, and to pick up after ourselves, and to work in the garden, and—"

"Yes," Mrs. Müller whispered.

None of them moved a hair.

"Yes," she said again. "I'll have you." The words came out louder than she intended. As she heard them though, she thought it better that way.

"You will?" Edmund said. While it sounded like a question, it wasn't, really. It was a declaration. A sigh of relief. A murmuring of the world's great wonders. "You will."

"Of course I will." Tears flowed down her cheeks and into Anna's hair. "Of course I will." She stood, setting Anna down and gathering Edmund and William to her in a fierce embrace. Neither of the boys found it awkward at all.

"Thank you," William whispered into her shoulder.

After a long while, Mrs. Müller released them. She wiped her own eyes, then each of the children's. Even Edmund accepted this most intimate of gestures. The four of them took their seats again.

Mrs. Müller sniffled. "It's me should be thanking you,

children. This is what I've wanted for—well, forever, I suppose—almost since the first moment you walked into the library, though I never let my mind speak what my heart was feeling. These past months, you children have been an oasis in a life that's been far too much of a desert. And while I've been ever so glad of the oasis, I've known all along—or thought I knew—that I'd have to trudge back into the sand one of these days, only . . ." She trailed off.

"That's a metaphor, the part about the oasis," Edmund explained to Anna.

Mrs. Müller laughed as none of them had ever heard her laugh before. "It is indeed a metaphor, Edmund."

"What's a metaphor, again?" Anna asked.

William opened his mouth to reply, but Edmund cut him off. "She's asking Nora, not you. Nora's the boss now. The chief. The top banana. The number one geezer. The mum."

William, feeling a lightness he hadn't ever felt before, found himself entirely glad of Edmund's being right.

Mrs. Müller re-defined *metaphor* for Anna, wiping her eyes again with the back of her sleeve, then giving the children a puzzled look. "Who is it you've been writing to all this time? Were you posting actual letters, to an actual person?"

"They were real letters," Anna said.

William nodded. "Our old housekeeper, Miss Collins."

"*Really* old," Edmund clarified.

"We should write and tell her," William said. "But it's Mr. Engersoll we'll need to speak to for the official bit."

Mrs. Müller was weak with the brilliant stun of it all. "Mr. Engersoll?"

"This was his idea. He's a solicitor," William explained.

"A solicitor?"

"He's got great clumps of hair growing out of his ears," Edmund said, by way of completing the picture.

"Honestly, Ed." William smiled.

Edmund pressed on. "But none on top."

"It's true," Anna confirmed.

"Indeed," Mrs. Müller said, as if Edmund had explained things entirely.

The children found themselves giggling, the way we all do when we suddenly find ourselves relieved of something that has weighed on our souls for far too long.

"We'll sort out the solicitor in the morning," Mrs. Müller said, still wide-eyed and dazed. "Just now, though, I think perhaps we should leave the dishes right here on the table and retreat to the snug for the evening."

Anna, Edmund, and William, still drifting in a sort of dreamish place between real and not real, all nodded.

Mrs. Müller took a deep breath.

"It's time to start a new story."

William, Edmund, and Anna's Recommended Reading List

For *connoisseurs* seeking *the diversion of a good story*... the books that William, Edmund, and Anna read in 1940–1941 are listed below. I have tried to provide original English-language publication information; however, these beloved classics have (lucky us!) been republished many times over since the children read them.

Blyton, Enid. *The Enchanted Wood.* London: George Newnes Ltd., 1939.

Burnett, Frances Hodgson. *A Little Princess.* London: Frederick Warne and Co., 1905.

Christie, Agatha. *Murder on the Orient Express.* London: Collins Crime Club, William Collins & Sons, 1934.

Doyle, Arthur Conan. *The Hound of the Baskervilles.* London: George Newnes Ltd., 1902.

Dumas, Alexandre. *The Count of Monte Cristo.* London: Chapman and Hall, 1846.

Grahame, Kenneth. *The Wind in the Willows.* London: Methuen & Company, Ltd., 1908.

Hunter, Norman. *The Incredible Adventures of Professor Branestawm.* London: John Lane, The Bodley Head, Ltd., 1933.

Lang, Andrew. *The Yellow Fairy Book*. London: Longmans, 1894.

Leaf, Munro. *The Story of Ferdinand*. New York: The Viking Press, 1936.

London, Jack. *The Call of the Wild*. New York: The Macmillan Company, 1903.

Milne, A. A. *Winnie-the-Pooh*. London: Methuen & Company, Ltd., 1926.

Montgomery, Lucy Maud. *Anne of Green Gables*. Boston: L. C. Page & Company, 1908.

Moore, Clement C. *A Visit from Saint Nicholas*. New York: James G. Gregory, 1862.

Nesbit, E. *Five Children and It*. London: T. Fisher Unwin, 1902.

Tolkien, J. R. R. *The Hobbit*. London: George Allen and Unwin, 1937.

Travers, P. L. *Mary Poppins*. London: Gerald Howe, 1934.

As for the *Encyclopaedia Britannica,* if any of you *bibliophiles* are considering reading it, end to end, I would so love to hear about such a magnificent quest. While, as far as I know, there is not a volume that actually starts with *HER(cules)* and ends with *ITA(lic),* all of the quotes included in *A Place to Hang the Moon* were indeed real entries from editions that would have been available to William in 1940.

ACKNOWLEDGMENTS

I love reading acknowledgments. I love them almost more than the books they follow. And yet, here I am writing my own, and I fear I can never be adequate to the task. I am filled with so much love and gratitude for the people who made *A Place to Hang the Moon* a reality. I hope you all can feel it.

I am indebted to that greatest generation—those who fought in the Second World War. Whether it was on the battlefield or on the home front, their spirit and sacrifice remain a continual inspiration. While it was C. S. Lewis's Narnia series—well, at least the part where the Pevensies got evacuated—that was the root of this story (hence, Edmund), it was the memoirs of actual evacuees, some truly extraordinary individuals, that made the experience real to me.

I feel tremendously lucky to be part of the Holiday House family. Huge thanks to managing editor Raina Putter, and to the fantastic marketing team—Terry Borzumato-Greenberg, Michelle Montague, Emily Mannon, Cheryl Lew, and Nicole Benevento—for all they do to get books into the hands of kids.

This book benefited in untold ways from Barbara Perris's copy editing. Her keen eye for detail was humbling—in the best possible way—and so very much appreciated.

From the moment I saw Jane Newland's portfolio, I kept my fingers and toes crossed that she would do the cover art for *A Place to Hang the Moon*. I fell in love with her lush portrayal of nature, her rich colors, and the gorgeous detail in her images. Thank you, Jane, for bringing Anna, Edmund, and William—and their library—to life so beautifully.

Kathryn Green, my beloved agent, championed this book from the start. Thank you, Kathy, for seeing promise in my story, for finding it the perfect home, and for your kind and clearheaded guidance and wisdom throughout this process. I am so very, very fortunate to have you in my corner.

Having Margaret Ferguson as an editor has been a gift from start to finish. Shaping this novel with her was an absolute dream come true. She is wise and kind—that rarest of combinations—and the level of thought that she put into my story left me routinely speechless. Thank you, Margaret. Your gentle spirit shines on every page of this book.

Endless thanks to those who were kind enough to read my words in their most primitive form. Thank you especially to Summer for planting the seed, and to Jill for nurturing it along the way. Thank you to Leanna . . . other than my own children, you were the very first to read this story, and hearing that you liked it made my heart sing. To other thoughtful early readers Wendy, Laura, Anne E., Bill, Ben, Anne A.O., Maya, Deb, Mark, and Rob . . . thank you for asking the required number of times, so I knew you really,

really meant it when you said you wanted me to send you those Word docs.

All the love to my family. To Bub, Sarah, Kat, Gracie, Libby, and Hannah. And most of all, to my parents—Jim and Brenda—for a lifetime of love and support, and for letting me read this story aloud to them so I could make sure it sounded right.

Luke and Olivia, my wonders, my real-life stories. . . . Sharing books with you is one of the great joys of my life. Thank you for countless magical hours of reading. I love you both more than I will ever have words to express.

And Matt. Thank you for being my rock. In all things, in all ways, at all times, your dear and loving heart is the center of my world.